THE SOVIET SOLDIERS JUMPED TO THEIR FEET...

Murphy stood a good six inches above his opponent and weighed almost twice as much. He charged into the Soviet serviceman before he could free his automatic pistol from its holster. Both men tumbled to the ground.

Murphy knelt on his struggling victim's chest, grasped a handful of his hair in his left hand and twisted his head back and to one side. With a quick easy motion, he drew the blade of his combat knife across the man's throat. The slit on his throat opened like a wide mouth.

As the Russian wrenched his body beneath the Australian's massive strength and weight, bright red blood squirted from the severed arteries in his neck.

> He died slowly, struggling
> like a farmyard chicken...

COBRA STRIKE

Also by J.B. Hadley

**THE POINT TEAM
THE VIPER SQUAD**

Published by
WARNER BOOKS

ATTENTION: SCHOOLS AND CORPORATIONS

WARNER books are available at quantity discounts with bulk purchase for educational, business, or sales promotional use. For information, please write to: SPECIAL SALES DEPARTMENT, WARNER BOOKS, 666 FIFTH AVENUE, NEW YORK, N.Y. 10103.

**ARE THERE WARNER BOOKS
YOU WANT BUT CANNOT FIND IN YOUR LOCAL STORES?**

You can get any WARNER BOOKS title in print. Simply send title and retail price, plus 50c per order and 50c per copy to cover mailing and handling costs for each book desired. New York State and California residents add applicable sales tax. Enclose check or money order only, no cash please, to: WARNER BOOKS, P.O. BOX 690, NEW YORK, N.Y. 10019.

COBRA STRIKE

J. B. Hadley

WARNER BOOKS

A Warner Communications Company

WARNER BOOKS EDITION

Copyright © 1986 by Warner Books, Inc.
All rights reserved.

Cover art by Morgan Kane

Warner Books, Inc.
666 Fifth Avenue
New York, N.Y. 10103

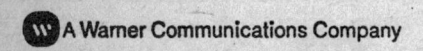

W A Warner Communications Company

Printed in the United States of America

First Printing: June, 1986

10 9 8 7 6 5 4 3 2 1

CHAPTER 1

Their only warning was a burst of machine-gun fire. The door gunner had opened up on them too early, giving them all a chance to dive for cover before the helicopter gunship swooped low over their position and strafed the ground. The chopper had appeared out of nowhere and disappeared again in seconds over the steep wall of the valley.

"Keep down!" Aga Akbar yelled in English to the three Americans. He had no need to warn his fellow Afghan tribesmen. They knew how the Russians operated.

In a few seconds more they saw a pair of jet fighters rise over the back rim of the valley, drop into it, and skim over the terrain. A white vapor trail squirted ahead of the lead plane, seeming to come right at them. A missile slammed into the ground one hundred and fifty feet from the prone, unmoving men, deafening them with its explosion and showering down stones on them like hail. A second missile hit maybe thirty feet closer to them than the first, and they felt the ground under their bellies tremble from its impact before the dirt and stones scoured by its explosion thumped down on their backs to tell them it had missed and they were still alive. The men waited a couple of slow, suspenseful seconds for the other plane to deliver its pair of missiles. They landed off the mark but close enough to shower their loads of stones on the prostrate men. Then the jets were gone. Silence returned to the valley.

"Everyone all right?" Aga Akbar shouted, but meaning only the three Americans, since he spoke in English. It was only after hearing that they were unharmed that he checked with his own men. No one was hurt.

"You see their accuracy?" Aga Akbar said to the Americans. "Those MIGs aimed their missiles exactly on the position where the helicopter door-gunner opened fire. If they had not made that mistake about our position, they would have nailed us for sure. All the same, the Russians are stupid—they do the same thing all the time. If the helicopter clears off after only one strafing run, you know it has called in MIGs. If the gunship comes back at you again, there are no planes close by."

"Won't the chopper come back?" one of the Americans asked anxiously, looking around the sky.

Aga Akbar shrugged. "Why should they? It will be easier for them to report us all as destroyed. If they come back, they might have to report that their attack was not a complete success. Why would they want that? We might even fire on them—if we had the weapons to do it. We don't, but they can't be sure of that. America might have sent us weapons. You haven't. But you might have. Someday maybe you will."

The Afghan tribesmen were standing again, readjusting the loads on their backs, which had become awkwardly positioned after their sudden dive to the ground. Dust raised by the four missile strikes still hung in the air, and four fresh gouges in the stony earth stood out like wounds in flesh. The tribesmen spoke among themselves and laughed, obviously at the unsuccessful Russians, then moved out in a long line on the path halfway up the valley's steep side. Aga Akbar gestured to the Americans to stay near him, about midway in the line of men, and they obediently fell in behind him.

Having spent eight years in Ann Arbor, Michigan, which

resulted in a doctorate in physical chemistry from the University of Michigan, Aga Akbar spoke very good English with a distinct Midwestern accent. Though the three Americans had known him almost a week now, they still found themselves startled from time to time to hear a home-grown American accent from this tall, skinny man with bronze skin, fierce dark eyes, and a flowing black mustache, who wore at all times an Afghan headdress that looked like two cloth pancakes flopped on top of his hair and a Kalashnikov automatic rifle hanging by its strap from his right shoulder.

By now the Americans were used to his bitter references to the scarcity of sophisticated weapons from the West, chiefly of rocket and missile launchers capable of downing choppers and jets. Indeed, Western countries had been very stingy with all weapon supplies while at the same time being very generous in verbal support for the rebels, words being cheap. Communist China gave the rebels as much aid as any Western country, so the rebels liked to point out. They knew that Peking was not helping them out of any real sympathy but only to irritate Russia, yet aid was aid and a helping hand still a helping hand, no matter what the real motive behind it was. The only trouble with aid from Peking was that the Chinese themselves did not have the surface-to-air missiles the Afghan rebels so badly needed. Without these weapons in the hands of the Afghans the Russians ruled the skies and selected their prey on the ground beneath without much fear of counterattack.

The line of men moved laboriously along the narrow path. In a little while they came to a ruined village. The mud-brick walls of the one-story houses were half collapsed, and their corrugated zinc roofs were stove in. Nothing moved in the single street lined by the tumbledown houses, and weeds grew knee-high in the middle of it.

"Only a year ago," Aga Akbar explained, "this was a busy village. Women kept their houses clean, their children played here in this street, the men worked the fields on the valley slopes. Today the ones not killed by Russian air strikes live as refugees in tent cities across the border in

Pakistan. The younger men still come back to fight as guerrillas. So long as any still live, they will fight."

The Americans listened sympathetically and tried to picture in their minds what daily life in the valley was once like for these colorful mountain people before the Russian communists reduced it to a desolate ruin. The Americans knew about the new "scorched-earth" Soviet policy in Afghanistan, by which the invaders hoped to destroy the food supply of the mountain guerrillas who resisted them so successfully and to break the fighting spirit of these brave warriors. Those they could not kill, they hoped to drive into exile. The Russians were determined to add this territory to their empire, with or without the people who lived there. And yet these hardy mountain tribesmen continued to defy the Soviet Union's massive war machine with mostly antiquated weapons and with hardly any outside help.

"This place looks deserted," Aga Akbar informed them, "but it is not. The Russians are meant to think that all the men have gone forever." He laughed contemptuously at the stupidity of such a notion.

Then he turned and shouted several times up the overgrown street between the two lines of mud-brick houses that were now mostly rubble. A thin form appeared from behind a heap of rocks and stopped, covering them warily with a rifle. Aga Akbar shouted some more, and the thin figure came forward again, only to stop once more and measure them with his rifle sights. Only when the lone villager was quite close did the Americans see that he was a boy hardly more than twelve. His rifle had a bolt action with a heavy wood stock, of World War II vintage at the very latest. Aga Akbar spoke with him and pointed to four goats high on a rocky slope above the village. There was much arguing between the two of them for some minutes as they pointed first at one goat and then another. Finally Aga produced a wad of Pakistani rupees, peeled off some notes, and handed them to the youth, who immediately raised the heavy rifle to his puny shoulder and picked off the second goat from the right in a single shot. The boy then went back up the village street toward the pile of rocks whence he had come.

"We've just bought our evening meal," Aga told the

three Americans. He added with a sly smile, "I hope you like goat. The boy says the men are all away attacking a government garrison two days march from here. He was left to guard their possessions. At first he thought we might want to rob him."

They climbed the hill to recover the carcass of the goat. None of the Afghans seemed to find it at all remarkable that the twelve-year-old with the cumbersome rifle almost half a century old had hit the goat in the eye and brain with his single bullet. The Americans had a feeling that this had not been just a lucky shot.

They waited till dark before lighting a fire in one of the wrecked houses so the smoke would not give away their presence to planes. They roasted and ate the goat, along with dry, hard bread they had to soak in water to make chewable. Then they slept deeply on the stony floors of several houses, their weariness so great and the comfort of warm food in their guts so strong, they were untroubled by the cold of the mountain night or the rough surfaces on which they slept. They woke before dawn, ate more bread soaked in water, drank warm tea. The three Americans walked a little distance away to watch the sun rise.

"I got to be the only preppie in Afghanistan this morning," David Baker said, massaging a stiff shoulder.

"Just what the poor Afghan mothas need right now—a fucking preppie from Yale," Clarence Winston said with a grin. He had once told David that Yale had turned him down on a football scholarship, which was about the only way the son of a black clergyman in Mississippi could hope to go there. Football hadn't worked out for him, anyway, and he ended by taking a doctorate in political science from Howard University. He had worked in the unsuccessful election campaign of a black Republican candidate for the House of Representatives before joining the Nanticoke Institute, which described itself as a nonprofit defense research foundation and which had sent all three of them to this part of the world.

The third American, Don Turner, as usual said nothing. He was more than twice the age of the other two, fifty-four, a retired Marine Corps sergeant who saw no reason not to be freshly shaved and neatly turned out even though they were thousands of feet up in the Hindu Kush Mountains. He was the last man anyone would have expected to find in a Washington think tank like the Nanticoke Institute. He explained his role there by saying: "All the clever shitheads here think everything they dream up is gold. Me, I'm strictly copper or lead. I graduated in Korea and did two tours of postgraduate work in Nam, and I just love to hear bright ideas from curly-headed children."

"You know, it's just beginning to occur to me," David Baker said. "That was a real Soviet gunship yesterday, those were real MIGs, that was the Red Army we were messing with. You ever find it hard to believe, Don?"

Turner nodded. "All the time, and it stays that way. Worse things get, the harder it is to believe what is going on in front of your eyes. That's what gets to a lot of men in the end. They can take it up to a certain point, then one day they wake up and they're not able to tie their bootlaces."

"And if that happens to me?" Baker asked.

Winston put a forefinger to his own head and fired an imaginary shot. "We'll have to put you out of your pain."

Turner nodded in agreement in the gray light now leaking through the cloud cover. There was going to be no splendid sunrise this morning, only gradual daylight in which they could first of all make out the tumbledown houses in the village, then the fields at the bottom of the valley, then the valley's far wall, finally the snowcapped peaks to the north and south of them.

"Yesterday I thought all this was beautiful," Baker observed ruefully. "Amazing how sore feet and a stiff shoulder interfere with one's enjoyment of scenery. You think we can trust Aga Akbar? I don't like the way he keeps harping about his people not getting any missiles while he knows damn well that his men are carrying missiles and that they are going to a rival rebel group."

"I think Aga sees the big picture," Winston disagreed. "He knows these weapons are needed more in the interior, where the Russians won't be expecting them, than here, close to the Pakistan border. I think we can depend on him. We don't have any other choice now."

Turner said nothing, but it was clear from the look on his face that he was placing his trust in no one—certainly not in Baker and Winston. Turner had been overruled back in Washington on this weapons business. He had willingly volunteered to accompany Baker and Winston on an information-gathering mission into Soviet-occupied Afghanistan and knew that he was being sent along to keep the other two from doing something dumb. It had been Baker who suggested that since they were going in, why go in empty-handed? Bring in armaments, bring out information. No point in wasting the first leg of the mission when they could be doing something useful. Turner had pointed out that reconnaissance and delivery of matériel were two different aims and that if you tried to combine them, one would interfere with the other—the end result being that you would neither deliver the weapons nor gather much information. For reconnaissance you needed mobility, which you lost if you were loaded down with a weapons delivery. For delivery of matériel you needed a secured supply route, which they obviously did not have into the interior of Afghanistan. Turner's solution was to bring the weapons across the border from Pakistan and leave the distribution to the Afghans themselves.

This made good sense, except that Turner was not allowing for one thing—the Nanticoke Institute, now that it had decided to deliver weapons, was not going to deliver the weapons to any old Afghan rebels. The think-tank intellectuals had their own star rebel, and no one else would do. This was a young tribal leader named Gul Daoud, who had proved himself less a Moslem fanatic and more a pro-Western anticommunist.

"What we can't allow ourselves to forget," a bald-headed professor with rimless spectacles and manicured fingernails said, "is that the Afghans are Moslems and that some of their leaders are pro-Khomeini and others grow poppies for opium. Those are not the ones we want to see with our weapons."

"What the hell does it matter who he is, so long as he

aims the thing at the Russians?" Don Turner wanted to know. "It makes no difference to a missile who fires it up some Russian asshole."

Turner was the only one who used impolite words in the sacred precincts of the Nanticoke Institute, a privilege allowed the battle-hardened veteran. But the thinkers had it all thought out—the weapons had to be delivered to Gul Daoud in person, with the compliments of the Nanticoke Institute! Turner could go along or he could stay home. Put that way, Don Turner had no choice. What they were going to do was foolish, but a fifty-four-year-old retired soldier doesn't get too many offers, so of course he went. And here he was. With two college twerps who had read all the books but couldn't hit a barn door with a shotgun at twenty yards.

At first Baker and the others could see nothing. Aga Akbar pointed at some place invisible to the Americans, at something he could see near the top of a boulder-strewn hill to the northwest. Aga laughed at their bewilderment. The rest of the Afghans also seemed highly pleased that the Americans could discern nothing on the scrubby rocky hillside. They climbed the hill slowly, breathless from the thin mountain air. Patches of old gray snow lay like litter among the stones, even as new grass sprouted greenly in the valleys only a few hundred feet below. Massive cloud banks lay pressed against distant jagged peaks. The sky was blue and empty, but all of them knew, as they humped their loads up the steep hill, that in a matter of seconds a gunship or jet might catch them in the open with only a few boulders for shelter on a barren hillside.

Baker and the other two saw nothing that stood out from anything else until they were almost on top of the perimeter of the fortifications and armed men emerged out of the ground practically in front of their noses. At first sight the trenches, breastworks, and bunkers looked carelessly and haphazardly built, but it was all to avoid a pattern easily seen from the air. The men were unsmiling and watchful, making no effort to welcome Aga's men. There seemed to be only a barely concealed friction between them, as if they had no liking for each other but hated the Russians more.

Aga spoke to a tall, heavy man with a bushy beard, dressed in three or four coats of different colors. He reminded Baker of a middle-aged hippie.

"This one's a real shifty-looking bastard," Baker said to Winston. "See the way he keeps taking sneaky looks in our direction."

"Man's only sizing us up. Can't blame him for that."

Aga parted with two sizable bundles of Pakistan rupees, and the big man handed the money to others, who immediately squatted down and rapidly counted the notes. Aga came across to the three Americans.

"This is Sayad Jan, headman of this place," Aga said. "I have bought six asses to carry the weapons—no more backbreaking work for you. He will send three men with you to the next stage. I am sorry but no one speaks English. But they understand everything. You will stay here tonight and leave at dawn. Now I and my men must go. From here we can reach a border crossing by nightfall and reach safe territory in darkness—it's a shortcut we could not take with the weapons. We must go now. I hope I will see you again. May Allah watch over your journey."

Aga watched the Americans shake each of his men's hands in turn. Allah would need to be very merciful if they were ever to see freedom again. Aga had done his best to try to make them less conspicuous, but they had not cooperated. Now that Baker had grown a dark beard, if he had worn the local costume, he might not have attracted immediate attention wherever he went. But what was he, Aga, to do with a big brawny black man and the other one who kept his head uncovered, his hair clipped short, and his face shaved clean? Those two might as well carry little American flags on sticks so they could wave them at the Russian helicopters.

Baker strode back and forth, back and forth. "Fucking asses. Donkeys, no less. What do we do when a Soviet gunship comes? You know what we're going to look like standing on some bare hill with six asses loaded down with missiles? What do we do? Shout at them to sink to their knees?"

"That's camels," Winston clarified.

"Right. Asses don't do anything except move their ears. They're too stupid." Baker looked at Turner. "I'm beginning to see that you were right, Don, when you said the weapons will weigh us down too much and restrict our movements. You might also have mentioned that they will make clay pigeons out of us."

Turner ignored him.

Winston said, "Don warned us, all right. Fact is, he was right and we were wrong. What do you want us to do, Don? David is right about it being crazy for us to drag asses loaded down with shit across these mountains."

"If we run into trouble," Turner said in an unconcerned voice, "we can always give the stuff away. We won't have no trouble getting them missiles off our hands. Donkeys and weapons is all the style here."

The three slept that night at the mouth of a bunker with the weapons inside. Like Aga's men, Sayad Jan's troops looked greedily at the mysterious six-foot-long cylinders and square boxes shrouded in camouflage nylon casing. That these weapons were being given by the Americans to another tribe, rather than their own, was probably an added annoyance. When Baker suggested that they take turns at keeping watch during the night, Turner told him that he wasn't going to lose any sleep over the weapons and that if Sayad Jan tried to take them, he was not going to stop him. Baker and Winston were too tired to really care anymore at this point, and they, too, sacked out for the night.

Yet it was Turner who slept light enough to hear, over the snores of the other two, the rasp of a footstep in the darkness. He did not move. Holding his head still, he darted his eyes back and forth to try to see something. He heard another rasp of a boot on soil—and nearly leapt up when something moved directly above him. But Turner checked himself and didn't move a limb. He saw now what was happening. Sayad Jan's men were quietly stepping over their sleeping bodies, going into the dugout and sneaking back out again with the missiles. When the Americans woke next morning, everything would be gone, and of course, no one would have seen anything. Maybe they'd blame the Russians for it. Turner silently pulled the zipper down inside his sleeping bag and reached for his Marine Corps combat knife. . . .

An Afghan toting a four-foot-long missile in his arms stepped carefully over Turner on his way out of the bunker. Turner shot his arm up and pressed the point of the blade into the Afghan's groin—not hard enough to cut flesh but with sufficient enough force to let him know that the message was urgent. The tribesman froze in midstep over the prone American. The other Afghans could not see Turner's extended arm and the threatening knife. Not able to make any sound in case they would wake the sleeping men, they quietly tried to push their way past their immobilized comrade.

Turner snapped on his flashlight inside his sleeping bag, and keeping the beam covered, he eased out of the bag fast so that he stood alongside the Afghan holding the missile. He switched the combat knife from the man's groin to his throat and kicked back the top of the sleeping bag from over the flashlight. The beam caught the flash of steel across the tribesman's throat. Turner knocked the man's headdress off and yanked back on his long, greasy hair to expose his throat in a sacrificial offering to the knife. The other Afghans could see everything clearly in the flashlight beam.

"You mountain motherfuckers, you put back all that stuff where you found it, y'hear?"

The Afghans did not need anyone to translate what Turner meant. They hustled back into the bunker with weapons they had been removing. In his hurry one of them stood on Baker's hand. All Baker did was moan and roll over. At least it stopped his snoring.

Turner had one of them take the missile from the hostage's arms and replace it in the bunker. He figured that although everything seemed to be there, they may have managed to sneak off some of the pieces before he woke up. There was nothing he could do about that. He could see the Afghans grinning at him in the flashlight beam. No doubt they regarded anything they had gotten away with as hard-earned and were not about to return it because he said so. He released the blade from the tribesman's throat and let go of his hair. The man scooped up his headdress and slapped it over the top of his head, as if he were covering something indecent and obscene. Then he smiled politely at Turner and left, along with the other tribesmen.

Baker was snoring again. Winston had never stopped. Turner thought about savagely kicking them but only laughed quietly to himself instead. Both of the younger men had been patronizing to him on the climb here. "You making out okay, Don?" and, "Need a hand on this slope, Don?" or, "Watch your footing here." Now the two young, red-blooded macho men were asleep like babes in the wood while a battered leather-skinned old soldier like himself had to take care of business.

He'd let that pair of snot-nosed kids hear about this tomorrow. Then again, maybe he wouldn't.

"Hey, Turner, you look like death warmed over," Winston said. "You have bad dreams during the night?"

Don Turner was too busy shaving to bother to reply. His shaving soap would not lather properly in the icy mountain water, and he scraped his straightedge razor along his bristly jawbone.

"You going to be all right, Don?" Baker asked in his patronizing tone, talking as the young jock to the old guy over the hill.

Turner ignored him.

"Shit! We're missing two missiles and one launcher," Winston called from inside the bunker.

"Sayad Jan's men took them," Turner said, and paused to scrape his upper lip. "Don't raise a fuss. Let's just get out of here as quick as we can with what we've still got."

Winston and Baker exchanged a look. It was dawning on them that things might not be running smoothly and that maybe they had missed out on something.

"All right," Winston agreed. "We can skip their Afghan breakfast and open our C rations when we get on the trail. That way we can get the animals loaded and move out of here within the hour. Where is everybody?"

The sun had risen. Although the valleys and cliffs all around them were still shrouded in mist, they could see the blue sky seeping through the gray vapor floating over their heads. It was going to be a clear day. Yet there were no men moving around among the stone-reinforced network of trenches, dugouts, and bunkers on the hillside.

"Maybe they've gone on a sortie against the Russians," Baker suggested.

"And were too polite to disturb us before they left?" Winston added doubtfully. "Where's the three men they promised us?"

Turner stared in his stainless-steel mirror and went on shaving.

"We can't go anywhere without those three men," Winston went on. "They know the way, they know the language. We can't go on without them."

"I can," Turner said.

"How?" Winston challenged.

"Find them six donkeys, tie this shit onto them, and head north-northwest into them hills. Simple as that. Either them three tribesmen show themselves when they see us go or they don't. Nothing much we can do about it. This is their turf and they do what they please on it. Things work a bit different out here in the real world than they do around a long table in the Nanticoke Institute. You boys are going to see some things out here that the professors back in D.C. never knew existed. That's why they sent you. So it's time you forgot about what you been told and start thinking for yourselves. These people up here don't have Pepsi, Kleenex, or TV."

"They've got Adidas running shoes," Baker said with a grin.

"Yeah, and they got combat boots and fatigues, too, but that don't make them think like you and me—if ever you two and me think alike, which can't be too often." Turner rinsed off his face before saying, "If both of you scruffy types are done with your morning wash, let's move out fast."

They found a group of asses tethered on the far side of the fortifications. They took six that had bridles and carrying harnesses on their backs. It took them more than two hours to balance the loads on the animals' backs and tie them securely in place so they wouldn't slip beneath the animals' bellies or otherwise shift in motion. The three men changed from hilarious laughter at each other's efforts to frustrated curses and back again to laughter. During all this time they never saw an Afghan. Although the trenches appeared deserted, the three Americans did not believe they were and so made no attempt to explore them. Winston and Baker saw the wisdom of Turner's advice—get the hell out while they could, without trying to stir up trouble for themselves or hanging around for it to find them.

As soon as the loads were secured, the three men checked their Kalashnikov assault rifles. These were old AK-47 models that they had bought in a Pakistan marketplace for the equivalent of fifteen hundred dollars each. Baker and Winston's pieces were battered, their mechanisms smooth from use. Turner's rifle wasn't any newer, but it hardly had been used. The poor fit of the gun's components and the sloppy finish had not been worn easy through use. Turner had to file away burrs from the magazine well and from some of the magazines to enhance reloading speed. They checked their thirty-round detachable box magazines before moving out and pushed their 9mm SIG-Sauer P220 pistols in their belts. These pistols were made by a Swiss firm in Germany because of Switzerland's strict arms export laws. They carried no American weapons, except for Turner's Marine Corps combat knife, and they figured that this hardly constituted direct U.S. arms aid to the rebels.

The animals went easy enough, head to tail, once they got them on the trail. Turner walked alongside the lead ass, Winston was rear guard, and Baker kept an eye on everything in between. The path zigzagged down the bare, rocky hillside from the fortifications. Turner periodically paused to check his map and compass, which wasn't necessary, since there was only one path in a northwesterly direction, and the six beasts of burden plodded steadily along it as if they, at least, had no doubts about where they were going.

They came down off the hill and followed the trail along the bottom of a valley where weeds grew high in what once had been small fields. There was no sign of life, only some crows or ravens that lifted off when they neared them, cawing loudly. The sun was high now in the blindingly blue sky and gleaming on the snows of the far-off peaks that they could glimpse occasionally from the valley bottom. When they saw a group of men some distance in front of them, Don Turner tried to slow the lead ass to a stop. The animal snapped at him with its large, yellow, chisel-shaped teeth and shouldered past him, followed by the five others.

Don cocked his AK-47, ground his teeth, and yelled at the lead donkey, "If it didn't take us so long to load you, ya skinful of shit, I'd drop you in your tracks. And the others are so stupid, they'd probably fall over you rather than stop." He kicked a passing donkey in the rump. "This whole fucking mess is unbelievable. We don't have to worry about no Russians—these jerk-off tribesman will waste us before any commies do."

Both Winston and Baker were surprised at Turner's sudden verbosity. The donkeys plodded relentlessly onward. The other two men cocked their AK-47 rifles. Hanging by a strap from their right shoulders, the gun could be fired from the hip at split-second notice. Turner glanced back at the other two, and it was clear that he was as much concerned about being shot in the back by his less experienced buddies as he was by the unmoving group of Afghans ahead. When they came closer, they saw that Sayad Jan stood at the front of this group of nine or ten men and that to one side another man lay on the ground, covering them with a light machine gun. The gun's barrel was raised on a bipod and was fed from a drum magazine beneath it, which might contain as much as seventy-five or a hundred rounds. It wasn't going to be much of a shooting match, but Turner swore quietly that he would nail the son of a bitch behind the machine gun if it was the last thing he did, which it probably would be.

The line of six loaded donkeys moved past the group of men along the path, but Sayad Jan stepped in the way of the three Americans. There as an uneasy standoff for a few seconds as the Afghans eyed the Americans and the three outgunned Americans tried to show that they could not be separated from their property so easily. Then Sayad Jan began speaking to them in an impassioned voice that rose and fell with his excitement. The Americans recognized the name Gul Daoud, but those were about the only words spoken by Sayad Jan that they could understand. Every time the headman mentioned Gul Daoud, the leader to whom the Americans hoped to deliver the weapons, he contorted his face with disgust, sometimes spitting on the ground, and, soon after, tapped his own chest with an approving smile. It did not take a genius to understand that Sayad Jan had a low opinion of Gul Daoud and a high opinion of himself and that consequently there was no doubt in his mind as to which of them could put the weapons to best use. Meanwhile the asses had disappeared around a bend in the mountain path.

"Looks like we just been relieved of our goods," Winston summed up. "Only question now is do we want to fight about it, and I think they're way ahead of us on that score too."

"Let's go quietly," Baker suggested.

Turner wouldn't budge. "These fucks ain't going to walk all over me. If we let them do this to us easy, we're not going to last long in these mountains. If we don't get the weapons back, they have to give us something in payment for them. Maybe an armed escort to Gul Daoud."

Baker and Winston agreed, and Turner went into a long harangue with Sayad Jan, pointing repeatedly to armed tribesmen, to himself and to the other two Americans, then to the mountains in the northwest, shouting, "Gul Daoud, Gul Daoud. We need nine of your armed men to go with us to Gul Daoud, you mountain moron." Sayad Jan either did not understand him or pretended not to, and yelled back at him, scowling or spitting every time he mentioned Gul Daoud's name and tapping himself on the chest with his self-congratulatory smile.

"This is probably something he can keep up for three days," Baker warned Turner.

"He's going to have to," Turner said, snarling. "The asses may be a hundred miles away by then, but he's going to have to give me satisfaction for having taken them."

The other two watched in surprise as the usually silent Turner repeated his demands over and over, accompanied by increasingly vehement obscenities. Sayad Jan showed no signs of relenting, though it was plain that he had to have understood the American's demands by now. The two men were still shouting each other down when something like a huge invisible snake rustled across the rocky ground close to them, its trail marked by spurts of dust and the sudden whine of bullets ricocheting off stone. One of the tribesmen went down with three dime-size red holes in a straight line across his chest. Then, in the same instant, they heard the gunship and saw its door gunner lining them up for another cut. They threw themselves down as the machine gunner sewed another seam of bullets across the ground, this time curling up two of the Afghans into howling balls of agony, twisting and kicking in the dust.

"Shithead commie," Turner growled, and loosed off his AK-47, which he had been primed up to use at a half second's notice, anyway.

The door gunner's head and shoulders flopped down over his weapon. They could see one of his arms hanging loose. By now the tribesman with the light machine gun had twisted it around. He sprayed the chopper. The pilot jerked his gunship up and down to evade the fire, maneuvering it from a side-on position to nose-on, in order to line up his rocket pods on them. But in turning to face them nose-on, the pilot exposed himself more fully to their fire. He desperately lost altitude in sudden drops and regained altitude in fast jumps to the left or right. The Russian gunship launched one rocket at them, a wild shot that exploded harmlessly a long way behind them. Then the Afghan's light machine gun splintered the chopper's plastic bubble into pieces on top of the pilot and copilot. This broke the Russian fly-boy's nerve, and he lifted his machine out of harm's way behind a massive shoulder of rock.

Two more gunships appeared out of nowhere. Before they could begin strafing or fire their rockets, the three Americans and the Afghan tribesmen had time to scramble back into a jumble of big boulders at the lower lip of an old landslide. The two gunships whapped into them with rockets, a pair from each ship, but all these did was crack open some of the boulders and send blasts of loose stones hurtling through the air. The men on the ground kept their heads down and got off with a few scratches and minor burns. Then the gunships swung sideways and raked the rocky landscape with their flex guns. The Afghan with the light machine gun emptied a couple of drums at the choppers, but they kept changing their hover levels, and their powerful guns forced him into only occasional short bursts from the cover of rocks.

Sayad Jan ran like a crazy man from rock to rock, the Russian gunners ripping the stone into white powder with a tearing staccato of bullets. He spoke a few words in each man's ear and moved on to the next. When he came to Baker, he twisted one hand above his head like a chopper rotor, pointed to his feet, made a small jump, and waved his Kalashnikov in the American's face. Baker nodded urgently that he understood.

He yelled to the other two, not far away. "Russian bastards want to keep us pinned down here while they land troops to take us on the ground."

The Afghans were already moving out, under the covering fire of the light machine gunner, who had now abandoned all caution and was trying to match Turner's feat of taking out a door gunner on one of the gunships. He didn't succeed, but he kept the two choppers from coming in close enough to prevent all ground movement.

Baker and Winston followed Turner. Bullets zinged off the rocks around them as they ran from cover to cover, not wasting time firing at the gunships but trying to keep solid rock between them and the door gunners. Baker and Winston blindly followed at first, believing that Turner was leading them to safety. In an instant of horror they realized that they were not running but attacking! It was too late now to back off—they had to keep going.

Three Russian slicks were unloading personnel. Two were settled on the landing zone, a small, naturally level area on the rocky, scrubby slope, and the third was hovering to the rear with no room to touch down till one of the others lifted off. It hovered thirty feet up with armed men in fatigues standing out on its skids, ready to go. Turner blew two of them off with a burst of fire from his AK-47, and they toppled headlong to the ground below. Baker knocked some of the men to their knees in the slick's doorway, and Winston drew zigzag lines across the bubble and either hit the pilot or took out one of the controls, causing the chopper to nose down. The stricken machine swung wildly sideways, losing altitude fast. The main rotor hit the ground, each blade snapping on contact, and the chopper's carcass thumped on the rocks like a landed fish.

Baker and Winston were kind of surprised that it didn't explode into flames, like downed choppers always did on TV. The three Americans cut down the men trying to crawl out of the wreck. They had forgotten all about the other Russians already on the ground from the other two slicks. Their blood was roused—they no longer thought of themselves as vulnerable; they no longer thought of themselves at all. They were now instruments of death against the Soviet invaders, fighting as much out of their own personal rage as for Afghan freedom. Lucky for the Americans, Sayad Jan and his men kept these Soviet troopers occupied.

One of the two slicks on the landing zone lifted off maybe fifteen feet into the air, but then landed again immediately. Maybe the pilot got radio orders to put down. The other chopper stayed where it was, resting on its skids on the ground, its rotors turning and whipping up dust. The gunships were nowhere in sight, leaving the firefight to the Soviet troops on the ground.

"The Russians are backing off!" Turner yelled to Winston and Baker. "They're going to be evacuated—they just want to fight their way back to the choppers. I say we go look for them goddam burros while the Russkies are keeping Sayad Jan busy."

The three Americans crawled on their bellies away from the firefight. The Russians, disciplined and trained, were moving to the slicks quickly and methodically, covering their rear. The mountain tribesmen were whooping and yelling and firing wildly. All the same, they nailed at least four of the Russian soldiers, whose companions dragged them away by the armpits, their heels leaving long lines in the dust.

Turner and the others found the asses farther along the path, being watched by an Afghan kid with a World War II

British Enfield rifle. Turner pointed at him and then back toward where Sayad Jan was. The two choppers had lifted off, and the tribesmen were firing up at them with their rifles. As the kid left to go back the three gunships came in for rocket runs. After ripping up the terrain for a while, they left without spotting the place where the six asses stood immobile.

Baker was impressed by the animals' wisdom in not moving. "A horse would have panicked and bolted. You think they're trained to keep still or is it instinct?"

Winston said, "I think they're scared so stupid, they've plain forgot how to run."

Turner was already moving out, poking the lead animal in the ribs with his rifle muzzle. When this ass moved, the other five obediently followed him. The Americans just kept going, leaving everything that had happened behind them.

But this was too much to hope for. Where the path rounded a big block of smooth, bare rock, they saw Sayad Jan and nine or ten men ahead of them, just like they had seen him before, with one of the tribesmen on his belly off to one side, training his light machine gun on them. The asses marched on. The Americans cocked their freshly loaded AK-47s. No one spoke a word.

Once again Sayad Jan let the six animals pass and stopped the three Americans—but this time to shake their hands, embrace them, and kiss their cheeks. He nodded to three of his men, who immediately went alongside the asses. The Americans waved farewell and hurried to catch up with the asses and their three-man escort.

One of the Afghans who was to travel with them gave Turner a toothy smile out of his unkempt beard. Turner nodded to him in recognition. He was the one Turner had held hostage in the middle of the knight with a knife to his crotch.

CHAPTER 2

What Mike Campbell knew about jet fighters could fit on the head of a pin. But Glasseyes McGee told him to keep his mouth shut and look wise. That would impress everyone. Mike was Glasseyes's guest aboard the U.S.S. *Constellation*, listed as "a civilian aviation consultant." The big Navy aircraft carrier was some hundreds of miles out in the Pacific from San Diego. Mike was just along for the cruise, as was his friend McGee. Commander Carlton McGee wore his nickname "Glasseyes" on the breast patch of his flight suit when he was in Arizona, but here on the carrier he wore regulation khakis. It wasn't hard to figure that McGee had earned the name from the fact that his eyes were about as warm and expressive as those of a long-dead fish from the deep freeze. He had flown carrier-based Navy fighters in Vietnam, but Mike hadn't known him there. They'd met when McGee was commander, as he still was, of the Bandits, a squadron that used Soviet tactics in mock combat with Navy flyers over the Arizona deserts. The Bandits used Soviet MIGs, which had come into American hands in various ways; French Mirages; rented Israeli Kfir-

Cis; old F-5s and A-4s; anything unfamiliar in order to give the pilots the feel of operating against strange aircraft with unknown capabilities.

"Some of the hotshot young pilots think they can take on anything—until they meet us," McGee had once told Campbell. "We kinda go a little out of our way to give 'em a surprise or two."

Campbell had once picked up a lost pilot in the desert who had ejected before crashing as a result of one of McGee's "surprises." The commander thanked him personally and, a few months later, telephoned Mike at his trailer-camp home to join a desert search for another downed pilot. Mike found him. Since that time Glasseyes had used Campbell's extensive knowledge of the desert terrain in many of his mock combats and genuine rescues. This "cruise" on the carrier was the Navy's way of saying thanks to Mike, even if the Navy was not informed that it was doing so. Since Glasseyes himself was a guest also, with no duties to perform, Mike was company for him.

Although the two men had gotten to know each other well over the years, McGee never questioned Campbell about what he did with himself. He knew, of course, that Campbell had been a colonel in the Green Berets and had made a name for himself in 'Nam, only quitting the armed forces in disgust at the fall of Saigon. Mike guessed that McGee knew all about his activities as a mercenary. He suspected that McGee, like some other military personnel he knew, was playing it cool for the time being with the intention of joining Mike on some missions after retirement. Mike knew how men like McGee feared the emptiness of their lives after being put out to pasture by the armed forces. If he had ever said anything, Campbell would have told him he was fooling himself to think he could be a merc. No doubt McGee would have his own strong opinions on this subject, but since he never gave Campbell any indication that he had heard rumors of him being a soldier of fortune, Mike said nothing.

Mike Campbell was tall and lean, maybe in his late thirties or early forties. His face was deeply tanned and heavily lined, and his calm gray eyes were in contrast to his active, restless manner. Most of the small, sharp scars on his neck and arms had been caused by shrapnel. A career officer in the Special Forces, Campbell had done back-to-back tours in Vietnam. As a colonel, he had led special missions and search-and-destroy forays all over Southeast Asia, earning the name "Mad Mike" in the process. When Saigon had been threatened after the main U.S. troop withdrawals, Campbell had energetically campaigned to go back in and this time do it the soldier's way instead of the politician's. He was ordered to shut up and shine his buttons. Instead he resigned and went free-lance.

Mike's first mission as a mercenary also ended in disaster. He fought against Cubans and local communists in the African republic of Angola, which had recently gained its independence from Portugal after a long struggle. Campbell had been lucky to escape alive after the CIA gave up on Holden Roberto and withdrew its support. Jonas Savimbi, who was not dependent on the CIA, continued to fight against the Cubans, but Roberto's men were scattered and killed. After that Mike swore he would work for no one but himself, and he saw that he had to scale down his operations so that he could keep them under his control. And he had stuck by these hard-earned decisions. He had stayed away from big, ambitious, heroic, but doomed efforts, concentrating instead on goals achievable by a small force. He had been in other parts of Africa, Central and South America, the Middle East, Asia—even back to postwar Vietnam. Nowadays his legend as a soldier of fortune was even greater than his rep had been as a Green Beret colonel. Mike cared for none of this. He was publicity-shy, an undercover operator—his idea was to be in and out with the job done before anybody realized what was happening. The last thing he needed was his picture in the paper.

The sun was completing a magnificent setting below the Pacific horizon as an elevator platform near them lifted an F-14 Tomcat from belowdecks. Five more Tomcats followed, then six F/A-18 Hornets, which were tiny in comparison to the Tomcats.

"Those big Tomcats show up real good on enemy radar," Glasseyes told Mike. "The Hornets are much harder to detect and are much more recent. That Tomcat wingspan is sixty-four feet, though, of course, it's a swing-wing aircraft. Those variable-sweep wings have small, movable foreplane surfaces housed inside the leading-edge roots of the fixed portion of the wings, and these can be extended forward into the airstream as the main wings swing backward during flight, which eases the pressure. I've flown Tomcats a number of times. Along with the Hornets, they're the Navy's official fighter planes. They would intercept any aircraft threatening this carrier."

"What's the Tomcat's combat radius?" Mike asked.

"About four hundred and fifty miles. It's armed with one M61-A1 Vulcan 20mm multibarrel cannon with six hundred and seventy-five rounds, in the port side of the lower front fuselage. Pylons beneath the fixed portion of the wings and recessed stations under the fuselage carry the air-to-air missiles." He pointed out the various locations to Mike. "It carries Phoenix, Sparrow, and Sidewinder in various combinations; for example, four Sparrow and four Sidewinder, or you could have six Phoenix and two Sidewinder."

"Six Phoenix?"

"Sure," McGee said. "The computer-controlled radar and weapons system can take on six separate airborne targets simultaneously and can detect targets out as far as a hundred miles. The pilot could shoot down six enemy aircraft all at once and become an air ace in a matter of seconds."

Mike laughed. "I've heard talk that the Phoenix is not all it's cracked up to be. They say it hasn't been tested properly under combat conditions."

"The missiles cost a million bucks each, so the guys ain't exactly encouraged to pop 'em off to see how well they work. The Sparrow is radar-guided, and it costs an arm and a leg too. So it all comes down to the heat-seeking Sidewinder for normal use. It was Tomcats using the Sidewinder that knocked those Libyan jets into the Mediterranean."

While Mike circled one of the big fighters admiringly, McGee came to him with someone, introduced them, and said, "Bill will be our LSO."

"LSO?" Mike asked.

"Landing signal officer," Bill said, obviously surprised at Mike's puzzlement.

Mike remembered what McGee had told him about shutting up and looking wise. "Of course," he said, shaking his head at himself for not remembering something as simple as LSO.

It truly did not dawn on Campbell that McGee intended to night-fly one of the Tomcats with Campbell along as his crew until McGee suggested that they suit up and head for the ready room where the pilots wait for their call. Then he began to fully understand the banter Glasseyes was exchanging with some of the pilots. It seemed that McGee and some of his experienced pilots in the Bandits had given some of the carrier pilots a rough time in mock combat over the Arizona desert. Now the carrier Tomcat pilots had challenged McGee to show his stuff by making a faultless night landing on the carrier. This was the supreme test of a Navy flyer, something that was not expected of any Air Force pilot. Mike fully understood the term LSO now. Bill, as their landing signal officer, would be guiding them in to the carrier by radio. It did not take much imagination for Mike to visualize the mess a high-speed jet could make of itself and its crew in a botched landing on the carrier deck. McGee was out of practice. What was he trying to prove by taking on these younger guys who flew off the carrier every day? This was just the sort of reckless bravado that Mike avoided. If he could have walked away from it, he would have. Trouble was, he had no place to walk away to on a ship, even a big one like this carrier. He had to see it through. He could not back out now.

"You said you've flown Tomcats before this?" Mike asked hopefully.

"Sure. When they're not on carrier duty, they're based at Miramar, near San Diego, and I've taken them up from there. I haven't flown one from a carrier, though, and it's been years since I've done a night carrier landing."

That was what Mike was afraid of hearing. He cursed McGee silently and wondered whether this whole thing had just come up after they had come on board, or whether it had been a long-standing challenge. If it had been premeditated, why the hell hadn't McGee taken one of his Bandit pilots along instead of Mike? Maybe none of them would go.

Campbell hardly knew what was going on during takeoff. He was forced back in his seat as the plane rocketed off the carrier, saw lights slide by in a blur, and heard meaningless instructions over his headphones. Suddenly they were up in the night sky, the carrier lights receding beneath them. He heard the familiar knocking sound of the landing gear being retracted. McGee was silent, concentrating on his flying, familiarizing himself with his instruments, increasing speed, slowing, swooping about in the pitch blackness. Strapped into his seat, with no landmarks out over the dark ocean, much of the time Mike had no idea which direction was up or down. But he was gaining confidence in Glasseyes's powers as a pilot. He had never been aloft with McGee before and also had never felt the head-lightening, body-pushing maneuvers of a jet fighter. Yet Campbell could feel the smooth motion and confident handling that McGee gave the plane. It was not unlike being in a Ferrari bucket seat with the wheel in the hands of a professional. This was not something Mike would have done from choice, yet now that he was here, he was enjoying it.

"What's the Tomcat's top speed?" he asked Glasseyes over the intercom.

"About 1,450 m.p.h. above 36,000 feet. But that's not the name of the game tonight, Mike. We gotta land this bird on an area about the size of your average carpet, and we do it in darkness at regular airport jet landing speed, from 110 to 135 m.p.h. In order to touch down on that exact spot, I got to come in at exactly the right level. Too high, I won't have enough room and I'll have to abort the landing. Too low and we've got a class A mishap."

"Class A?" Mike inquired.

"Half a million bucks or more damage and/or death."

"When you come in too low—"

"You hit the ramp."

Mike decided to change the subject. "What did you mean when you said you fly Soviet-style tactics over the desert?"

"Well, you have to understand the difference between the American training and the Soviet. Every U.S. fighter pilot has to be very skilled with high-technology aircraft and weapons. He's taught to fly in pairs and to confront any number of enemy aircraft with just these two planes, using his talent, brains, and the latest hardware. The Russians don't take this approach. They put up a dozen aircraft against two. Their planes may not be so sophisticated, but there's more of them. Their pilots may not be so well trained, but they're closely monitored from the ground and blindly follow orders instead of using their own initiative. So we fly kinda dull and uninspired attacks against the hotshots in their Tomcats and Hornets—that's what makes it sting all the more when we beat them."

"So half the pilots with us on the carrier are hoping you make a fool of yourself tonight."

McGee laughed unconcernedly. "We got a few bucks riding on it too. Last I heard, it was three to one against me making a perfect landing."

"I take it the definition of 'perfect' is that you don't smash us like insects into the steel deck."

"Hell, no, it's more skilled than that," Glasseyes said, sounding offended. "There are four steel cables stretched across the deck. If my tail hook catches the third, that's perfect. Or the second, they can't argue. If I catch the first wire, I was coming in too low, and the fourth wire, I was coming in too high. Way too high, I just touch the deck with my wheels and take off again." They had already discussed what happened when the plane was much too low. That was class A. "You were asking how fast this bird went," Glasseyes continued. "Strange thing is that these supersonic planes do all their important things at regular speeds—takeoff, landing, fighting. It's only for getting to the scene fast, or getting the hell out fast, that supersonic capability is useful. That was a mistake the Navy made with its first fast fighters. Everyone thought that the day of the aerial dogfight was over, that now aircraft were only mobile missile launchers. So what happened was that during the first part of the Vietnam war, the Navy was losing one plane for every two enemy aircraft downed. Compare that to the Korean kill ratio, which was seventeen to one, and to World War II, which was fifteen to one. We were down to two to one. So we re-equipped the planes and developed a new pilot training philosophy, with the result that for the second half of the 'Nam conflict the Navy blew twelve MIGs out of the sky for every one of theirs downed."

A stream of instructions came over the radio from the carrier. They were to fly in a holding pattern with the eleven other planes, about twenty miles from the carrier. The planes were called in one by one. All of the first three aircraft aborted their landings, one of them three times. They learned over the radio that the fourth plane in caught the fourth wire from a high approach. Glasseyes and Mike were fifth.

"Look out for the meatball on the port side of the carrier," McGee told Campbell. "If I'm coming in at the right level, we'll see it as a yellow light. Too low, it will look red. Too high, green."

McGee began his approach about ten miles from the carrier's position, at 1,200 feet. Mike noticed that he flew by instruments alone, never once peering anxiously ahead for a sign of the carrier's lights, as Mike was doing.

Bill, the LSO, was talking Glasseyes in over the radio hookup. Three miles out, McGee began his descent. With less than a mile to go, he looked up from his instruments for the first time and checked to make sure that he was lined up with the drop lights at the aft of the carrier.

Mike stared at the meatball, which shone yellow. He wondered momentarily if it was in working order, since he had never seen even a flicker of red or green. Now was not the time to distract the pilot with thoughts like that.

Bill called him down, the wheels touched the deck, and McGee applied full power as he waited for his tail hook to make a trap on a wire. The jolt of the aircraft suddenly hooked at more than 100 m.p.h. pitching them forward and then backward into their seats. Mike heard the declining scream of the engines as Glasseyes cut down the power. They were home.

"Third wire!" McGee announced proudly. "I'm in the money!"

* * *

It was a few minutes before midnight when McGee's Tomcat touched down on the carrier. By chance, at this exact moment, a few minutes before eight A.M. on a cold, wet morning in western Lancashire, an old friend of Mike's, who had accompanied him on many missions, was also busy with a jet fighter. He lay shivering in the long, wet grass, under a low, cloudy sky, at the perimeter of an airfield. If they tested the plane today for ground observation, it would have to be at relatively low altitude because of the low cloud ceiling, which would be ideal for him to get good video footage of maneuvers. He had his bird book and binoculars and had taken the precaution of using a few feet of tape on a lark rising up out of the grass, so that if he was apprehended before he actually filmed the plane, he could claim that he was an ornithologist doing a study of the larks of northern England and that he had just wandered in through a hole in the fence, which, of course, he had not made himself. He could claim no knowledge of anything secret going on in the big red hangar on the other side of the airfield.

Andre Verdoux had been in Warton for a week now, living quietly in a bed-and-breakfast place on a side street. The landlady was a nice-looking widow in her late forties, six or seven years younger than himself, and she developed a great curiosity about his comings and goings. Apparently Warton was not accustomed to visits by French bird-watchers. At least, he was the first one she had seen hereabouts, or so she said. Andre did what was expected of a Frenchman in these parts, and now she visited him in his room every night for a few hours. Besides relieving his frustrations and passing the time very pleasantly, their romantic sessions kept her mouth sealed. When anyone asked what the Frenchman was up to, she responded vaguely, as if he were so insignificant and uninteresting that such a question had never occurred to her. Andre felt he could lie low here for as long as he had to without being discovered. The only problem was that he did not have much time. Results were needed back in France without delay.

This aircraft deal was going to be a big source of rivalry

between France and Britain, much bigger than the Thomson-Plessy communications network rivalry. That was worth maybe $5 billion, while the aircraft could be worth $30 billion and even more. Thomson in France and Plessy in Britain were competing to see which would be the one to supply the Pentagon with a supersophisticated battlefield communications system. With this network a soldier on reconnaissance can draw a map of enemy positions and insert it in a slot of equipment in his jeep. A coded, digital version of this map passes through several mobile radiotelephone exchanges and in seconds is reproduced at HQ miles distant. At the same time dozens of direct-dial messages are coming in from officers in the field, along with other teleprinter messages, which are automatically graded according to urgency. The HQ commander has constantly updated data supplied to him, such as ammo and fuel expenditure and supply. For the first time ever in warfare the commander would know what the hell was happening!

But that was chicken feed in comparison to the aircraft deal. The Euro-fighter could expect a thousand orders worth $15 billion from Western Europe's air forces, plus another fifteen hundred orders from other countries. What made this fighter special was that it would be an unstable aircraft; that is, one that could not fly according to the laws of aerodynamics. The plane would fly by wire, which meant that its wing and tail flaps and its engine thrust would be totally controlled by computer-guided instruments that would make constant rapid readjustments to prevent the craft from breaking up.

The advantages of such a fighter would be enormous. An ordinary stable aircraft is designed to fly in a straight line and has to be forced to climb, dive, or bank. But an unstable fighter would have no steady flight path and could jump in almost any direction with incredible speed, thus outmaneuvering a more conventional aircraft.

British Aerospace, a government-owned firm, and Avions Marcel Dassault, the maker of the Mirage and controlled by the French government, were bitter rivals to see who could come up with the Euro-fighter first and grab all the orders. Needless to say, Andre was working for the French. And for a very fat fee. It was pure and simple greed that urged him to take these videotapes by himself; he didn't want to share with others if he didn't have to. What he was required to do sounded simple enough. The British were testing an unstable aircraft at Warton in Lancashire. Still photos were of no interest since this was a regular British fighter, a Jaguar, destabilized by fattening its wings and adding half a ton of lead in its tail. What the French wanted was either film or videotape of a number of key maneuvers made by this unstable plane.

So Andre got himself a light video camera and a bird book. What had gone wrong during the past week had been nothing he had foreseen. He was a lousy cameraman. He could not keep the speeding, crazily wobbling aircraft in the viewfinder. Everything he had shot so far was valueless because the aircraft kept jumping out of sight in each sequence. Either today would work because the low cloud ceiling would keep the plane in a more restricted area so it could be observed by experts on the ground, or Andre would abandon his solo effort, undo the purse strings, and hire a professional cameraman and a group of men to spirit him around and protect him. If it came to that, Andre would call Mike Campbell and let him put a team together. This would be a change from their usual type of mission, hopefully a bloodless effort and more an espionage stunt than a paramilitary mission. Andre guessed Mike would welcome the challenge of something different. He knew Campbell well, having been on missions with him everywhere from Angola to Vietnam to Nicaragua. Crawling around in the damp English grass just might be one of the few things Mad Mike hadn't ever done! But Andre wasn't ready to split his fee yet. If things worked out this morning, he'd get to keep everything for himself.

The door was being slid open in the big red high-security hangar across the airfield. Tiny figures in white coats or in brown mechanics' overalls moved around swiftly. In a few minutes a little yellow tractor would tow the aircraft out. Andre watched intently from his hiding place in the long grass, ignoring a lark singing its little heart out a short distance away.

He also did not notice something else: two German shepherds bounding along inside the perimeter fence. The animals had sighted him and were eagerly straining after him with little yelps of anticipation. As Verdoux peered through his binoculars at the hangar door, his sharp hearing registered one of these yelps, which were changing now to more deep-throated growls as the two animals neared their prey. He took the binoculars away from his face and glanced around him, listening. He saw the tan fur of the two shepherds coming at him through the high grass. He jumped quickly to his feet with the lead dog no more than fifteen yards away, its jaws agape, the lips peeled back from the long fangs.

Andre had no weapons or even anything that could be used as a weapon, except the wire cutters he had used on the fence. The Frenchman was a cool, fast thinker in an emergency, but even he could think of no way to use a small pair of wire cutters against a trained attack dog. He was wearing a heavy tweed jacket and a gabardine raincoat against the damp cold, and he merely stood where he was, since it was way too late to reach the hole in the fence, waiting to meet the dogs with his left forearm held horizontally before his face.

The lead shepherd took a flying leap at his throat from six feet away. Andre looked at the gaping jaws and glistening teeth, heard the rumbling, savage growl of the beast, and thrust his left forearm between its jaws. He felt the dog's teeth puncture the sleeve of the gabardine raincoat, then pierce the heavy tweed and knife into the flesh of his arm. But it was only the long canines that could penetrate this far, two on the dog's upper jaw, two on its lower. Verdoux's fright deadened the pain.

He looked into the crazed, bloodshot eyes of the dog, its jaws clamped tight on his left forearm, then brought down the edge of his right hand in a sharp karate chop that caught the dog across its muzzle at a point midway between its snout and eyes. The animal's neck snapped, and it hung lifeless for a few moments, its teeth caught in his sleeve.

The second shepherd attacked around the body of the first one. The dog's teeth sank into the side of Verdoux's raincoat. The animal held on to the coat and used its momentum to knock the man off-balance. When Andre fell, the shepherd went for his throat.

He lay on his back while the big dog, forefeet on his chest, repeatedly took savage snaps at his throat. With his injured left forearm under the dog's chin Andre managed to force back its head for a moment. He used that instant to wrap his right forearm over the top of the dog's muzzle, covering the animal's eyes in the process. His right hand grasped his left elbow, and his left hand his right upper arm. He squeezed his forearms tighter together, the dog's muzzle caught in between. Trained to attack, the shepherd made no effort to withdraw its head from this tightening vise until it was too late—its jaws were firmly clamped shut, and it could not extricate its muzzle from between the man's forearms, no matter how hard it pressed down with its paws on his chest and violently shrugged its shoulder muscles and shook its head. Andre lay on his back in the long wet grass and held on.

He let the dog play itself out a bit and tire before he rolled on his right side and applied a scissor lock with his legs just below the animal's rib cage. The dog threshed in agony and died slowly under the constriction.

Winded, hands trembling, Andre Verdoux picked up his video camera, binoculars, and book. He left the two carcasses of the dogs where they lay and this time did not wire up and conceal the hole in the fence after he had passed through. Now there was no way he could conceal the fact that a breach of security had taken place. He examined the teeth punctures in his left forearm as he went and discarded his shredded raincoat. He could be out of Warton in a half hour, and after he reached Liverpool, he'd put in a call to Mike Campbell.

CHAPTER 3

Baker, Winston, and Turner were four days into Afghanistan, four days of constant climbing, descending, picking their way along rocky mountainside paths, weakened by the thin air of the high altitude, as wary and watchful as rabbits as they awaited a sudden attack from the air, ready at a shout or signal to instantly throw themselves facedown on whatever they happened to be walking on, be it snow or sharp-edged broken stones. First their minds had to accept these conditions, and now their bodies were coming around slowly—getting hardened, leaner, toughened. They moved out at sunup and were constantly on the move till sundown, when they lit a fire and made a stew of whatever was available, which they ate with flat cakes of unleavened bread, their only food at times other than the evening meal. Each night they slept where they could and woke shivering from cold before dawn. Yet all three of them were having a great time.

The professors of the Nanticoke Institute had chosen well. The three men now worked as a close-knit team, an outcome that would have surprised many at the beginning of their journey. After Sayad Jan's three-man escort had passed them on to another group, and that group to another, Winston and Baker had impressed Turner with their military analyses of each group's standing against the Russians. Turner saw that these two men, whatever their other faults, had brains and could see things with their trained minds that even he, a combat-hardened veteran, had missed. Baker and Winston, for their part, had begun to learn what no textbook ever taught anyone—that it takes a lot more than brains to survive in an enemy-occupied zone. Their courage, willpower, and good spirits were tested at least several times every day. As the two college men responded well under pressure, Turner became more friendly to them. They in turn learned to respect him for his tough-minded common sense and his experience, things they now saw as essential to their survival and here, in Afghanistan, more valuable by far than a theoretical knowledge of the latest Soviet infantry tactics.

They were now with another guerrilla band, though these seemed to be small farmers first and resistance fighters second. Unlike the men they had met before, these rebels had their women and children still with them, worked their land, and did not operate back and forth across the Pakistan border, being too far from it. The area's headman was too old to fight, they were told, and so whoever happened to be around worked it out among themselves who was leader for any particular clash with Russians or the puppet-government soldiers. Baker, Winston, and Turner were stuck with Mohammed.

Mohammed knew no English, not a word, but that did not stop him from talking to them continually, arguing with them and shaking his head sternly, nodding in smiling agreement with things never said, urging them to follow him.

"I think we got ourselves tied in with the local cowboy," Turner opined.

"Yeah, I think he wants to show us his stuff," Winston said.

Mohammed wanted to show them things, all right. He brought them into a ruined village, similar to the many they had seen before. The people had not fled their land in this case, and they now lived in caves scooped by hand out of banks of earth with a blanket or carpet hung across the opening to keep out the heat and dust. The mutilated were everywhere, hopping or sidling or dragging themselves around. Men, women, and children had one or more feet blown off by the tiny anti-personnel mines dropped randomly by the Soviet planes. Small children had hands blown off by the booby-trapped toys the Russians dropped. The Americans had heard about this dirty warfare against harmless people, young and old, but it was a different thing to see it. Mohammed wasn't such a crazy, after all—he was insisting that they see firsthand what the invaders had done to his people. What the Russians did to other tribesmen in other valleys might not be of so much concern to him, but these were *his* people, this was all that was left of *his* village, and he wanted the Americans to see that.

The asses were loaded, and they set out on the next stage of their journey in the early afternoon, having had to give the beasts of burden longer than usual to rest between their daily hauls. All six animals had been slow and droopy-headed when they arrived the previous day. The plentiful mountain grass and water in this place, along with the rest, had made new animals of them. Instead of being listless and docile, as they had been in their exhausted condition, they were back to being independent and contrary again. Turner swore at them and claimed that was the last grass they'd eat or the last rest they'd take as long as he had control over them. It was true that a few of the animals seemed deliberately to defy Turner on some kind of donkey principle.

Mohammed signaled for everyone to stop. Baker went forward with him and two other men, leaving six Afghans behind with the two Americans and the pack animals. Baker soon saw what this was about. They had to cross a tarred road, which Baker understood, from Mohammed's gesticulations, led to a pass in the mountain range ahead, a pass they, too, would have to use but at a higher, more difficult level than the road and during darkness that night. First they had to cross the road, which Mohammed feared might expose their slow-moving asses to the sight of government or Soviet vehicles. They returned, and Baker explained the problem in English. The Afghan answer to this problem was demonstrated to them. The twelve men divided into six teams of two, one team to each ass. The front man clutched the creature's bridle and attempted to drag it forward at a run, while the rear man beat the animal's rump, in the absence of sticks in that area, with the butt of his Kalashnikov rifle.

Baker had an attack of laughter. "I'm going to play this one up in my report on transportation techniques."

But as soon as they got out into the open and his animal balked, Baker lost his sense of humor. Looking anxiously up and down the road from time to time, he and Winston half pushed and half carried their ass across the tarred surface and heaved it down the slope of a ravine on the far side, where it had to stumble and find its footing. No more than half a minute after they had gotten the six animals and themselves out of sight in the ravine, they heard the roar of a heavy truck pass by on the road above them. This close call highly amused Mohammed and the Afghans.

Baker's sense of humor had totally evaporated by now. "This fucking joker is going to get us wasted, Turner."

Turner didn't bother to respond, being too busy brushing dust off his pant legs.

Two of the Afghans were walking along the ravine bottom with the asses. When the Americans made to follow them, Mohammed urgently beckoned to them to creep up to the side of the road.

"You think they're trying to steal the pack animals?" Baker asked Turner as they went where Mohammed directed, and crouched out of sight of the road behind loose rock.

He heard the metallic scrape of Turner cocking his AK-47 and took this as an answer that Turner thought this might be what was going on.

When Baker saw Mohammed load a rifle grenade, he began to change his mind.

Winston knew it. "It's an M60 HEAT. You see the slim, streamlined shape, the round-nosed body, and the rounded stabilizing fins? The Yugoslavs make them, and they're the only weapon of this type that a communist country makes well. The Polish PGN-60 ain't worth shit. But this baby has a range of a hundred and fifty meters. I think that's an old M48 rifle he's using."

They waited. Mohammed gestured to them from his hiding place, and Baker, who had a talent for interpreting sign language, explained to the others, "He's very excited for some reason about that truck or whatever it was that passed. From what I understand it's only when the Russians are feeling very confident that they allow vehicles to travel singly on this road. He desperately seems to want to show us something, and it's not just him blowing up a truck. I can't understand what he's trying to tell me, though. But I don't believe they're keeping us here in order to steal the asses."

"I was hoping they were," Winston muttered.

They waited for another twenty minutes before they heard anything. A truck came traveling north at high speed. Mohammed waited till it was less than eighty yards away before he fired the rifle grenade, which hit the truck square in the radiator. The antitank grenade blew the engine off its bearings and knocked it into the roadway almost opposite, where the three Americans were concealed. White-hot fragments of metal emerged from the blinding white-and-yellow flash of the explosion and skittered off the rocks around them.

The engineless truck rolled down the road a way. When it stopped, soldiers poured out of the back of the canvas-covered vehicle. The Americans were about to fire on them as they leapt over the tailgate onto the road, until they noticed that Mohammed and his men were not firing. The soldiers were not ethnic Russians. They appeared to be Afghans but had military-style haircuts and no tribal headdresses. When they walked on the road, they had the unmistakable gait of city dwellers in the countryside.

The soldiers from the disabled truck began to stack their rifles by the roadside and threw ammunition, pistols, and other gear on the ground beside them. Then they walked back into the middle of the road and shouted slogans and raised their fists in the air. Mohammed and his men chanted back the same slogans and raised their fists. After that, the disarmed soldiers set out on foot along the road.

Mohammed winked at the Americans and came over to shake their hands. He sent one man with them to bring them along the ravine to the asses while he and the other eight men went to gather the stacked arms before another vehicle came.

The pathway left the ravine and traveled more or less parallel to the tarred road, sometimes coming very close to it and then veering away again. The ground was bare and dusty from the passage of many feet, and it was obvious that this alternate route was heavily used by people with no wish to meet military vehicles on the road.

At one place where the path neared the road the Afghan walking beside the lead ass's head grabbed his bridle and yanked him to a savage stop. The others piled up behind, and gradually the whole line came to a halt. Ahead, over a roadside bank of earth, the camouflaged canvas roof of a military truck was visible. If they continued on the path, any soldiers with the truck could not miss seeing them. And there was no other route for them to take across the rocky hillsides except this path. One Afghan remained behind to keep the animals still, and the other two stealthily advanced toward the bank of earth, rifles at the ready.

Before Turner could stop them, Winston and Baker had joined the two Afghans in stalking the truck's occupants. Turner cursed silently. The job he had been sent to do here was to stop Winston and Baker from getting involved in things like this. They were here on an intelligence-gathering mission and not to trade lead with the Russians. But since Turner saw that he was too late this time to stop them without causing a dangerous disturbance that might give their presence away, he decided to join them and thereby increase the chance of their success. He was in time to see two Russian soldiers standing next to the truck, talking and smoking—and these were definitely Russian, with high Slavic cheekbones and fair hair—before the two Afghans riddled them with automatic fire. The soldiers clutched their guts, dropped their cigarettes, and crumpled to the tar, one managing a few steps before he fell.

They cautiously made their way around to the back of the

truck. It was filled with cardboard cartons stamped with lettering in the Russian alphabet.

Baker looked them over. "C rations," he said, and then mimed putting food in his mouth for the two Afghans.

One of the tribesmen pointed at Baker, then to the truck, then across the road and down a piece, where there was a steep slope downward for some hundreds of feet. The Afghan twisted an imaginary steering wheel and pointed at himself and the other tribesmen and shook his head. They didn't drive. Baker was pleased to start the truck, drive it down the road a little, and jump out after steering it toward the slope. It caused a miniature landslide down the slope and banged and rattled but stayed on its four wheels till it came to the bottom, where it flipped on its side and scattered some of the cartons.

The Afghans were hiding the soldiers' bodies in the rocks. One remained behind, and the other went back for the asses so they could continue their journey toward the pass.

Aleksei Rybakovich Ustin was taking a peaceful leak among the rocks, following instructions to be modest and not give offense to the locals by pissing in public. His pleasurable relief was strangled by a burst of gunfire from the roadway. He froze, prick in hand. When he heard nothing else after the first burst of automatic fire, he guessed it might be one of his comrades horsing around. But Aleksei had been long enough in Afghanistan—four months—not to make any assumptions. He eased his head slowly around the rock and saw his two comrades lying still, on the road in front of the truck. Two Afghans were looking into the back of the truck, along with—Aleksei could hardly believe this, but there they were, no more than fifty meters away—two white men and a black man, all clearly American.

If he could shoot one, he knew he could demand to be sent home as a reward. He would be a hero. He might even be on television, for he had heard that the newspapers and television back home had begun to admit the existence of this war. It was rumored that so many Soviet soldiers had been killed here—some said more than ten thousand—that

COBRA STRIKE 41

the Party could no longer hope to keep it quiet. He glanced back at the lifeless bodies of his friends, who had been so full of life and jokes such a short time ago. Some Party committeeman would say at a meeting that they had died fulfilling their internationalist duty on Afghan soil. And that would be that. A few bottles of vodka and reminiscences among their friends. That was not going to happen to him! He was going home! Back to Natulya in her warm bed... And these Americans were how he was going to get home. If only he could shoot one. But he had left his rifle in the truck, which, of course, was against regulations, and he had only a pistol against five men with automatic rifles.

He watched one of the Americans ditch the truck and the two Afghans drag his friends' bodies among the rocks. One Afghan stayed behind, and the other left with the Americans. Then he saw a sight that surprised him even further, although he would not have thought it possible. The Americans reappeared with a train of six asses loaded down with camouflage-fabric-covered cylinders that looked very much like some kind of missile to him. This was it! He didn't need a dead one. His information alone was worth an immediate transfer home.

Aleksei thoughtfully put his prick back in. It was an easy thing for a Russian soldier to lose in Afghanistan, and he was going to be needing it for Natulya in a few days time.

Colonel Matveyeva placed the aerial photos on the lieutenant's desk, walked across the office, and gazed out the window at the bare, stony soil that stretched levelly around the barracks. The lieutenant carefully looked at each shot. There were six separate stills that a low-flying jet had taken on two passes over the target at first light that morning. The other fourteen or fifteen photos were all enlargements of details from these six photos. They showed six asses laden with tubular objects, two Afghans, and three American-looking Westerners—two white, one black—exactly as the private had described everything. The lieutenant was pleased to be vindicated after all the fuss he had raised.

"How did these pictures come to be taken, Comrade

Lieutenant?" the colonel asked. "I heard you were responsible."

She had spoken without turning around from the window, and her voice was neutral. Perhaps she was playing a game with him, hoping to make him worry whether he had followed the correct procedure. If this was what she was doing, she was wasting her time. He was an officer, sure, but he was a draftee, just like the private who had started this whole thing, and like him, all he wanted was to be out of this place and out of the army as quickly as he could. So he looked at the way the sunlight from the window outlined the shape of her body, her narrow waist, swelling hips, and long thighs in her military skirt, and he took his time before replying.

"A private who survived an ambush saw them and realized they were heading for the mountain pass to cross through it during the night. He stayed where he was until a truck convoy arrived with a military escort. They radioed in his report. I was on duty and spotted it. I had him flown in by helicopter so I could personally verify the incident. From there it was easy to estimate how far they could have traveled during the night and to locate them by jet on the other side of the pass at first light this morning."

"Has this private ever been abroad before serving in Afghanistan?"

"Never, Comrade Colonel. He's from a small town near Rovno, in the Ukraine. He's never even been to Moscow."

"Interesting," she said, still without turning around. "I asked that because there are some who think this is some kind of deliberate provocation—three very obvious Americans appearing like this in a slow-moving group with weapons. How could they have come this far from the Pakistan border without being observed before this?"

"I don't know, Comrade Colonel."

"Neither do I," she said, finally turning around to face him. "Do you think this private told you the truth about what he saw?"

"Absolutely. He's very proud of himself and is demanding to be sent home without delay as a reward, along with an honorable discharge."

"Offer him a promotion if he stays on here."

"I did," the lieutenant said. "I told him he was sure of making sergeant. He turned that down."

She smiled. "See that he's posted to a barracks near his home. But he has to serve out his time in the army." She came over and sat on the edge of his desk, her skirt hiked up to bare her knees. "He probably has someone at home he's anxious to get back to."

The lieutenant glanced at the smooth skin of her legs and wondered what she was up to. Why would a colonel bother with him when she could have a general?

"Who designated this incident as top priority?" she asked softly.

"I did," he told her firmly. "I thought the chances of it being true were slim but that it was worth making an effort to check out."

She looked at him appraisingly. "Through normal channels this would have taken about three days to get such a decision from career officers. You showed unusual initiative, Comrade Lieutenant."

"Do I get a reward?"

"You want to go home too?"

He nodded.

"We could use officers like you in the Red Army. You would go far if you decided to stay with us." When he said nothing, she sighed and rose from the desk. "I'll see what I can do for your transfer. If we can take these infiltrators alive, you'll be a people's hero and get a good job and a large apartment, even a car. But first we must capture at least one alive. Orders are being sent out to deploy men behind them to cut off all possible escape routes back to Pakistan. With the Soviet Union to the north of Afghanistan, and Iran to the west, they have to head east or south to return to Pakistan. They seem to be heading northwest now. Any idea where they are going?"

"They could be bringing those weapons to any of maybe twenty tribal leaders. But there are so few passable routes, they should not be hard to ambush now that we know they exist."

She nodded. "I want all villages who help them severely punished."

The lieutenant nodded back wearily.

The sergeant in a Pakistan army listening post across the border from Afghanistan placed a sheaf of intercepted messages on the major's desk. "More of the same, sir."

"Nothing new at all?" the major asked.

"No, sir. A lot of them have the exact same wording as the ones I brought earlier. All in everyday codes that they know we can crack in less than an hour. The Russians are going all out on this one, sir, and they don't give a damn who knows."

"But it sounds crazy, Sergeant. I think those three men must be a television team, and all that stuff on the asses' backs is equipment, such as cameras and microphones and so on. You know all the stuff they drag around, making a nuisance of themselves and expecting to be treated like the American ambassador."

"I just heard locally that they bought those missiles in Peshawar, sir," the sergeant said in a respectful voice, as if reluctant to destroy the major's last illusion.

"So they are missiles?"

"Yes, sir. And they are Americans. And they did buy the weapons in Pakistan and transport them across our border."

"The Russians will blame the Pakistan army for allowing this to happen," the major said thoughtfully. "That is why they want to take these Americans alive—so that they can accuse Pakistan."

"Maybe they will be more interested in blaming President Reagan," the sergeant suggested tactfully.

"Of course, you are right! Pakistan is a mere pawn in the game Moscow and Washington play. Tell Abdullah to telephone the American consulate in Peshawar and connect me to Mr. Dobbs. He will want to hear about this."

The six asses were content to lie inside hillside caves all day, out of the glare of the sun, munching on little piles of grass and leaves foraged for them by Baker, Turner, and Winston. They traveled by night—sometimes quite short distances. But according to the local men acting as their guides, they had no other choice. The Russians and government troops were everywhere, questioning people about three Americans, offering rewards, making threats, bombing villages the Americans were thought to have passed through, executing individuals suspected of having helped them. The Russian message was clear—these three Americans were a plague and would bring sorrow and misfortune on everyone who went near them. But it was not the local people they had to worry about, according to Baker's interpretation of the men's signs. It was the soldiers lying in wait for them. They no longer traveled by path at all, trudging instead across rocky slopes in pitch blackness, their guides leading the front ass and the others following. They relied more on hearing than on sight and ended each night trek with bruises and cut legs from banging against unseen rocks. While they were preparing to move out at the onset of darkness for the fourth successive night, a local man came to their hiding place and spoke with the other Afghans. They shook their heads and pointed to the asses. They could not travel tonight.

After a lot of signaling by oil lamp inside the cave, Baker summed it up for the others. "Last night cattle, goats, horses, and asses were shot during the night by helicopters with floodlights. I guess we were lucky they happened not to hit the area we were in at the time. The people hereabouts were warned today to bring in all their livestock tonight. It sounds like the Russians must be using some kind of infrared heat-sensing device and dispatching the gunships to where they pick up signals. The door gunners in the choppers probably just shoot whatever they see for the hell of it. These six asses of ours would give off an awful lot of body heat. If they can pick up a single horse in a field—and that's what they were doing last night—they can hardly miss us. Our Afghan friends here want to stay put, and I can't say I blame them."

So they stayed put in the cave all that night and all the next day. Then the next night and day. Then another night. They were all ready to kill one another by this time. Fortunately the cave was large enough for them to put some distance between themselves and the six animals, but they now had the added restriction of the Afghans pleading with them not to leave the cave by day, even to stretch their muscles and breathe some fresh air. The Russians were conducting sweeps through the hills. They were photographing from the air (by now the three Americans realized they had been photographed by the jet that had swooped down twice on them as they left the mountain pass at first light). They would be safe where they were, even if the Russians or government troops came close, because the cave entrance would be found only by someone who knew where to look.

Cooped up in a dry, dusty cave, with only primitive oil lamps for illumination, Turner, Winston, and Baker succeeded in avoiding arguments with one another, which in a way only served to build up the tension between them and the irritation they all felt with one another. They were prepared to wait the Russians out, if it took them a month, and knew they had the discipline to do so, even if they did take to biting their nails.

On the morning after their third night in the cave, a local man brought news of a rebel victory close by—they had heard the gunfire—in which ten government soldiers had been captured alive. They had learned by then that government troops deserted to the rebels all the time, bringing their weapons with them or just throwing down their weapons and refusing to fight their fellow countrymen, like those they had seen after the truck was hit by the rifle grenade. But these government troops held captive were different. They had been guilty of atrocities, and the local people were demanding that they be executed.

"I think he's come up here to invite us to the execution," Baker said. "One day they say we can't step out of this damn cave to take a breath of air, and the next day they're inviting us, no doubt as guests of honor, to a public execution."

"Ask if they can give us six of them alive," Turner said, sensing an opportunity to break out of their entrapment in the cave. He rapidly explained to Baker and Winston what he wanted. It took Baker a long time to get the Afghans to understand that they needed six of the prisoners, unharmed

COBRA STRIKE 47

and blindfold. The local man left, still puzzled and doubtful. Baker persuaded one of their escort to go with him to make sure they got the men. Turner was already adjusting their small radio receiver and stringing an antenna wire out of the cave mouth.

It was early afternoon before the prisoners began to arrive, brought in one by one, twenty minutes apart, hands bound behind their backs, electrical tape across their eyes. Turner raised a finger to his lips upon the arrival of the first one. He wanted no more English spoken, and within earshot of these prisoners the Afghans knew they were not to mention that Americans were present.

Turner chose the prisoner with the darkest skin to represent Winston and picked two others with light skin. With a scissor he clipped the hair of all three into brush cuts, although Turner himself was the only American with extra short hair. Then he shaved off the mustaches and beards of all three, although both Winston and Baker had two weeks growth of beard by this time. Then he ripped off their clothes with his Marine Corps combat knife, giving each of them a few minor cuts and scrapes. All three prayed aloud to Allah for mercy. Then he forced on them a spare set of his, Baker's, and Winston's clothes. He looked them over critically and nodded with satisfaction in spite of Baker and Winston's smirks.

It was late in the afternoon when the six new asses arrived, and Turner paid generously for them from a wad of Pakistan rupees. He examined the long, empty burlap sacks draped over the animals and put Baker and Winston to filling them with dead grass and whatever they could find. The animals were assembled outside the cave entrance, calling to and being answered by those inside the cave, when a group of Afghans arrived with four bound men who were gagged but not blindfolded. Turner was furious.

"Ask them why they brought them here," he ordered Baker. "They've seen us. I didn't want that."

He watched impatiently as the Afghans gestured to the burlap sacks and Baker waved his arms. "Baker, they can't put those four assholes in the sacks because they'll struggle."

Baker signaled some more and finally shrugged. "They say they won't move. Don't ask me why."

One of the Afghans demonstrated why. He pulled a long blade from under his loose tunic and very casually sliced it across the throat of the prisoner next to him. Spurts of blood leapt out over the crimson blade, and a gallon of it ran down the man's front. His eyes rolled and he fell on his side.

The Afghan with the knife slit up along the leg of the fallen man's pants. He swept the blade in a short, sharp arc, hacked twice, and lifted out the man's penis and testicles in a single blood-dripping lump. This he stuffed in his victim's mouth.

Turner heard Winston behind him gag, then vomit. He glanced at Baker, who was as white as a sheet.

The Afghans carefully inserted the mutilated corpse into a sack, tied the neck, and lifted it onto an ass's back.

Turner felt sorry for the other three men who had to stand and see what was in store for them. They were gagged, but their eyes expressed the agony of their terror. The man with the blade went about his work as methodically as a pork butcher, stopping to laugh and light a cigarette and, from time to time, winking at his American friends for whom he was clearly putting on this special show.

Turner said in a low, nasty voice. "This is a big chance for you students of war to do a little fieldwork."

Winston and Baker said nothing.

When all four prisoners were cut and bagged, Turner led the other six out from inside the cave. Their hands were still bound behind them, and electrical tape covered their eyes. Kalashnikovs hanging from their shoulders, Turner and Winston set out with the Afghans and the six asses. Baker stayed behind to watch over the missiles and their own asses, still safely stashed in the cave. They came to the edge of a broad, low valley after a twenty-minute walk, and one of the Afghans pointed. A group of military vehicles was clustered on the far side of the valley floor.

Turner studied them through binoculars. "Tents. Armored personnel carriers. And Russians." He watched some more in silence. "They're Russkies, all right. No sign of Afghans there. This looks good."

Turner nodded to the Afghans, and he and Winston concealed themselves behind rocks. The Afghans stripped the tape roughly from the men's eyes, which made them howl. Then he cut loose their wrists. They put headdresses on the three unshaven prisoners and left the three "Americans" bareheaded. Four of the Afghans held sniper rifles with telescopic sights on them as they marched the six asses across the valley. Turner noticed the bloodstains on four of the sacks. The Russians soon saw the men and animals, and a vehicle came out to meet them.

Turner said, "Chances are those dumb Russians have never seen a real American in their lives and won't be able to understand what those six are saying. Maybe they'll think they're talking English! We only need a few hours to slip out of here."

Back at the cave, they loaded the missiles on the asses while Baker, who spoke Russian, monitored the radio channels to see if that Soviet unit announced its capture of what had been reported to be Americans with missiles. Just a few hours of confusion...

CHAPTER 4

When Mike Campbell first went to live in the Arizona desert, he'd hoped to find a deserted rancho in a lonely box canyon which he could fix up. But desert is desert, and he found very little of anything in the scrubby lands. Then he met Tina. Like a sensible, practical woman, she refused to live without electricity and running water and with only coyotes, rattlesnakes, and cactus for company. Mike refused to live in a town. So they made a temporary compromise by buying a mobile home and setting it up in a trailer camp a way out in the desert. Most people there were retired couples who now devoted their lives to growing miniature lawns in the desert and to keeping alive sickly shrubs imported from Michigan or New Jersey or wherever they had spent their working lives. Campbell's prolonged periods of inactivity and then sudden disappearances for weeks on end led to a lot of talk. The general agreement was that he was a criminal of some sort, with various factions favoring particular activities such as drug smuggler, hitman, seller of Mexican babies. They were lavish in their sympathy for Tina being stuck with such a brute, while trying to pry information from her. Born in Arizona, Tina had cousins and friends all around, and the trailer camp folk's constant gossip and questions amused her more often than annoyed her.

The truth was that she had no more idea than they did of where Mike went and what he did there. She knew, of course, that he was a merc and that each time he left he was leaving for war and that she might never see him again. Some of the old Southwest lingered in her attitude in that she did not find it odd that women stayed home and worried while their men did crazy, dangerous things. She knew Mike told her nothing in order to protect her. And it had to be nothing. She never even knew what continent he was leaving for. None of Mike's associates, even his close friend Andre Verdoux, knew her name or where to find her. A couple of times each day, Mike checked with a phone-answering service in Phoenix for urgent messages, and he picked up his mail there once a week.

That was plenty of contact for him with the outside world. Increasingly he had come to enjoy near solitude, except for Tina and his nosy neighbors in the trailer camp. They bugged Tina but mostly let him alone. They knew he practiced with automatic weapons out on the desert and still remembered with gratitude the time he single-handedly chased off a marauding biker gang from the trailer camp with a machine gun. The retired folk felt they hadn't too much to worry about alone out on the desert, so long as Campbell was around, though this did not stop them from bitching about his not earning a decent, straightforward, nine-to-five living.

When Campbell got back from his week-long cruise on the aircraft carrier, there were a half dozen phone messages from Andre Verdoux at the answering service. Mike drove twenty miles to a tavern, loaded the box with quarters, and phoned England, only to be told that Andre was not in his hotel room at the moment. A few drinks and one hour later, Mike phoned again and this time got him.

Andre was brief and careful about how he worded things. When he had finished telling Mike what he had been doing and what had happened to him, culminating in the dog attack at the airfield, he mentioned the finances and suggested, "You might consider coming here, Mike, with some of your associates. I can supply the two cameramen from this side. I don't think any special equipment will be needed, apart from a few standard pieces, which should be fairly easy to obtain in Liverpool. Three men and yourself should be enough. No need to bring the Aussie."

"I'm confused, Andre." Mike's voice was humorous, yet had an edge to it. "Is this your mission or mine?"

Andre paused. "Well, if you come in on it, you're the chief."

"Then I'll be the one who decides how many go and whether or not the Aussie goes, won't I?" Mike was not going to tolerate the continuing feud between Andre and Australian Bob Murphy.

"All right, Mike, you call the shots," the Frenchman said in his accented colloquial English. "I suppose I will have to consider myself lucky if you include me."

"I also want to put things together over here, not in England."

Andre did not want this, but he could not argue with the logic he knew was behind it. A merc mission was best organized far from the field of operation, so that when the team arrived, they knew what their roles were and more or less what would be expected of them. To bring in an unorganized group of men and to try to set things up in the field of acton was to court disaster. Even though this photography thing would hopefully be a noncombat mission, Andre knew Mike would organize it as if they were going inside the Kremlin. That was how Campbell succeeded where others failed.

"Mike, I'm in a big hurry with this. It would be much quicker if you and the others could come straight to Liverpool. We could go to the Lake District or the Yorkshire moors, even the Scottish Highlands, to get ourselves in shape—"

Mike interrupted, "I want a look at everyone before we ship out, not after. You know how it's done, Andre. Give me a call in three days time, I'll give you the meeting place, and we'll be ready to move out one week after that. Ten days. I can't do better than that and you know it."

Andre knew it.

Mike hung up and dug more quarters from the supply he had brought with him. He had left one other number to call from this public phone because he did not like the sound of it. A Mr. Lowell from the Nanticoke Institute in Washington, D.C.

Lowell took some time to come to the phone. "Mr. Campbell? Good of you to return my call. Could you spare us one day of your time as a consultant? For a fee, of course."

"In about a month's time I'd be pleased to, Mr. Lowell."

"I was thinking about tomorrow."

"Sorry."

"I forgot to mention the fee, Mr. Campbell. Five thousand dollars. Can any of us turn down that for a single day's work?"

"It's tempting."

"You will have to leave this evening in order to join us for breakfast at eight tomorrow. Tonight you will find a room reserved in your name at the Hay-Adams Hotel, across from the White House on Lafayette Square. In the morning a car will be sent to fetch you at seven-fifteen sharp."

Mike guessed that everything about Lowell would be sharp. He replaced the receiver. His curiosity was aroused, and five thou was five thou. One thing sure, this Nanticoke Institute, whatever it was, was too much of a big spender to be federal government. He thought for a moment about bringing Tina with him for the trip, then realized that this thing could not be as clean, safe, and aboveboard as Lowell had made it sound. No one paid five thousand dollars for that.

Campbell buttered his toast and let the distinguished-looking gents at the long table have a good look at him. There were thirteen of them nibbling toast, sipping coffee, and chatting the usual "in" talk of long-familiar colleagues in the workplace. Although there had been no introductions, Campbell recognized two of them from newspaper photos or TV. Plainly they were all "experts" of one sort or another, the kind never elected to anything but who seemed to run the country all the same. Lowell, gaunt, skin like parchment, his hands trembling, sat beside him but never said a word to him. Mike worked on his toast, butter, and grape jelly and left it to them to get things going. He smiled a little to himself at the thought that these egghead professors might think they could intimidate him by ignoring him in the stately surroundings of this breakfast room. The ceiling high above the long table had plaster decorations, marble busts of grim-faced men stood in alcoves, the service was silver, and the waiters were formal, and at one end of the vast room hung a huge painting of someone in a cocked hat on a rearing white horse, holding his sword in the air, leading his troops into battle. Mike thought that the place should have been good for scrambled eggs at least, if not eggs Benedict, but all they were served was this well-done toast and very so-so coffee.

Lowell began the presentation without warning in the form of a loud, one-sided conversation with Campbell. He referred to the three members of the Nanticoke Institute in Afghanistan as "fine young men who had gone there on a goodwill mission."

Lowell concluded his account by saying, "It is simply out of loyalty to these fine young men that the Institute is trying to organize a clandestine rescue party to get them out and, of course, for the good name of America."

Mike looked at his coffee cup and said slowly, "This stinks of a government mission gone sour. What's your relationship with the CIA?"

"Since this incident we've been on very cool terms with the gentlemen at Langley," Lowell answered in his precise voice. "We did not consult them before sending our three men in, which they now regard as a breach of etiquette."

"Is this Institute a CIA front?" Mike asked.

"Certainly not. No doubt some members of the Institute are also members of the CIA or NSA. I wouldn't know."

"What did you send the three to Afghanistan for?"

"To study conditions there."

Mike smiled at the evasiveness of this answer. "I'll be frank with you. It sounds to me like you deliberately sent in those people to have them trapped and caught by the

Russians. Right now I'm second-guessing you to try to figure out why you did that. And why you want to involve me."

Lowell looked angry, but a heavy man on the opposite side of the table laughed and said, "I think it's reasonable for you to suspect us of some convoluted conspiracy in which things that seem to be one thing turn out to be another. Yet you would be surprised at how easy it is for clever men, confident of their own abilities, to do something stupid and irresponsible. But that is what we did, and now we are trying to extricate ourselves with a minimum of damage to the Institute and, of course, to our own precious reputations."

Mike was satisfied with the sincerity of this answer. He next asked, "Were your men armed?"

"They may have smuggled in a few rifles and sidearms in a spirit of youthful irresponsibility," Lowell said hurriedly at Campbell's side.

Mike looked across the table at the heavy man. He said, "They brought in missiles. Not U.S. manufacture, but all the same, we don't want them caught with them."

"The Institute has no official knowledge of this," Lowell added primly, "and certainly does not condone its members carrying out such activities."

"Just as you would not hire mercenaries to rescue them," Mike suggested.

"Exactly," Lowell agreed without a trace of humor. "Mounting a clandestine rescue effort to free these fine young men is an entirely different approach."

"Suppose they can be located but not rescued."

"Then they will have to be terminated in such a way that their remains cannot be identified," Lowell said in his stiff voice.

Mike looked across the table at the heavy man to see if he would disagree, but the man looked away from him.

Now Mike had the truth of the offer: Rescue them if possible; if not, scorch them into the dirt before the Russians can use them. It was not the three men who were to be saved as much as the reputation of the Nanticoke Institute.

Mike sighed and played with his coffee cup. "A million dollars," he said.

Campbell returned to Arizona that evening with the matter resolved in his mind. He would go to Afghanistan after he completed a prior commitment. His team would be ready in three weeks to a month. The professors hadn't liked this at all. They couldn't see why their problems weren't more important than everybody else's. All Mike would say was that he was committed to a mission but that he would do theirs back to back with it since the first mission would probably go easily. He wouldn't tell them where or what it was, and he left the mansion and walled grounds of the Nanticoke Institute under a cloud of disapproval, which didn't keep Mike awake that night back in Arizona with Tina.

She was kind of surprised to see him show up so soon. He had left to make some phone calls and had been gone only a day and a half. Sometimes it was for six weeks. He went to a shopping center with her next morning and fixed things around the mobile home in the afternoon—always a sign that he was having the guilts. Tina wondered whether it was another woman or because he was leaving again soon and would be away for a while. She hated it when he was gone for a long time, but when he came home, it was almost worth it because he was loving and peaceable. It was when he was around and inactive for months on end that he became almost impossible to live with. So she took what came and hoped for the best.

Tina picked up the phone when it rang, listened for a moment, and said, "For you. He says it's Andre."

Campbell's eyes flickered with anger at a merc phoning him here. How had Andre gotten the number?

"They picked me up coming through Kennedy Airport," Verdoux's familiar French-accented voice told him. "I've been given no reason and have been locked in a tiny windowless room for five hours now. Then a gentleman arrived and gave me a piece of paper with your name and this number on it. I'm standing at a private phone I'm sure is tapped. I've no idea what's going on. Have you?"

"What's the name of the man who gave you my number?"

"Oh, yes. He left a card. Here it is. T. D. Lowell, Nanticoke Institute. Mean anything to you?"

"Who did you tell I was going to work with you?" Mike asked.

"No one. Except the two cameramen. I had to persuade them by assuring them of protection. I said Mad Mike Campbell would look out for them. The Frenchman hadn't heard of you, but the American cameraman had."

"You bet. He also reported back home, which is why you are being held."

"The pig!"

"I'm afraid Mr. Lowell wants his mission to take priority over yours, and he seems to have certain powers of persuasion," Campbell said. "What do you say?"

"Can I come?"

Mike laughed. Andre Verdoux was an old soldier who wanted to go to war, and it no longer mattered very much to him which war.

The Russians reacted like Turner guessed they would. After sending the three fake Americans along with the three other Afghan puppet-government soldiers and six loaded asses into the Soviet encampment, Turner, Winston, and Baker hurried back to the cave. While Winston and Turner loaded their asses with the missiles, Baker monitored the Russian-language broadcasts on the radio. What they were listening for came soon: the proud boast of the Soviet unit that it had captured the three wanted Americans. Other transmitters picked up the news right away, and the relief could be heard in the tone of the Russian voices.

"The pressure must have been hard on the bastards to find us," Baker said in an almost sympathetic tone. "Wait till they find they've made a mistake."

"They might find that out sooner than we think," Turner snapped. "Let's move out while we can. It's dark enough now, and we can make a few miles while the Russians are still relaxing and congratulating themselves. We could have all night to travel if the Russians decide to kick the shit out of their 'American' prisoners and the three Afghans with them, instead of questioning them. Either way, we better make tracks."

They gained a little more than an hour before the first warning transmittal came through, and then it was only a caution rather than a warning that the Americans were still loose. Apparently the Russians were finding the bad news hard to believe. Baker had the radio strapped on the donkey next to him, with its loose wire antenna extended forward to the donkey in front. Confusion continued. Reports were denied, then confirmed, only to be denied again. There was more resentment than urgency in the voices over the radio, and it was plain to Baker that it would be some time yet before Soviet troops close to them on the ground started an earnest search for them. Having kept on the move all night, they managed to clear the exit of the mountain pass. Now they were in open country again and would be much harder to locate, even traveling by known trails. They spent the daylight hours hiding in a gully and covered a lot of ground the next night. Gul Daoud's men escorted them from there, traveling now by daylight and consequently traveling much greater distances with relative ease. After two days of backbreaking trekking, they reached Daoud's territory. All three of the Americans looked at one another with genuine surprise. They had made it.

Gul Daoud was tall, skinny, bearded, and looked a little like Abe Lincoln with a heavy tan. He spoke good English and told the three Americans that they had just achieved what his own men rarely had.

"We have never brought in anything nearly as big as this," he said admiringly of the missiles. "I didn't think it could be done."

Baker was interested in Daoud's accent. "There's only one place on earth you could learn to speak English like you do, and that's New York City."

Gul grinned. "I bet you never knew us Afghans are big in the fast-food business in New York. Like the Koreans are taking over selling vegetables, the Afghans are moving into the grilled chicken business. One man started it all. He was an engineer from Afghanistan, and the only job he could find was as a cook in a fried chicken place. He saved his money, developed a recipe for his own special sauce, and then opened his own place after a few years. It succeeded, and he opened others. Then he helped other newly arrived immigrants by giving them jobs in his places, and in time they went out on their own. For a long time in New York, the only English I knew was words having to with chicken parts."

He smiled. "I never really learned the language until I fell in love with a girl who spoke only English. We were just about to get married, and I had qualified for a bank loan to open my own chicken place when my father and eldest brother were killed by the filthy Russians. I still did not come back here. I was the youngest. I said they don't need me, I have two older brothers here. Then another brother was killed. I said I will come back for a short time—only on a visit. I delayed my wedding and the buying of my store. I swore I would be back in two months. I really thought at that time I would.

"While I was here, my last remaining brother lost his right leg to a Soviet anti-personnel mine. He survived but could not fight anymore. My father had been headman of this region, then each of my brothers in turn; now it passed to me. Everyone looked at me to know what to do next. I tried to tell them about what I wanted to do in America, but they could not understand why I would want to marry a Christian girl who did not even speak our language when I could pick and choose from the prettiest girls in the mountains and make an important alliance with a powerful family through my marriage. They could not understand why Chase Manhattan Bank wanted to give me money to cook chickens for people—why couldn't they cook their own chickens? But really the question they were asking was this: Has the Daoud family, famous for its warriors and leaders, produced a coward and a weakling youngest son? My mother and sisters did not reproach me, my brother was too sick to care. But the people in the fields and on the roads avoided me until they knew whether I would run away or stand and fight.

"Since then, as I think you have heard, I have been making up for my slow beginning. I am the Russians' public enemy number one, as your FBI would say. So long as I am free and alive to continue to fight against the invaders, I am a hero and a symbol of resistance for everyone in Afghanistan. But I often wake up alone in the middle of the night and wonder how someone who really wants to open a fast-food chicken outlet in the Bronx can be a rebel hero to fierce mountain tribal warriors."

The three Americans liked Gul, and he showed his gratitude to them for the missiles through his hospitality. Winston admitted to having wanted to dump the missiles and said he now thought it was worth the effort to bring them all the way to Gul Daoud. Turner suggested that if Gul got back to New York City and ran for mayor, Turner would vote for him in the unlikely event that he happened to be living there. This was by far the biggest compliment Baker and Winston had ever heard Turner make about anyone, living or dead.

The military situation was desperate. Gul told them, "A Soviet helicopter unit has established on a plain a base that controls this region. Their engineers are now building an airstrip to allow MIG fighters to refuel and Antonov transports to fly in supplies. If they get that airstrip completed and fortified, they will be able to drive every Afghan rebel from this whole area and use it as a stepping-stone to put pressure on other places inaccessible to them up to now. It's not just my turf that is in danger here—though that's an important propaganda element in it for both sides—it's the question of whether this entire part of Afghanistan can successfully resist the Soviet war machine or whether it will crumble and be ground under. If we go under, no one can hope to hold out. If we succeed, everyone will gain hope from our example and fight all the harder."

"So we have to take out that Soviet base," Winston concluded.

Gul Daoud looked at him with interest. "You're here to fight?"

"No way," Turner put in. "I'm here to keep these two suckers outta trouble."

"We'll go along and just watch," Winston conceded.

The missiles had been unloaded and the asses set free to

COBRA STRIKE   61

find grazing where they could. The big missiles, which made Gul Daoud's eyes gleam, were eight DKZ-B free-flight projectiles, each a little more than six feet long and a hundred pounds in weight.

Gul Daoud hardly bothered with the SAM-7s they had brought also, saying only, "They are no good against very fast jets, and when the gunships keep very low, we can't hit them, either. This is why we ask for the American Red Eye or the British Blowpipe."

They knew that the Soviet-made SAM-7 heat-seeking surface-to-air missile was limited by its lack of radar target acquisition and the small size of its warhead. It could also be easily outmaneuvered by alert pilots or diverted by flares or metallic chaff dropped by the target craft. Still, it was Russian-made, easily bought, and Uncle Sam could not be held responsible for its presence in the hands of the rebels. There was poetic justice in using Russian-made weapons against the Russian invaders. On finally counting the missiles, they found that Sayad Jan's men had stolen three SAM-7 missiles and one launcher but none of the DKZ-Bs, which were the real prize.

"Up to this, we've never been able to get near the Russian chopper landing zone," Gul Daoud explained. "They are able to see us five miles away across the bare valley floor. We have had nothing to hit them with from that distance, and they have had lots of time to counterattack before we could get within range of them. Now they are so confident, they are putting up buildings and laying down a runway for their jets. But the DKZ-Bs you brought us will change all that." He glanced at his watch. "Time we were going."

Each man picked his burden—one of the eight six-foot, hundred-pound rockets or one of the two eight-foot launching tubes, which each weighed about fifty pounds, or one of the two folded tripod mounts for the tubes, each about three feet long and weighing sixty pounds. The Americans and the Afghans toted their loads along winding paths in the dry, stony hills, sweating like pigs under the blazing sun. A path led them through a narrow gorge and out onto an arid valley floor covered with small stones and knee-high scrub.

"Snake country," Baker said grimly.

Gul Daoud nodded.

No one had to point out the Russian installation to them. It was a cluster of cinder-block huts in the middle of the valley, next to a chopper LZ with maybe forty gunships and slicks parked in rows of four. Yellow bulldozers crawled slowly nearby, gouging the earth with steel jaws and blades, presumably clearing and leveling it for the jet runway.

"It's impossible to gauge the distance," Baker muttered, squinting his eyes. "Five miles is as good a guess as any, and it's nicely in range for our DKZ-Bs."

"Yeah, I can see how they'd pick you guys off if you tried to cross this scrub to get at them," Winston drawled. "If the snakes didn't get you first, them Russians would."

Gul Daoud nodded. "You can fire from here? Good. I will get my men ready. They are behind those hills."

Winston and Baker went to work mounting the tubes on their tripods while Turner growled and complained that this was the strangest fucking "intelligence-gathering" mission that he'd ever been on. He also said that the Nanticoke Institute had made a mistake in thinking that idiots could gather intelligence. Winston and Baker ignored him, and he shut up fast when he saw the expert way in which these two greenhorns handled the Soviet equipment. They knew what they were doing, much to Turner's surprise. Another thing that Turner noticed was that the Afghans all seemed to know exactly what these missiles were capable of, perhaps through having been at the wrong end of the launcher tubes previously.

The Soviet DKZ-B missile launcher was really only a single tube taken from the well-known truck-mounted BM21 multiple-tube rocket launcher. Obviously the single tube could be taken into back country while the multiple-tube configuraton was limited mostly to easily accessible territory in friendly hands. These HE fragmentation missiles had the longest range of all single-shot launcher missiles, about seven miles.

The two Americans set the nose-mounted fuse of each missile to explode on impact instead of delayed-action detonation. Then they checked each missile's folding stabilizing fins, the six jet nozzles set in the base, and the small lug, up from the base, that imparted spin to the missile by catching in the rifling of the launcher tube. This rifling, along with the panoramic sight and fitted quadrant, gave the launcher better accuracy than most rocket and missile tubes and allowed reasonable shooting at relatively large targets at long ranges. With a missile fitted in each tube, and the tube's angle of elevation carefully calculated, Baker and Winston waited for Gul Daoud to return. The Afghans helping them were now openly excited, laughing among themselves and occasionally shouting fierce-sounding things at the Russians far across the valley. When Gul Daoud showed, they quieted and watched in tense anticipation. Gul nodded to the two Americans, and Baker counted to three.

The 122mm missiles left the tubes in a roar of flame and smoky exhaust, two dark pencils of death streaking across the sky above the valley floor. The Afghans stuffed two new missiles into the launchers while the first pair were still in flight. Baker and Winston hung back, waiting to see the point of impact of their first shot before deciding whether an aim adjustment was needed. Winston's missile hit the runway, lifting a yellow bulldozer up into the air and throwing it against the side of the cinder-block building. The impact of the heavy machine caused the wall to collapse, which made the roof crumple and collapse into the interior.

Baker's missile landed among the parked choppers, its exploding warhead disintegrating the helicopters nearest the point of impact. The force of the blast knocked over the choppers it did not destroy, snapping off their rotors as they keeled over. The Afghans raised a great roar as they saw the Russians' air capability destroyed with a single shot.

They did not adjust the aim, knowing that the kick from the first shots had slightly adjusted the angle of the tube on the tripod mount, anyway. The third and fourth missiles landed among the buildings and raised debris in the air. The fifth, fired by Winston, struck the middle of the longest cinder-block building. They saw the orange ball of its blast expand, shattering and melting the structure, only to be dwarfed by a much larger orange ball of flame it had initiated, then another and another.

They could feel the shock waves on their cheeks, traveling through the air across the valley from the chain of huge explosions triggered by the DKZ-B missile.

"That had to be their ammo *and* fuel dump," Turner murmured with reverence.

The seventh missile was a dud. It flew, its warhead did not explode, but the sixth and eighth projectiles carried safely their load of death and destruction into the Soviet installation five miles away across the valley floor.

Gul Daoud raised his right hand above his head. At this signal sixty or seventy mounted tribal warriors galloped their horses from behind the hills, waving their AK-47s and yelling like a Comanche war party in an old Western movie.

"What the fuck is this?" Turner snarled. "They going to ride in a circle around the commies like in Custard's last stand?"

"Yes," Baker answered. "Except this time we get to be the Indians."

There was no way Turner could have prevented Baker and Winston from going, except by shooting them down, which even he had to admit was not the best way to protect them from harm, although it had a lot to be said for it otherwise, in his opinion. Turner was beginning to lose the team spirit that had united them for a while and was getting back to looking on himself as the reluctant watchdog for two unruly half-wits who were geniuses with textbooks and instruction manuals but had the street smarts of kindergarten graduates. He mumbled some obscenities as he put his foot in the stirrup and threw his other leg over the back of a horse being held for him. Winston and Baker were already way ahead of him, galloping across the scrub-covered valley floor toward the burning Soviet installation, whacking their horses and whooping and waving their AK-47s in a pretty good imitation of the approved Afghan mountain style.

The crowd of horsemen raised a huge plume of dust behind them as they crossed the valley toward the even bigger column of black smoke rising into the clear mountain air above the burning installation. The tribesmen raced one another to get there first, and little more than halfway there—after about three miles—the fiercest young warriors on the finest horses had left the main crowd of horsemen behind. Gul Daoud and two of his lieutenants hung back deliberately to stay with the Americans, for whom breakneck riding over rock rubble and thorn scrub was a new experience. Baker and Winston had quieted down their war cries by this time and were concentrating on staying in the saddle.

A small group of Russians pulled away from the wreckage in an open jeep-style vehicle. Some of the lead riders branched off to give chase, their horses making slightly better time than the jeep over the rough terrain, so that they slowly gained on the escaping Russians and would catch up with them if their horses did not tire or something else interfere. The other leading riders galloped straight toward the destroyed installation, trying to best one another to see which of them would be first man to ride into it. An explosion snapped the front legs and ripped open the belly of the lead horse. Its rider was thrown, and he was unlucky enough to land headfirst on another mine, which severed his head from his shoulders and rolled it like a wet ball in the dust. When it lay still, grime coated the open eyeballs and unmoving lips.

The second and third horses were too close behind the first to avoid the mine field, and the two mines detonated by the first horse and rider panicked their two horses beyond the control of their riders. One horse bolted and killed itself and its rider within ten yards. The other threw its rider and was destroyed when it, too, tripped a mine. The thrown rider tiptoed out of the mine field with fear-widened eyes and a prayer to Allah on his lips. He made it out safely, promptly forgot his prayers, and went back to cursing the Russians.

The other horsemen had time to rein in and circle the installment, looking for a way in through what was probably a nearly closed ring of protective mine fields. The hard, stony ground had tire tracks in several places that appeared to lead into the camp, but the Afghans knew that these tracks would have been deliberately made before the mines were laid down and that only one or two entrances would have been left clear for travel.

The other group of lead riders were closing in on the jeep. When one Russian tried to operate the machine gun mounted in the rear of the vehicle, he was picked off by a sharpshooter and fell over on top of the weapon. Another Afghan rider drilled the Russian driver in the back of the head, and the jeep slid sideways and its engine stalled. Before the other Russians could pull the dead men off either the steering wheel or the machine gun, the Afghans had the vehicle surrounded and, from horseback, looked down their rifle barrels at the four surviving Russians, three enlisted men, and an officer. The Russians raised their hands and tried to look like decent friendly guys who were there by mistake.

By the time the advance horseman brought back their four captives and the vehicle, the main body of horsemen, including Gul Daoud and the three Americans, had arrived outside the installation. They were taking sporadic rifle fire from inside, nothing heavy, and were responding and keeping their horses moving to avoid presenting themselves as stationary targets.

"Officers are more cowardly than regular soldiers," Daoud said with a sneer. "Sit this Russian captain on the hood of the jeep, tie his ankles to the front fender, free his hands, and let him point out a safe route into their camp."

Baker started to protest that this was against the international rules of warfare. Gul Daoud seemed genuinely suprised to hear that any such rules were in existence and ignored Baker, of course. Gul lined the three Soviet enlisted men abreast behind the jeep, in case its four tires missed any mines in its path. The captain did a good job directing the Afghan driver after Gul promised him, in quite good Russian, that he and his men would be handed over to the International Red Cross for transporation to Switzerland after being displayed first to Western reporters. The captain said he wanted to go to Canada.

"No problem," Gul told him. "From Switzerland you can go to Paris if you want. Canada. Hollywood. Wherever you like."

The captain led them safely inside where it soon became apparent that the Afghans had no intention of burdening themselves with more prisoners. They did not waste bullets, either; they simply cut the throats of the uninjured or lightly wounded and left the badly wounded to die where they lay. They circulated rapidly, stuffing undamaged weapons, ammo, and supplies into large sacks, which they tied to their saddles. As time passed, they speeded their already feverish pace. In a little more than twenty minutes Gul Daoud gave the signal to leave. By that time, in Baker's estimate, at least one hundred and twenty Russians were dead or mortally wounded, perhaps as many as a hundred and eighty, with only four survivors. While the Afghans killed and looted, the three Americans worked to one side on the bulldozing equipment, placing charges of plastic explosive at vulnerable points in the heavy structures. The detonations damaged the equipment beyond repair. They had time to divide their remaining supply of *plastique* into the relatively small charges needed to explode the fuel tanks of the lightly damaged choppers. They set these off as a farewell fireworks display.

Nearly all the horsemen made it across the valley floor into the protection of the hills before the first wave of MIG fighters hit. The only riders caught in the open were those escorting the four Soviet servicemen in their jeep. One of the seven planes in the second wave of fighters scored a direct hit on the jeep with a rocket, instantly frying all four of his fellow countrymen. Then the first wave of fighters hit again, scattering the horsemen.

Not far away, behind the cover of big rocks, Gul Daoud shrugged at the three Americans. "You Yanks'd do anything to free American hostages. Now you see for yourselves that these Russians would sacrifice four of their own to deprive us of a single jeep."

CHAPTER 5

The gun show was on the outskirts of Bakersfield, adding maybe sixty or seventy miles on his trip on Route 5 from Los Angeles to San Francisco. As he drove, Lance Hardwick dialed in a temperature of sixty-eight degrees on the Automatic Climate Control system of the Volvo 760-GLE and then fiddled with the graphic equilizer, which balanced the weaker set of front speakers with the forty-watts-per-channel pair in the back. It was like he had Bruce Springsteen singing in the bucket seat beside him, and the band in the backseat, except for the drums, which were halfway up the rear window. He was also doing ninety in the fast lane, depending on his Whistler Spectrum to detect stationary, moving, trigger, even pulsed police radar from behind hills, around curves, or wherever the highway patrol could squeeze into. The Spectrum was his own equipment and not part of the rented Volvo. It flashed a red light when it smelled police radar and clucked like a Geiger counter next to an atomic bomb.

Lance smiled at the idea of a decent sound system on a mission with Mad Mike Campbell. Campbell would have him in a Chevy or a Honda—something unobtrusive. But this was one of Lance's solo jobs, something he kept up in spite of becoming one of Mike's regulars. Maybe it had something to do with him being an actor, or more accurately, an out-of-work actor. He had been used to scuffling for a living. His only so-called acting jobs had been as a stuntman on TV series and low-budget movies. Mostly he had worked as a bodyguard for L.A. rock musicians. It had not turned out as great as he had once hoped, but at least it was sunshine and palm trees—and he was Lance Hardwick with an apartment in West Hollywood instead of being Miroslav Svoboda from Minneapolis. True, when his mother had named him Miroslav, she had expected the family to return to Czechoslovakia, and how was she to know, anyway, hardly talking any English herself at that time, that you couldn't make it in America with a first name like Miroslav. Lance. That was more like it. The other part of his stage name, now his legal name, was a stuntman's joke. And why not? His whole life in a way was a stuntman's joke. Yet his mother had never been able to accept his new name. She still wrote him as Miroslav Svoboda c/o Lance Hardwick. Like Mr. Hyde c/o Dr. Jekyll. But imagine calling a kid Miroslav . . .

Mike Campbell had been a consultant on a war movie in which Lance and others had filled in for the stars when things got rough. He knew Mad Mike by his rep and bugged him for a chance to go on a real-life merc mission. Then, when Mike finally gave him a chance months later, he had almost literally blown the opportunity with cocaine at the training camp before they left. That wasn't so long ago, yet now he looked back on himself then as just a dumb kid.

This mission he had accepted dealt with what he guessed was an even dumber kid, only seventeen. The boy's father was a Los Angeles studio musician Lance had known for years. As a backup and often lead guitarist, he sat in on recording dates with name bands in order to help out on the musical end of things, which was not the strong point of quite a few famous rock bands, and he took instant bucks instead of credit and royalties. Because studio musicians soon lost the drive and desperation to strike out and make a big name for themselves, the work was a treadmill in a way, but a comfortable high-income treadmill with all the perks.

This guitarist's son had dropped out of high school and then disappeared four months previously. He knew his son had at least six thousand dollars and thought he was in Mexico. He heard nothing until five days previously when the phone rang late at night. It was his son's voice, from an outdoor pay phone with trucks passing in the background. His son talked fast in a frightened voice, then hung up the receiver when he saw someone coming—or so his father figured. The boy admitted he had come to grow marijuana, that the plants were in the ground, that his partners wouldn't let him go till after the fall harvest. They had already killed one kid who had stood up to them. He told his father not to come personally for him—reasonable advice since the guitarist was six foot three and his body weighed no more than his long, bushy hair and beard. His son said to find someone tough who knew how to use a gun and to tell him that he was at Noddy's near Alderpoint. His son interrupted himself after a few more words with "I gotta go" and hung up.

The guitarist gave Lance $25,000 and asked if he wanted more. Lance said no. He found Alderpoint on the map off Route 101, less than two hundred miles north of San Francisco. He would have flown to San Francisco and hired a car there were it not for this gun show in Bakersfield, where he knew they would have what he was looking for.

He was in a hurry, having a long way to drive, and so he did not go into the show itself. Three different guys in the parking lot had secondhand MAC-10s for sale. Since they were not new, no government paperwork was involved. Anyway, presumably they had been illegally converted from semi to full automatic; certainly the silencer that came with the one he bought was a homemade job. He also bought a thousand rounds of .45 ACP for the gun and some spare thirty-round detachable box magazines. He was on the road again in less than a half hour and drove north on Route 5 to Oakland, crossed the Bay Bridge to San Francisco, and took the Golden Gate Bridge north again without stopping. It was dusk when he turned west off Route 101 toward Garberville, which was the only sizable town fairly close to Alderpoint.

He found himself a motel, ate a meal, and let a local cadge drinks off him in a tavern. He heard about how the federal government had been financing raids on the local pot growers: For the past two summers cops in fatigues and bulletproof vests carrying automatic weapons had been ferried by choppers into the hills to cut and burn the illegal crops.

"It's too early yet for you to see them," the man at the bar said, " 'cause the plants ain't growed enough yet for them to spot. But even this early in the year we have undercover types floating in and trying to find out what's going on." He paused and gave Lance a long look, as did a couple of other men in peaked caps along the bar.

"It's fine with me if you want to talk about baseball," Lance said.

"We don't have much ball between Frisco and Seattle," the man grumbled. "I wouldn't cross the road to see a game." Lance said nothing, and the man was soon back on his favorite topic. "You see any garden supply stores coming into town?"

"No. It was near dark when I got in."

"When I first arrived here near twenty years ago, there was only one garden supply store. Now there are thirteen. Who do you reckon is doing all this cultivating in a place like this with nothing but mountains and pine trees? Dang right, it's them that used to be hippies, came up here in rags without a dollar or an acre of land to their name, and now they're driving Cherokee wagons and flying planes while they grow that stuff on public land. You stay away from them if you're planning on staying on here for a spell. Some of them's flower children and wouldn't harm no one, but there's others that'd cut your throat as soon as look at you. They got million-dollar businesses out there on those state and federal lands. They been a whole mess of hikers disappearing in these hills in the past few years. There's some who reckon maybe they saw something they weren't meant to see. Hell, you couldn't get some of those game wardens to set foot *near* some of those places back in the hills—and it ain't the grizzlies they're afraid of."

Lance played the dumb tourist a while longer, left before he attracted attention, and got a good night's rest. He drove back toward Route 101 shortly after seven the next morning, and then he took the small, winding blacktop road east off the main highway. Alderpoint was in about twenty miles, on the Eel River, deep in what was known locally as the Green Triangle. The road wound around the mountainsides, and Lance got some nice views down hundreds of feet over the edge. Valleys filled with redwood and pines nestled between jagged peaks. Alderpoint itself was no more than a general store and a tavern named the Bum Steer, along with a few cabins. Lance kept driving till he saw a bearded man in a work shirt and jeans standing by the road, doing nothing in particular. Lance braked. "Noddy's?" The man pointed down the road. Lance waved.

Since hardly anyone lived around this area, it took him some time to inquire and finally get to Noddy's, down a pair of wheel tracks to a cabin deep in the woods. He stayed in the car with the engine running, and after a while, when nobody showed, he tapped the horn lightly a few times. A barrel-chested man with a long mustache came out on the veranda, a shotgun cradled in his right arm.

Lance called out the window, "You Noddy?"

"Could be."

"I'm up from L.A. I'm looking for an opportunity to invest."

"We don't need no investors up here, mister."

Lance smiled. "Tell Tony Wood that an L.A. investor is here."

"Does this Tony Wood know you?"

"Tell Tony the guitar man sent me." Lance took a chance with this, figuring that if Tony was mad at his father, he would not have mentioned him much to anybody.

"Where you staying?"

"I spent last night in Garberville. Some nosy people there. I don't think I'll go back."

Noddy twirled his mustache. "How come you came to me?"

"Man, you're famous."

Noddy could barely repress a pleased smile. "Drive around, then come back in an hour."

Lance drove back along the tire tracks a ways until he saw

COBRA STRIKE

a stand of heavy brush where he could hide the car. He beat the ground with a branch to hide his new tire tracks cutting away from the old. Taking the MAC-10 from the trunk, he pushed a loaded magazine into the magazine well in the pistol-grip handle of the submachine gun. After that he screwed on the silencer and slipped three other full magazines into his pockets. Then he headed back through the trees toward the cabin, keeping off the car tracks.

Before he was near enough to see anything, he heard someone yelling and pleading. Lance quickened his pace through the trees. Noddy sat on the veranda steps, his shotgun across his knees, placidly watching a squat, burly man beat and kick a skinny youth who was shouting that he didn't tell anyone to come to this place and didn't know any guitar man. Lance recognized him from photos he'd seen.

Noddy didn't stir when Lance walked into the clearing with the MAC-10 ready to go. The squat man quit beating the kid and waited to see what was going to happen now. Lance saw the heavy revolver stuck in his waistband, and he guessed that Noddy might be carrying slugs instead of bird shot in that shotgun. They probably had other men in calling distance, and that was a long, dangerous walk back to his car through the trees. Lance thought about killing them but decided it would be dumb to do so with the kid as a witness, in case he decided later, for some reason, to turn on his rescuer.

Lance said to the kid, "You and I are getting outta this place and we're both going to forget we've ever been here."

"They have my money." The kid was getting snotty now that he saw the respectful attention Noddy and other man were giving this dude with the submachine gun. "Make them pay me back before we leave."

"Forget your money, kid," Lance said. "Write it off to experience. You don't remember a thing about this place. Anything that goes wrong here, they will blame you for it, and you may not be as hard to find as you think." Lance said this loud enough for Noddy and the other man to hear. He wanted them to understand that he intended to make this kid keep his mouth shut so there was no need for them to pull some kind of dumb attack to prevent them from leaving. "You learned you shouldn't deal with folks like Noddy, and he learned you got connections and can't hold you here against your will. Both of you are damn fools if you don't let things rest like that."

Noddy didn't move a muscle or say a thing.

But the kid was furious. He said in an undertone to Lance, "Three weeks ago Noddy had an argument with a twenty-year-old guy from Cleveland. We were out in a growing area at the time, putting in seeds. Noddy knocked him down and beat him to death with a stone. One side of his head was all stove in. They left him out in that field till we had finished planting it, as a warning to the rest of us. The body was out there four days, and each morning we'd see more of it gnawed away by animals during the night.

"Noddy picked on me to bury the head and bones and other pieces. He made me do it by myself, which made me figure that maybe I was a marked man too. They might have used me as a slave laborer till harvest time if I didn't give them too much trouble, then get rid of me. We got a flat in the pickup on the way in to Garberville to get supplies, which is how I got to use the roadside phone to call my pop. If they had seen me, they'd have killed me then for sure. I know where that body is buried and I seen Noddy do it. He ain't going to let me walk out of here with you."

Lance had a decision to make. He had been satisfied up to this point with how things were going—saying to himself that even Mike Campbell couldn't have handled things more smoothly and professionally—and he was hoping to extract the kid without bloodshed. In and out without a shot fired, that was what Mike said always to aim for, but that was a hard thing to achieve. Lance hoped that Noddy would have the good sense not to interfere, but if what the kid said was true, and Lance believed it was, Noddy was not going to continue resting on his ass on the veranda steps while they tried to leave. He could probably radio ahead to someone as well as give chase himself, after picking up some serious weapons to match the MAC-10.

"Bring over that pickup," Lance ordered the kid. Noddy put down his shotgun when told to and the second man lifted the revolver from his waistband with two fingers and dropped it at his feet. Lance had them sit in the truck bed with their backs to the driver's cab. He sat on the tailgate, covering them with the submachine gun, and waved to the kid to drive forward. Lance had the kid stop the pickup and go into the trees and fetch his Volvo. When the kid was back behind the wheel of the truck, Lance spelled it out for all of them: "You two stay put while the kid drives. If you try to jump out, you better be fast as greased lightning because I'll be driving right behind you, and some bushes and branches won't be enough to protect you from a stream of .45 bullets from this gun."

The two men sat quietly as the pickup bounced over the trail through the woods. Lance stayed close behind. As soon as the pickup was out on the blacktop, the kid speeded up and went too fast for them to jump out. The pickup suddenly slowed at one sharp corner where the side of the road dropped off in a precipice. Lance had to brake the Volvo to avoid hitting the rear of the truck. He was wondering what was happening when he saw the pickup door swing open and the kid try to take a running jump out of it and instead bury himself in the tar surface of the road. The pickup went over the edge. Last thing Lance saw was the surprised look on Noddy's face as he sank out of sight.

The kid was cut and bleeding, but he had no broken bones. Lance didn't bother to cuss him out since he himself would probably have done something similar under similar circumstances. However, he didn't relax until after he reached the San Francisco airport, bought him a ticket to L.A., called the boy's father to meet him at LAX, and waited to see him on the plane. Then he dialed his home number, used the tone while his recorded announcement answered, and picked up the messages from the answering machine. No name was given with one message, but he recognized Andre Verdoux's New York City number.

Colonel Matveyeva smoothed her fair hair and looked down to see that her knee-length military skirt was straight before entering the general's office. She knocked and went in. He was sitting behind his desk. He had a big head with short, grizzly hair, and bulbous eyes that ogled her body.

Colonel Matveyeva let him enjoy himself by strutting a little before his desk. She saluted. He smiled and waved her to a chair.

"Comrade Colonel," he began, "I have been busy, as you can imagine, explaining the circumstances of the heavy losses we took at the forward helicopter assault post in Gul Daoud's territory. Moscow was particularly critical, because only last week I was reporting progress on the runway there and being a bit overly optimistic, it seems. The fact that the three Americans were almost certainly personally involved, as well as supplying the missiles used, makes their capture essential. I managed to keep your name out of the disaster."

"Thank you, Comrade General." She sighed with relief to show him she knew what he had done for her. To have her name tied to a sizable slaughter of Soviet soldiers would mean the end of promotions and a job out on the taiga, steppe, or tundra. She supposed she would be working off this favor to the general on her back for as long as she was posted to his staff. Still, it was worth it.

"These three American adventurers have teamed up with these Afghan bandits," the general was saying. "This time there is no way for me to protect you further. You must catch these three men. And Moscow wants them alive."

"All escape routes for them to Pakistan have been cut behind them. They used up all the missiles in that attack. It will be only a matter of time before we capture them. If I didn't have to take them alive, I could have eliminated them already."

"Moscow will not accept that explanation, Comrade Colonel."

"They won't have to accept any explanation. I will deliver those Americans, and Gul Daoud as well."

"That would be a glorious day for the Red Army," the general said, beaming. "But before you start on those endeavors, I hope you are free tonight so I can toast you from our new vodka shipment. Will you come, Yekaterina?"

She smiled her assent. She never called him by his first name while he still had his uniform on.

* * *

The two jet bombers circled as their pilots tried to make visual contact with the village they knew from their maps to be somewhere below. On the ground the Afghan men, women, and children raised their faces to the sky and stood still, knowing that movement could give away their presence. The small houses, made of mud bricks, were not easy to see from the air—something that had preserved them from attack up until this. But now things were different. The planes had come to find them specially and would stay up there circling, beyond the reach of their rifle bullets, until either the pilots found what they were looking for or just dumped their bombs somewhere in pretense of following orders. The people had been warned. Other villages through which the Americans had passed were being bombed.

The time the three Americans had come through the village, everyone had come to their doorways to see them. Mothers had held up their smaller children and shouted, "Look, look." The children did not know, of course, what Americans were, except that they looked different from Afghans and that their parents were happy to see them, unlike the Russians. Now the Soviet planes were circling overhead, ready to punish them for helping the Americans. They had been warned but had no place else to go. They had lived all their lives on this mountain slope. This was theirs, not someplace else. They belonged here, no matter what happened. They had to stay. The two Soviet bombers spiraled overhead, like eagles lazily riding an updraft.

First one plane and then the other broke their circles and pulled away. It seemed like they were leaving, but the Afghans knew better and rushed from their houses dragging the very old and the very young with them before the planes streaked in on their bombing run. Some of the old men and women, perhaps too senile to understand what was happening or else too weary to care anymore, refused to budge from their houses and had to be left behind when their obstructive tactics endangered the entire family. Some small children managed to get lost in the rush and, frightened, ran back to their homes.

The two jets screamed in, flying low, almost wingtip to wingtip, and tumbled down their load of bombs on the mud-brick houses. The bombs, specially designed for such work, were not charged with high explosives like those used to destroy steel-and-concrete structures, since the mud-brick buildings of Afghan villages were easily knocked down by much less powerful shocks. Thus the bombs could be made into a mixture of incendiary and anti-personnel devices. The initial shock blew the mud-brick walls apart, the flaming chemicals spread over a wide area, scorching through living flesh down to the bone, and the anti-personnel shrapnel ripped through the bodies of those the flames had missed. The Russians had put a lot of thought into some of their dealings with the Afghans.

More than half the houses in the village were demolished, and the burning chemicals lay in glowing trickles and small puddles on the dusty, unpaved streets. Groans came from those buried out of sight beneath the debris. Burned children screamed for their mothers. Old semicripples hopped around with an agility they had not been capable of for decades as the combusting liquids seared slowly through their muscles and nerves. In the street lay one dead baby, cooked through by the heat like a suckling pig, its eyeballs burst.

The villagers rushed back to tend the wounded and dying, regardless of the possibility of another attack. But the planes did not come back on a second run. This time the Russians were just sending them a warning.

Joe Nolan gave two of his first cousins their full costs for two years at college, just handed it to them in cash and said, "You can blow it or start to get yourself educated, whatever you want." They both picked school. Nolan bought more than a half dozen tombstones and had them erected over the resting places of cousins. He paid dentist, doctor, and hospital bills for others and for one wedding reception, two funerals, and a big Thanksgiving Day bash for everyone even vaguely related to the family, regardless of who was on speaking terms with whom. Car repairs, a leaky house roof, clothes for a kid's First Holy Communion. Joe Nolan took care of everything for everybody—while the money lasted. Now he was nearly broke again.

Being broke was a common condition for many people these days in the once-booming steel town of Youngstown,

Ohio. No one wanted to buy American steel when the government let them import cheaper foreign steel from places where workers were paid less than a dollar an hour. Men who had never been idle in their lives now stood bewildered on street corners and watched yuppies on TV lecture them on "developing new skills" and joining "the service economy." No one seemed to be asking awkward questions about what happens when everyone is part of the communications and service industries and no one is making anything anymore. If nothing is being manufactured in the U.S., what is being communicated? If all these people are employed in providing services for other people, where is the cash coming from to provide these services? They saw news footage of Tennessee factory workers doing Japanese exercises and wondered what was coming over the good ol' boys down South. People talked first about the Sunbelt, and now they were talking about the Rustbelt, in which Youngstown was prominently featured. It was almost like one of those mysterious things that killed off ancient civilizations, leaving empty cities intact to slowly smother under layers of dust. Or like those Western ghost towns, except that there everyone picked up and left for a richer mine somewhere else while in Youngstown folks stayed on, unwanted in their hometown and unwelcome elsewhere.

Joe Nolan's last paycheck from Mike Campbell had been a hundred grand. It hadn't taken long for the problems of his large family to eat up even that amount of cash. He hadn't heard from Mike in some time and didn't know how to contact him. He didn't even know if he ever would hear from Campbell again or maybe tomorrow get two days notice before leaving on a six-week mission. He didn't begrudge his relatives the money they needed and always knew he had their affection and loyalty to fall back on if things went bad for him. People still looked out for one another in the old neighborhoods in Youngstown. It was that kind of place.

Joe's face was long and sad. He was thin, with fast reflexes. He had very bright blue eyes, long teeth that some people said looked like a dog's, and lifeless brown hair. His father had come north from Kentucky during World War II to work in the steel plants, and he could get real mad if someone called him a hillbilly. His folk were mountain people, and he still had their fighting blood in his veins, if anyone was curious enough to test it. Mostly he was peaceful, having seen enough in Nam for any man's lifetime.

Like Mike Campbell, he had been in the Green Berets, but unlike Mike, he had not been an officer. After coming back he had gone from job to job, woman to woman, drink to drink... Nothing had quite worked out. Going on missions with Mad Mike had given him a new purpose in life—he was good for something again. And his newfound wealth gave him status in the community, even if there were dark rumors as to how he got the cash. It amused Joe that none of the rumors ever approached the reality of what he did. He was still a badder boy than they even could imagine!

"Fella in here last night is a bail bondsman down at the courts," the barkeep at the Bunch o' Shamrock told Joe Nolan when he came in for a beer. "You know what he was saying? It made me think of you, only you weren't here, so I took the guy's number and said you'd call him for sure." He handed Joe a crumpled piece of paper with a name and number on it. "This fella is looking for a bounty hunter. He'll pay twenty percent of the bail skipped plus your expenses if you catch the guy. If you don't catch him, he pays zip. So if some guy jumped a fifty-thousand-dollar bond and you caught him, you'd collect ten thousand plus what it cost you."

Joe grinned. "Soon as I stop being a big spender in this place, you figure it's time I went back to work."

"Nolan, I don't know what you do for a living, and believe me, I don't ask. But what I'm talking about now is legal work for big money. It's legal. That means you won't be breaking the law. You heard of the word?"

"I thought it had something to do with having to pay taxes."

"In a place like Youngstown, that's a good complaint to have."

And so Joe Nolan became a bounty hunter. The barkeep's judgment was good. Nolan proved to be a natural at the job.

It didn't turn out to be such a big-money job as it first sounded, but then, few jobs ever turn out to be as good as they first sound. Mostly the bail jumped was much lower than fifty thousand, and the time it took to trace someone could be counted in weeks instead of days. Also, as a newcomer, Nolan was not given any cushy jobs. There were lots of psychos who had jumped bail for five thou and no one desperate enough to go after them. Joe soon found what he liked to do best.

"I take an assignment that involves a ten-thousand-dollar bail minimum," he explained to the barkeep at the Bunch o' Shamrock. "That gives me two thou plus expenses. So even if it takes me three weeks to find the guy, it's not bad. And I figure I have to be lucky every now and then and collar the guy in a matter of hours or a day or two, which really pays off."

"Nolan, are you saying you can assault some bum in the street and drag him against his will down to the local jailhouse?"

"To hell with the local jailhouse. I can do more than any cop can. I can bring him across a state line without extraditing him. There's a law going back to the last century that permits a bounty hunter to subdue and take his prisoner across state lines."

"You can hit him over the head?" the barkeep asked, impressed.

"Only when he won't come quietly," Joe said.

Nolan didn't talk about the creeps and weirdos he had to go after. The sane ones who jumped bail vanished. Only the loonies hung around, convinced that once they were no longer behind bars, they were free. The character Nolan was tracking down now qualified in the mad-dog category. Joe was waiting in the bar for a call from a plainclothesman who had a hot tip that the fugitive was in a farmhouse just over the Pennsylvania border. The cops were anxious to cooperate on this one because he had recently evaded capture by kicking the shit out of an off-duty officer in a saloon and stealing his shield and gun. The Youngstown, Ohio, police had their hands tied on the far side of the state line, and they saw Nolan as a quick way to bring back the fugitive without weeks or even months of legal bickering.

Errol Nelson was a real asshole, with a sheet that listed everything from assault and wife beating to burglary, car theft, and extortion. He was out on a twelve-thousand-dollar bail bond on an armed robbery charge. The owner of the store that had been held up had been murdered since Nelson's release on bail, and now the two other witnesses to the crime, both willing to testify against Nelson, lived in fear for their lives.

Nolan waited for the call in the Bunch o' Shamrock and sipped on his beers, taking it real easy. He guessed that some of the Youngstown cops, friends of the one who'd gotten beat up in the bar by Nelson, against regulations were maintaining a watch for him across the state line. Nolan asked no questions. The call came. Nelson was in the town of Pulaski in Lawrence County, Pennsylvania, a half-hour drive from where he sat. He was driving a red Toyota, the scrapes on its right side making it look as if it had sideswiped something. Nolan had seen his mug shots, a fair-haired farm boy with a crazy look and a Neanderthal brow. He would be armed with the cop's stolen gun, at least. He could also be expected not to want to be taken back to Youngstown.

It was dark by the time Nolan drove into Pulaski. He found the red Toyota in the parking lot of a closed bank, and for a moment Nolan thought that maybe Nelson was breaking into it, but then he guessed that the car was stolen and that Nelson was putting it out of plain sight. Nolan parked down the street from the lot. After about an hour he saw a lone man get in the Toyota, having come in the back way. The car's headlights flicked on and it started moving. Nolan started his engine, and in the few seconds the Toyota was out of sight behind the bank building, he switched on his lights and drove to meet the Toyota, which stopped at the parking lot exit to yield him the way. Nolan eased his car to a stop in front of the Toyota and yelled at the driver if he knew the road to New Wilmington, another town not far off.

The Toyota's driver stuck his head out the side window. It was Errol Nelson, all right, or else his twin brother. He yelled back, "Outta my way, shithead!"

COBRA STRIKE 83

Nolan let him go and scratched the side of his head so Nelson would not get a good look at his face in case he was suspicious. If things had gone well, he would have lured Nelson out of his car. Things hadn't worked that way, just as earlier, when he hadn't seen Nelson approach the car until he was almost to it. Nolan wasn't going to force things—just wait till the right moment came and then step in fast. He could see the Toyota's taillights ahead of him, nearing the edge of town. Even at this early hour the whole place seemed deserted. Then he saw the taillights brighten as Nelson braked and pulled over to the side of the road. The lights went out. Joe waited ten minutes before driving past. The Toyota was outside a tavern. He made a U turn and drove back, parking behind the Toyota. Should he go in or wait outside? Normally he would have gone in. But Nelson was probably carrying a piece and would have friends inside to interfere with Nolan and give him time to use it. Joe decided to wait outside. He got out of the car and walked up and down the roadside.

It was a short wait, no more than ten minutes. By now that seemed like nothing to Nolan. He limped along past his own car, dragging his left foot. Nelson paid no attention to the handicapped, slightly built man passing him as he dug in his pocket for his car keys.

Nolan whacked him in the nose with his right fist, blinding him with his tears and pain. He kneed him in the groin and rabbit-punched him when he bent over double. He took a step back and booted Nelson in the face, which straightened him out and knocked him flat on his back. Nolan grabbed his right arm in a lock and slapped him down fast for a gun. He wasn't carrying. So Nolan released his arm and hauled him by the left ankle along the road surface to his own car. He snapped one end of the cuffs on Nelson's right wrist and the other on his door handle. Then he went back to where Nelson had dropped his car keys.

The cop's gun and shield were in the glove compartment. He left the VCR and stereo amplifier in the car trunk. They were probably stolen, but he had no proof of that and would risk robbery charges himself if they turned out to be genuinely owned by the fugitive. But he had the shield and gun—and that was what the Youngstown cops cared about.

Errol Nelson was on his feet when Nolan came back. He was big and menacing and was trying to rip off the door handle on the other end of the cuffs.

"I ain't going nowhere with you, scumbag," he said, snarling. "You're a Youngstown cop operating over the state line, and so long as I keep you here, you're the who's going to be busted, not me."

Nolan went around to the other side of the car while he told Nelson who he was. He put the cop's gun and shield in the glove compartment and drew out some papers that he showed Nelson across the car roof by a streetlight.

"Here's your surrender piece, Nelson. Know what that is? It's from the bail bondsman you cheated by skipping town. And this paper here is a certified copy of the bond on which you were released. Now, these two papers together make a warrant a bounty hunter can use. I could take you to Seattle from here if that's what these papers said, but lucky for me, I just got to run you in to Youngstown."

"I ain't going nowhere and you can't make me. You come around this side of the car, I'll tear you apart with one hand and kick your head in. You won't catch me by surprise this time."

Nolan smiled and climbed in behind the wheel. He started the car and moved out into the road at six or seven miles per hour. Nelson ran alongside, shouting and cursing. When he fell, Nolan slammed on the brakes, but he wasn't in time to prevent Nelson's right arm from being nearly wrenched out of its socket. Blood flowed from his wrist where the metal had cut the skin and soaked into his pants at his torn kneecaps. Nelson took a second fall before he agreed to be cuffed and sit quietly in the back.

Joe was feeling pretty good about his night's work when he arrived back at the Bunch o' Shamrock.

"There was a phone call for you," the barkeep said. "Guy with a foreign accent. He's called for you here before." He gave Joe a severe look like he should stay on the straight and narrow now and not go back to whatever it was he had been doing before.

Joe guessed it might be Andre Verdoux. "He didn't leave a number to call back?" Joe asked, surprised.

"You told me you were coming back later, so I told him to call again. I'm not your fucking social secretary, Nolan."

The phone rang and the barkeep picked it up and nodded to Nolan. But it was not Andre Verdoux on the phone, as Joe had hoped, nor was it Mike Campbell. It was the Youngstown plainclothesman who had tipped him that Errol Nelson was in Pulaski.

"You brought him in a little more than an hour ago, right, Joe? You're not going to believe this. Even I don't believe this, and I see bullshit from morning till night, week in, week out. The Nelson guy jumped twelve-thousand-dollar bail and allegedly wasted that store owner who was to testify against him. Do I have the facts straight?"

"Those are some of them," Nolan agreed.

"Some half-assed judge has just released him again on a seven-thousand-dollar bond."

"Jesus!"

"Not even Jesus would have turned that sucker loose."

This time Joe ordered a whiskey at the bar. When Andre's call finally came, as usual all Joe said was, "Count me in. Just tell me when."

CHAPTER 6

The big Australian looked out of place on the rear deck of the fancy motor yacht purring into dock at the exclusive resort colony on Hilton Head Island in South Carolina. His cropped straw-yellow hair was only slightly longer than the several days growth of yellow stubble that covered his red jowls. His broken nose, cauliflower ears, and blubbery lips looked like those of a sparring partner in a pro boxing training camp. His long powerful arms hung from broad shoulders on a stocky body. His fists were huge and gnarled. Definitely not the portrait of an average luxury yacht owner. That was how men saw Bob Murphy. Women saw him differently. They noticed that he liked them, that his brown eyes were soft and understanding, that he actually listened to what they had to say.

Murphy was a loud, raucous Australian outbacker with a tranquil marriage to a wealthy New England socialite. She was no beauty, any more than he was, and to the continuing amazement and envy of their friends they kept their romance going strong despite years of marriage. They spent summers in the Green Mountains of Vermont at his wife's old family place. They wintered in Palm Beach, at another of his wife's old family places. And now they were cruising north with the spring in his wife's family's luxury yacht, registered these days in Bob Murphy's name, with stopovers scheduled for Hilton Head, Charleston, the Chesapeake, Manhattan and Montauk, with a few days social activity at each place before dropping anchor in summer waters at Newport, Rhode Island. Bob liked life aboard the yacht when it was moving; Eunice put up with that in anticipation of the social gatherings she could organize at each port of call. Bob hated the parties on board, with some clown tinkling on the white baby grand, the crew serving as champagne waiters, and people in new deck shoes whose names he could not remember saying to him, "So *you're* Eunice's husband."

Bob didn't give a damn that most of them regarded him a some sort of leech or parasite on a poor little rich girl. Eunice herself knew that he cared little for money and was happier with a gun on a duck swamp or a rod and line at a good fishing spot than he was hobnobbing with wealthy trendies or old-money horsey types.

Few people knew that Bob more or less paid his own way from his merc work with Mad Mike. Campbell and he went back a long way. They had met while fighting the Cubans in Angola. Murphy had been in Vietnam with the Australian army but had not known Campbell there, and before that, he had fought communists in the Malayan jungles with the British army. As a Green Beret colonel fresh from the Southeast Asia conflict, Campbell had thought when they met in Angola that no one could show him any new tricks in combat. Bob Murphy had shown him some and had saved his life more than once by coming up with something neither Campbell nor the enemy had ever seen before. Eunice had been on peace marches to Washington while Bob was fighting in Vietnam; they had yet to meet. Now she dismissed his merc activities along with his hunting, fishing, and drinking. It was just something that men did. The nature of the beast. She was pleased at the fact that womanizing was not also on the list and a bit disappointed that Bob could be very unpleasant to her distinguished guests.

But this night at Hilton Head he was on his best behavior and apparently more or less sober. He chatted with people and even remembered some of their names while he introduced them to others. Eunice did not complain when he eased away early to their stateroom for a long night's sleep. He was up two hours before dawn, stalking up and down the dock, until a battered station wagon arrived and he climbed in the front seat with two other men.

"Good to see you, Bryce," Murphy said.

"This here is Don Crockett," Bryce said from behind the wheel, and Bob shook hands with the man between them. "He's the county man where we're going this morning."

Bob Murphy had contacted Bryce Cummings by radio-telephone while the yacht was still offshore, and it was looking forward to this day's trip with him that had made Bob so agreeable to guests the previous evening. Bryce had been invited but laughingly declined the invitation to the plush party aboard the yacht, which many others would have given their eyeteeth for. Bryce was a tough Georgian whom Bob had once fought outside a bar in Savannah because Bob was drunk and had acidentally bumped against him, and Bryce hated liquor and anyone carrying it in his gut. Bryce lost that fight, but the two men got to talking down at the police station and were soon amused at each other's absurdities.

Bryce Cummings was an agent for the Federal Bureau of Alcohol, Tobacco, and Firearms stationed in Beaufort, through which they drove. Don Crockett was an alcoholic-beverage officer for Colleton County, immediately north of Beaufort County. Murphy had been out with Bryce a few times over the years, yet hadn't met Crockett before, although it seemed as if the two men worked together very often. They kidded each other like old friends as the station wagon wound down tiny back roads in the half light of dawn.

"Hope you feel like a good walk this morning, Bob," Bryce said. "Where we're going is right deep in the woods. We was back in there yesterday morning, and the mash was just nice and ready to go. We're betting they'll be working there this morning, wanting to finish the run before the heat of the day."

"That mash'll turn sour if they don't run it today," Crockett confirmed, "unless they was to add more sugar, and they have no call to do that."

Bob listened to their tales of busts they had made together, both red liquor and white liquor. For Bryce those were the only kinds of liquor. Red liquor covered all legitimately manufactured whiskey sold by bootleggers after hours and on Sundays in wet counties, or at any time in dry counties. White liquor was moonshine, made often by families with generations of tradition in the business. This morning they were after a still that had been accidentally pinpointed in the woods from an aerial forestry survey photo.

"What gets me, Bryce, is I ain't got no idea who's running this still, and damn, I pride myself on knowing everyone in this part of Colleton County who might be tempted to let anything more than a glass of apple juice ferment." Don Crockett was taking this still almost as a personal insult.

"They always come up with something new," Bryce said, "which is how we get to keep our jobs. Best one they done on me recently was over near Govan in Bamberg County. Fella there turns the rooms of a nice big ranch house into vats by nailing plywood to the floors and up the walls to just below window level. He's got four rooms with thousands of gallons of mash at different stages, and his cooker, doubler, and cooler are set in a central room so he can run each vat of mash as it comes ready. I don't like to even think how long he was operating there right under my nose. Last place I ever thought of looking, a nice suburban house with children's swings out on the lawn."

"How did you discover it?" Bob asked.

Bryce grinned. "By chance I caught a local fella redhanded at his still. He was mad as hell, not so much at me but at who might have given him away. I didn't tell him no one had, that I had come across him by smelling his still at work in the woods—it smelled like a bakery, all yeasty like. I said to him, 'You got some mean competition in these parts, my friend.' So, sitting in the car, he got to thinking which of his competiton turned him in to get rid of him, and he ended by giving me a name that was new to me and that led to the still in the house."

"You're a real nice guy," Murphy said. "Been shot at lately?"

"Sure. All the time. But no one's hit me in the past eight years. They don't like revenuers hereabouts."

The federal, state, and county agents were known as revenuers because the illegal sale of red liquor and the making and sale of white liquor was treated not as a regular crime but as the evasion of taxes. That's what bootleggers went to jail for—not for making moonshine but for cheating the government out of tax revenues.

"You know whose side I'm on in all this, don't you?" Bob said once to Bryce.

"When you're with me, Murphy, you're on the revenuers' side. When you're not with me, do as you please. Only remember, if I got to thinking you was making white lightning, I'd bust you fast as I would some old redneck out in the woods."

"All I drink is twelve-year-old Scotch," Murphy said.

They left the station wagon at the end of a trail through the woods and set out on foot. Bryce checked his .38 Smith & Wesson and Crockett patted a long-barreled .45 in his shoulder holster. Bob Murphy was unarmed, which Bryce always insisted on since he was present only as an observer. They plowed through endless woods, the thorny undergrowth tearing at their skins and the mosquitoes droning after them. Although it was full daylight by now, it was dark in some of the evergreen forest. Crockett was hoping the moonshiners would show and bring their car long, saving them a return walk back this way like they had yesterday. Murphy knew that Crockett, as the county man, got to seize whatever vehicle the moonshiners brought along. Because of all the stuff they would have to move in and out from the still, including the finished product, wherever the still was located would have to be accessible by some kind of track a truck or car could be driven over. Murphy knew that Bryce and Crockett were taking him along a cross-country back-

COBRA STRIKE

entrance way that only a hog or a revenuer would think of using.

When it seemed like they had been walking through the woods for hours and only occasionally emerging in a field or a clearing, Bryce turned to Bob and said, "Go easy from here on and no more talking."

Murphy nodded tolerantly. In spite of his height and bulk, he could ease across woodland without snapping a twig, which was more than he could say for his two companions. They came to a path, and Bryce pointed down at what looked like fresh tire marks on a damp patch. Bryce sniffed the air. There was no smell of wood smoke or mash cooking. He listened. There was no sound of men working. Then he plucked a tall fern and felt his way with it along the grassy path, a few paces ahead of the others. When he stopped, they did too. He jiggled the fern to show them the length of green thread it had picked up, almost invisible, stretched across the path a few inches above the ground. Murphy saw that the thread was tied at either end to saplings and was not set to release some diabolical weapon if broken, as it would have been in Nam. The three men stepped over the thread and left it unbroken behind them.

In a small clearing at the end of the path, a steel drum lay on its side across two cinder blocks. Wood ash and some half-burned logs filled a pit beneath it. A pipe connected the steel drum to three wood barrels, which in turn served as cooker, doubler, and cooler. The cooler was filled with water, and a spiral of copper pipe, called the worm, ran through it. A pump head was installed in a well shaft the bootlegger had sunk.

Bryce pointed to a neat pile of cut logs. "They brought these in since we were here yesterday." He ambled over to six oil drums standing upright, their tops covered with burlap held down by lengths of board. He lifted one burlap cover, ran his finger through the mash, and tasted it. "Ready to run," he pronounced. "I reckon those boys are going to be along here today."

"Maybe they're still recovering from last night and are a bit late in starting," Crockett responded. "You want to wait?"

"Do no harm. If they ain't here in a couple of hours, they ain't coming."

Bob Murphy had done enough walking and hoped the bootleggers would show so they wouldn't have to trek back all the way through those woods again. Murphy dipped his finger into the dark clear liquid and tasted it. It was sour and tangy. Dust and dead insects floated on its top.

"Sometimes you'll find a rat or a coon drowned in it," Bryce told him as he tasted the mash in the other five oil drums. "Two of these barrels are ready to run. The others are still sweet and sticky with scum on top—they'll be a few days yet. It takes the mash longer while it's still not too hot. In summer it could be ready in three days." He carefully replaced the burlap and boards. "This stuff ain't too bad, as white liquor goes in these parts. In each of these fifty-five-gallon drums there's, say, fifty gallons of mash, which is probably about forty-five pounds of cornmeal, thirty pounds of sugar, two pounds of malt, and a one-pound cake of yeast. The rest is water. Depending on a lot of things, including the skill of the moonshiner, out of fifty gallons of mash he could get five to ten gallons of whiskey."

Crockett had been foraging around and came back with a pint bottle of clear liquid. "I found this hid in the bushes yonder." He shook the bottle vigorously, and both he and Bryce looked closely at the bubbles on the surface. "About a hundred and ten proof, I'd say," and Bryce nodded his agreement.

For liquor of a hundred proof, the bubbles would sit exactly half in and half out of the liquid. For weaker liquor, the bubbles rode higher; for stronger liquor, lower.

Bryce took the bottle and sniffed it. "Most white liquor comes in at a hundred proof, even if the bootlegger has to add rubbing alcohol or paint thinner to get it there. Another thing they add is beading oil, which makes the bead or bubble sit just right, like it was a hundred proof. Don't seem like anything's added to this stuff, though, not by the smell of it."

Murphy knew Bryce Cummings had not tasted liquor in many years, and he noticed that Crockett was not tasting it,

COBRA STRIKE

either. So he took the bottle and swallowed a generous mouthful. He immediately felt the jolt of the fiery liquid.

"I bet this baby packs some hangover," he said.

"Yeah, it's the impurities in the alcohol more than the alcohol itself that gives you the hangover," Bryce explained. "Wood alcohol breaks down in the body partly into formic acid, which ants use to sting. You better stick to your expensive aged whiskey, Bob. At least it has a lot of the poisons leached out of it." He walked toward the bushes at one side of the clearing. "Maybe we better quiet down some. Those boys is likely to come along any minute."

All three of them were big men and, none too comfortable, crouched down in the bushes, along with mosquitoes, deerflies, and assorted other bugs to keep them close company. They stayed put for more than an hour before they heard voices coming down the path. Four men walked into the clearing, each toting a fifty-pound bag of sugar on his back. That was all the evidence the two revenuers needed against them. Both men sprang out of the bushes at the two nearest them, knocking them down and walloping the hell out of them, as well as taking some powerful counter blows themselves. This left Bob Murphy to handle the other two moonshiners. At this moment it was clear that Bryce no longer expected him to behave as an uninvolved observer.

Neither of them had seen Murphy yet in his hiding place. The nearest one to him dropped the sugar sack he was carrying and tried to jump in to help his buddy struggling with Crockett on the ground. Before he managed to lay a fist on the county revenuer, Murphy burst out of the bushes like a tiger. His roar scared this moonshiner, and his right boot did a lot worse. It caught the man in the ribs, snapping a few of them like chicken bones. He was already sinking to the ground when Murphy's left fist hammered into his right cheekbone. All he could see were bright patterns before his eyes and feel the sharp pain as he went down and instinctively curled to protect himself from further blows.

None were coming. Murphy was too busy handling the fourth man, who dropped his sack and drew a hunting knife with a six-inch blade. Murphy was kind of relieved to see that it wasn't a pistol, though he had a lot of respect for any kind of knife. The man made a running lunge at him, and Murphy backed away so fast, he fell over a bag of sugar. Before the blade could reach him as he lay on the ground, his big hands grabbed the fifty-pound bag and held it out on his long powerful arms. He felt a blade thrust penetrate the tightly packed paper sack and climbed to his feet propelling the sugar sack forward and keeping it between him and the knife-wielding moonshiner. Then he heaved the heavy sack, and it took down his adversary with it, flattening him on his back beneath it. Bob gave him a swift kick in the nuts, which made him drop the knife and lose the will to fight.

Bryce and Crockett handcuffed all four together and got busy busting up the still, turning over the vats of mash, smashing the pump head, and throwing stuff down the well shaft. Murphy felt a bit sorry for the four bootleggers, handcuffed and bruised, watching their equipment being smashed by a pair of experts, so he found the pint bottle of white liquor and offered it to them.

One shook his head in disdain. "We make that shit to sell, not to drink. You'll find a new bottle of Wild Turkey in our truck back along the path. We'd sure appreciate that."

But Bryce put his foot down about that. Crockett said the bottle *and* the truck were now state property. He told Murphy that since he had never seen these fellas before, he didn't want to go encouraging them to stay in *his* county by treating them too soft.

After leaving Don Crockett and the four bootleggers at the courthouse, they took the seized truck around to fetch Bryce's station wagon, returned the truck to the courthouse, and then headed back to the yacht at Hilton Head.

"You see the amount of work goes into this job?" Bryce demanded to know on the way.

Bob said that he did.

"You ready to come out again tomorrow? I'm going to help a county man over in Allendale County."

"Sure, I will, but only if you come aboard and talk with the god-awful folks coming aboard this afternoon."

Bryce was agreeable until he got to the dock and saw the socialites chattering on the rear deck. "I ain't going to be able to go through with this, Bob," he said in a sorrowful voice.

"You ain't got no backbone, Bryce."

"Not for that kind of stuff, I don't."

"See you next time I'm passing through."

Bryce waved and yelled, "Thanks for your help."

Eunice hustled him down to their stateroom to change into something suitable. "You had a call from Andre Verdoux." Eunice had met Andre and knew what the call probably meant. "I'm going to miss you while you're gone." She sighed. "But at least since you will be away for a while, you have no excuse now not to be nice to the guests. And I'm afraid they're a dreary lot."

They both laughed and kissed.

Baker, Winston, and Turner sat silently on the hillside sipping tea with Gul Daoud. The three Americans had previously agreed on what they had to do. This time they would not let Gul Daoud dissuade them as he had done before. As usual, Baker was their spokesman.

"Having us here with you is costing you too much, Gul," Baker said.

"Without you we could not have destroyed the jet runway," Gul replied graciously. "With jets landing there we would have even more Russians everywhere than we have now."

This was hard to credit. At present all the mountain passes to the east and south had been sealed. Soviet and government troops were conducting sweeps over suitable terrain and house-to-house searches of villages. Where the terrain was too rough and rock cover too heavy to make ground sweeps feasible, helicopter gunships patrolled and single-engine observation planes flew along planned coordinates.

"If we three leave this area," Baker said, "and show up somewhere else, it will take the heat off you. They're so damn anxious to catch us alive, they'll forget about their revenge for the men you killed and choppers you destroyed. And it's not just your fighting force we have to consider. Practically every man, woman, and child in this region has been made to suffer in some way because the Russians know we're still hiding here. Once we go, they'll follow."

Gul Daoud shook his head. "I could never allow you to give yourselves up to ease the pressure on us. Never."

"We're not giving ourselves up," Baker argued. "Give us an escort of armed men and we'll lead the communist forces away from you. It's a military tactic; look on it that way."

They finally prevailed by promising the rebel leader that they would come back again.

"I know you will," Gul said with a sly smile, "because there are not many other places you can go."

Two days walk from Gul Daoud's territory, they and their four-man Afghan escort came across a small army outpost of government soldiers. It reminded the Americans of a miniature version of a French Foreign Legion post in an old movie. It was only a single-story flat-roofed building surrounded quite closely by a twelve-foot-high wall with miniature towers at each of the four corners. Slits in the towers' curved walls allowed the occupants to fire outside, and a walkway ran inside the wall near the top so that those inside could stand behind it and fire over its edge. A heavy wood door protected the entrance. Considering that it all seemed to be built of sun-dried mud, it was an impressive structure. At most, a dozen soldiers could be stationed there.

The four Afghans had not brought them here by accident. They seemed to know all about the outpost. All seven of them remained most of the day observing the place from an outcrop of rocks a quarter of a mile away. Through what they saw they were able to interpret what the rebels had been trying to tell them, and they couldn't understand, Baker being unable this time to make head or tail of their hand signs and facial expressions. They saw that the officer of the outpost had established himself, probably against regulations, in a small private house a few hundred yards from the outpost and at the edge of a small village. No doubt he was eating better food here than his men at the outpost, and perhaps he had even arranged for some other comforts to ease the loneliness and rigors of a military life. The men, about nine in all, and the officer continually went

COBRA STRIKE　　　　　　　　　　　　　　　　97

back and forth between the house and the outpost. It was obvious that discipline was slack and none of them felt much threatened.

All that was really necessary was that the three Americans let themselves be seen by some of these government soldiers. But plainly the four rebels with them had higher hopes, and even Turner, with all his responsibility for Baker's and Winston's safety, found it hard to pass by this sitting duck.

Turner and Winston sneaked down to the house with two of the rebels after dark. Through a lighted window they saw the officer squatting on the floor, eating with his fingers and being waited on by three women. The back door had been left ajar, and all four men eased their way into the kitchen at the back of the house and from there into the room in which the officer was eating. His mouth stopped chewing when he saw the four AK-47 barrels pointing at him by lamplight. The three women were terrified but knew better than to scream. Winston and Turner herded them into the kitchen and spoke soothingly to them in English. They would make good witnesses that the Yanks had been here.

In the kitchen they heard hammering in the front of the house. Turner went to investigate. The two rebels had driven a nail into the wood crosspiece above the front door and were now stringing up the officer from it on a short length of rope. Gagged by a cloth stuck in his mouth, with his thumbs tied behind his back, all the officer could do was kick desperately against the wood door in his last moments of life. Then he hung limply, swaying and revolving at the end of the rope, his toes almost touching the floor and his nose almost touching the closed door.

A soldier at the outpost may have heard the kicks on the door; anyway, he was soon outside shouting. When he tried to push the door inward, something unseen prevented it from opening. The soldier heaved it inward, and his hanged officer banged into him face-to-face. A second later the soldier was hauled inside and knifed deeply in the chest. He was left to die on the floor, gasping, convulsing, choking on his blood.

After a while, when the soldier did not come back, a

floodlight came on atop one of outpost's corner towers. Three men emerged from the big wooden entrance gate and headed for the house. Baker and the other two rebels were hidden nearby but saw no opportunity to get inside the little fort. The three men approached the house cautiously, yet remained in full view in the floodlight. The two rebels inside the house became agitated. Winston and Turner nodded to them, and they opened fire with their AK-47s, taking down all three government solders in a single burst.

Baker and the others joined them behind the late officer's house. He said, "Forget the outpost. There's maybe five guys in it, but they could hold out against us for a week. And you can bet they've already radioed for help. I'm starving. You think there's anything to eat in this burg?"

Guns at the ready, they walked down the village street. The people stared at them with curiosity and seemed careful to show no support for them. All the same, they showed no hostility, either. They helped themselves to lamb kebabs still on the skewers. When Turner tried to leave Pakistani rupees as payment, the man shook his head, genuinely frightened at such proof that he aided the Americans. He did accept gladly several handsful of AK-47 rounds. Then he whispered something about Allah, which the four rebels whispered back to him.

Winston said, "Right on, brother."

Harvey Waller wanted to kill him—strangle him with his bare hands—as soon as he saw him, but the crowded Wall Street sidewalk in the middle of a business day was neither the time nor the place for that. Even Harvey could see that, and Harvey liked to kill people in places where they least expected to die. Another thing threw Harvey also. The guy seemed glad to see him, and this was a guy he had sworn to kill for having gotten cold feet and betraying him. He had never even known the joker's last name before. He just knew him as David when they were both members of an ultraright society trying to save America by eliminating known communist agents operating there. David and others had accused Harvey of getting out of control. When the FBI net started closing in, they all bolted like frightened rabbits, leaving Harvey to face the music. Harvey often thought about how surprised they must have been when he eluded the FBI, and on his own, continued liquidating those on the society's hit list. He had completed the job solo, without their funds or inside information, after they had all scampered off to hide in the woodwork. He didn't know their last names, but neither could they locate him. He didn't need the likes of them to zap fucking commies. Harvey could manage right well on his own.

He still had some high-level contacts in Washington, D.C., and other places who thought like he did. Recently Harvey had read Winston Churchill's *The Gathering Storm,* about how nice-guy English politicians had been no match for Hitler, Ribbentrop, Himmler, and Mussolini. Harvey could see himself today, if he had been rich and educated, warning his fellow members of Congress about the Red danger creeping onward all around them, and they yawning during his speeches and leaving the chamber for a smoke, like they did to Churchill. Only difference between him and Churchill was he would have waylaid them in the corridors and kicked their butts.

Harvey Waller had gone into the Marines as a kid and found himself in Vietnam. He came home to his New Jersey town "funny in the head," as his stay-at-home friends liked to say. They sneered at him when he pointed out to them that their heads were empty, and soon quit tangling with them because he saw that it was a waste of his time. He kept himself honed and in fighting trim by working as a soldier of fortune, nearly always with Mike Campbell, whom Harvey respected as a man and a soldier, even if they did not see eye to eye on most things. With his regular army combat experience and his skills as a merc, it was only natural that Harvey became the executioner of the nameless ultraright group. This guy David was the only one he had ever seen after they had ditched him, and Harvey was sorry it turned out to be on a crowded city sidewalk.

The coffee shop where David brought him was not a good place, either. Harvey only stopped thinking about how to kill him immediately when David pushed his business card across the table to him.

"I'm a corporate lawyer with a big financial house on Water Street. I have a job for you that needs doing right away. Fifteen thousand, half in advance, to cover your expenses and so forth. This man is a dangerous communist plant, Harvey. A mole."

They met once again, and Harvey picked up half the cash and all the details. He was to hit the target while David was on a three-day cruise out of Miami. Piece of cake.

On a plane from Newark to O'Hare, Harvey began to wonder if he hadn't been maneuvered into all this too easily by that smooth-spoken Wall Street lawyer. By the time he rented a car with a forged driver's license and Visa card and found his way onto Route 90 northwest out of Chicago, he was convinced he had been suckered into something. It would all have been so much simpler and cleaner if he could just have strangled David without ever getting to talk with him again.

He drove through the flat farmland of Wisconsin and exited from Route 90 at Madison. His target was a student at the University of Wisconsin who lived in the student residential area on Langdon Street. Harvey Waller found a motel near the edge of town, an inconspicuous place. He left nothing in the room, since he would not return to it if he got his work completed today. The danger of working in a small town like Madison, more than fifty miles from any other sizable town, was that if something went wrong, there was no place to hide and escape routes were easy to cut off. Waller knew he didn't look like a student at the university or a civil servant working at the State Capitol, and there didn't seem to be much else happening in this town. But to Harvey, considerations like that only added spice to an otherwise bland job of work.

He leafed through the copy of the *Wall Street Journal* he had bought at O'Hare airport. Harvey used this newspaper only because he could usually find it anywhere he happened to be in the country, not because he had an interest in or knowledge of the financial market. It had only been a coincidence that he had met David on Wall Street: Harvey was in the downtown area to visit an electronics store. He found what he was looking for in the classified ads: BUSINESS OPPORTUNITIES.

COBRA STRIKE

He scanned the ads in this column, looking for coded messages. Each of his contacts had their own format, and taking an ad here for a few days in succession was the only way they could signal him. Then he contacted them. His eye settled on one item: ARIZONA DENTAL PRACTICE —Root Canal Work a Specialty—Partner Wanted. He nodded in satisfaction. That was from Andre Verdoux. He'd get this job done fast, then phone Andre from Chicago. He didn't trust the phone exchanges of anything less than a big city, where everything was beyond control.

He had to pull into the driveway of the house on Langdon Street because he could find no place to park on the street. From one clapboard house, amplified rock music blasted from a stereo. Not far behind the house, a lake stretched in a calm sheet. Everyone on the street looked nineteen years old. Bicycles were stacked against porches. All these kids looked friendly. They looked like they were having a good time here and had big hopes for the future. Harvey thought that if he had been given a chance, he would have liked to have come here.

So who or what was this kid he had come to kill? Arthur Putnam. He pressed the bell, one of six with names alongside each. A head and shoulders stuck out of a window upstairs. A big guy, a jock.

"Who're you looking for?"

"Arthur Putnam."

"That's me."

Waller pointed to the rented Chrysler in the driveway. "We got to talk."

The big lug clumped down the stairs, came out the door in shirt, jeans, and sneakers, and got in the car without asking a question, such as who Waller might be and what he was here for. Did the kid think he was a communist contact? Was he used to strangers showing up like this? He looked more like a naive, well-behaved youth who was used to obeying adults without question.

Waller backed the car out of the driveway and drove down the street without saying anything. They passed through what appeared to be the main campus center on the lakeshore, with a lot of high-rise buildings. He just kept driving, making random turns, not saying anything.

"Where're we going?" Arthur Putnam finally asked.

"Just driving around and around."

Waller saw out of the corner of his eye that Putnam was finally giving him some suspicious looks. It took most people about two seconds to start doing that. Waller knew he struck most people as "creepy."

"What do you want?"

"You a communist?"

"A what?"

"Communist. A believer in Marx and Lenin. Maybe you never heard of them."

"I know who they are," Putnam said indignantly. "Can't say I've read anything by them because they're not on any of my courses, and I've got a big enough workload as it is—"

"You ever heard of David Forbes?"

"Sure. He's my mother's brother, lives in New York City."

"Has he any reason to kill you?"

A long silence now. Finally Putnam asked in a hesitant way, "Are you a cop?"

"No. A hit man."

Another long silence.

Waller snapped, "I asked you a question. Has he some reason to kill you?"

Short silence. "I suppose so. We're the only two left in the family. My parents were killed in an air crash three years ago. They left me a lot of money. I'm not allowed to touch it till I'm twenty-one—my father stipulated that in his will—and I won't be that till next year. David is the trustee of the funds. He knows all about those things, being involved in the stock market and such. He paid you to kill me?"

"Fifteen thou was all you were worth, body dumped in a bad neighborhood of Chicago. Make it look like a street crime, he said. He's on a three-day cruise to the Bahamas. Left early yesterday."

"Why aren't you going to kill me?" Arthur Putnam asked.

The kid was maybe not so dumb, Waller decided. "I kinda like this place, college and all." Waller smiled his sinister smile. "I enjoyed killing a guy in Harvard. I didn't like that place at all. But this is all bullshit. I don't kill people for money, that's all."

"That why you were asking about me being a communist?"

"Don't ask questions. What is this place?"

"Aboretum. Like a botanical garden," Putnam explained.

Waller parked, got out, and looked around him at the lawns and trees. He took a large, extra strong plastic garbage bag from the trunk and told Putnam to bring the Polaroid camera that was on the backseat. Waller lit a Viceroy and stubbed it out after a few puffs. He made a round black mark the size of a bullet entry wound on Putnam's left cheek, then another on his right forehead.

"I don't have nothing to make you look pale. You're too fucking healthy-looking. Get into that sack with your head and shoulders sticking out—maybe one arm—like I was stuffing you into it so your corpse wouldn't mark up the trunk of the car or leave hairs or skin traces that lab guys could analyze."

Waller spent some time getting his arms and head into unnatural positions.

"You always know a dead guy by the way he lays," he instructed Putnam. "No matter how bad a guy is hurt and unconscious, so long as he's still alive, he lays in a natural way. Only after he's dead does he get what they call a broken-doll look. Yeah, now you're doing good. That's better. Much better."

He took three shots from different angles quickly. Then he uncovered the Polaroids in turn without bothering to count off seconds. They could have been better photos, but one thing all three of them plainly showed was a dead youth half in a garbage bag with two bullet holes in his face.

"David's gonna love them," Harvey said, gloating.

Harvey Waller was wrong. David Forbes didn't love the photos. When Waller thrust them before his eyes, the lawyer made little gurgling sounds like he was going to throw up. They were walking west on Wall Street, after Waller had waited for him to arrive that morning at his place of work on Water Street.

"I believe you, Harvey. I don't need to see that. Please destroy them."

Waller produced a lighter and touched it to all three photos held together. They burned fiercely, and to save his fingers he tossed them in a steel mesh trash basket. The contents of the basket caught fire.

"This is just what my reputation needs, Harvey, to be caught setting fires before my day's work. I know what you're here for. Your money. I don't have it. No one in this city walks around with seven and a half thousand in their pocket."

"So we go to your bank," Harvey suggested.

"My bank is where I live, in Connecticut."

"I know someone who will take your IOU and pay me on it." Harvey pushed him down the subway steps of the Lexington Avenue IRT, ignoring his pleas to take a taxi and that he had an important appointment in fifteen minutes. Waller had tokens and pushed Forbes through the turnstile ahead of him. They stood on the uptown platform, and Forbes complained to the silent Waller but made no effort to disobey him. When they heard the grinding of steel wheels on steel rails as the approaching train rattled toward them at speed, Harvey began shouting over the din.

"I don't want your fucking money! Forget the second payment! Those photos were fake! I didn't kill the kid because he was no commie! You're the rotten bastard, not him! You stabbed me in the back once! Think I had forgotten that?"

Harvey Waller waited only long enough to see the fear in the lawyer's eyes and then pushed him headlong in the path of the train.

CHAPTER 7

With Andre Verdoux it was a case of "old soldiers never die," except he had no intention of fading away, either. The Frenchman was in his fifties, but he considered himself fitter in many ways and a hell of a lot wiser than when he was in his twenties. Mike had been trying to ease him out of missions recently and, when that didn't work, shunt him into a noncombat managerial position. In his wily way Andre had turned that ploy against Mike by taking on as much responsibility and undertaking as many arrangements for each mission as he could possibly handle. That way he knew who was going to be where and when, and so included himself in an indispensable role. Although Andre was definitely included on this mission, he found all the same that he was saddled with all the arrangements.

Besides Campbell, Andre was the only member of the team to know where they were going. And he had just now found out where they would train.

"Now, I want you to repeat for each man before he goes," Mike said, "that it's illegal for U.S. citizens to plan within U.S. borders to violate U.S. neutrality in the internal affairs of another country. Since none of them will know where they're going, they can't plan to violate the place. But we take no weapons, no military gear—it's strictly running shoes and shorts."

Andre nodded.

"There's another problem," Mike went on. "The Nanticoke Institute people pointed out to me that they consider their big mistake was in sending in a three-man team who did not know Afghan languages and customs. They said they now have an expert on the area working for them, and they want to send him with us. I said I'd have him checked out by one of my men and warned them that he was not to reveal the mission's destination to this man. So I phoned Bob Murphy before he left Hilton Head Island and told him to try to find out where the mission was to, that this guy knew it. Bob called me an hour ago. He said the guy was a beanpole but real smart—he had been able to find out nothing from him about where we're going. So that's good. I asked Bob what else the guy could do. Bob said, 'He can swim.' 'Anything else?' I asked. Bob said, 'No. I gave him a rifle to shoot and he didn't know how to hold it. He admitted he'd never fired a gun in his life.'

"Well, I blew up at that, hung up, and dialed the Institute. I screamed at them that we weren't taking any helpless egghead with us, regardless of how many dialects and folk dances he knew. They told me that they would work with him nonstop, beginning in ten minutes from talking with me, and all they asked in return was for me to give him a chance at training. If he flunked that, he's out. So I said okay."

"I see the problem," Andre said. "We know that all the other team members are proficient with weapons. All they will need is some physical toughening up and discipline. But this one will need testing with weapons. There is no way around it. But I agree with the Institute members—I think his knowledge of the region's languages and customs make him worth including if he can pull his own weight at all."

Mike smiled, knowing that Andre prized his own linguistic abilities and regarded them as important to the success of some past missions. The Frenchman knew none of the Afghan languages, nor did Mike or any of the others.

"We'll see how he turns out," Mike said, resigned to the worst.

A merc in the field was often only as good as his hardware. It was not that difficult for any soldier of fortune to infiltrate someplace with civilian status. Only when he made contact with his hardware was he burning his bridges. This was nearly true, because some missions were already dead before the mercs left home base as a result of leaked information about the mission. However, so long as they did not collect their weapons, they could only be charged with conspiracy, which was a lot more vague than being accused of possession of military-grade weapons. The point of purchase of the weapons was often the weak spot. When somebody bought a quantity of serious hardware, it was obvious what he had in mind, and often it was not hard to guess where. Some of the more unscrupulous arms dealers regarded selling such information to interested parties as a bonus to their deal; first they'd sell the guns to one party, next they'd sell the information to the other party. Sometimes the information brought in even more profit than the guns.

Quality was another problem. A merc leader could order from a shiny catalogue with four-color pictures in one location and accept delivery of rusty weapons with parts missing in another. When that happened in the field, it was usually too late to replace the weapons, and the mercs would be goddamn lucky if they survived to complain.

Point of delivery was even more risky than point of purchase. Kind old ladies don't go into the business of delivering arms. If the mercs had not already been sold out to the local authorities, they were liable at this point to be murdered by their suppliers—killed with their own guns and bullets. The popular notion of mercs arriving in rubber rafts by moonlight, with blackened faces and weapons draped across both shoulders, did not correspond much to reality. Parachute jumps and frogmen stealthily creeping onto a beach were nice notions, but the preparations necessary for any of these maneuvers would be bound to attract far more attention than the low-key arrival by commercial aircraft at different times of a number of unremarkable men who picked up their hardware from a reliable source close to the scene of the action.

Mike Campbell normally took all of these problems to Mobile, Alabama. Colquitt Armaments was composed of a small office building and a big warehouse in an industrial estate on the edge of the city. Lawns, azalea bushes, and live oaks took the harsh edges off the factory environment. Inside the glass doors, a startlingly pretty girl sat at the reception desk. Mike hadn't seen her before, which was no surprise to him since Cuthbert Colquitt's receptionist-secretaries never seemed to last more than a couple of months.

"Mike Campbell is the name. Mr. Colquitt is expecting me."

She pushed her chair back from the desk to give him a view of her legs and shook a wave of her long black hair from in front of her dark eyes. "Cuthbert said he didn't want to be disturbed."

"Please tell him I'm here."

"Cuthbert don't feel so good this morning. You sure you don't want to come back some other time?"

"Tell him Mike Campbell is here."

Instead of using the intercom, she stood in her high heels and sashayed back into the office, wiggling her cute butt in a tight black skirt. She was gone awhile. When she came back, she raised her eyebrows and said in an arch voice, "Mr. Campbell, Mr. Colquitt will see you now."

Mike heard her snigger as he went in.

As well she could. Cuthbert Colquitt looked a sight. At the best of times his jowls and double chin, the rolls of fat on his neck, and his great bulk hardly presented a picture of health. This morning his little bloodshot eyes had almost disappeared above his bloated, reddened cheeks, his hands trembled, and his stomach audibly rumbled across the room.

"Been burning the midnight oil, Cuthbert?" Mike asked pleasantly, and shook his hand.

"I been drinking the midnight oil, least that's how it feels." Cuthbert made no move to rise from his chair and greet him, which was not typical of this usually courteous man. "You could perform a big service for us both if you'll take out that bottle of Jack Daniel's and pour us two generous measures over the ice you'll find in that spittoon over there.

"That dingbat gal keeps insisting I need a blow job more than I need a drink, but my pecker don't seem to agree. He ain't jumping to attention for anyone till I get a drop of good liquor in me. Way I feel right now, I'd be surprised if either of us ever move again. Been on a three-day jag, boy. I met some friends unexpected like, and everything just fell in place and I kept going. I've no idea what happened to them. They just fell by the wayside or went home. I kept going." He slurped greedily on the Jack Daniel's and held out the glass to Mike again, his shaky hand rattling the ice cubes. Mike poured him another three-finger measure. Cuthbert swallowed half that. "Oh, yes, I believe I'm beginning to see the light at the end of the tunnel. What brings a cunning Yankee like you down among us Confederate chickens?"

"I'm thinking of a vacation in Afghanistan, Cuthbert."

"You really know how to pick them, boy. I see likely fellas head out to places only half as dangerous as you like to pick, and sure they go, but they don't come back. You keep coming back all the time with never a scratch nor a gray hair, while even stay-at-homes like myself, who don't feel comfortable more than twenty miles outside Mobile, die like flies on the highways and in other people's beds. It's like those folk who tell you flying is safer than driving to the airport. You're out there beating on the heads of savage, wild men and you don't break a fingernail, while I'm liable to slip in the shower and crack my skull. It don't seem fair, but the Good Lord giveth and the Good Lord disposeth. When my time comes, I hope to go gracefully. . . ."

"I know there's going to be a big discount on prices for my having to nurse you through this crisis."

Cuthbert cackled and reached out himself for the bottle of Jack Daniel's. "Don't you go pulling your fast ones on us easygoing Southern people. You know you're not going to the cheapest part of the world so far as hardware is concerned. A Kalashnikov assault rifle you could buy for two-fifty in some places will cost you twelve to sixteen hundred on the Afghan border. I can get them for you for less than a thousand, of course, but that's still four times the price elsewhere."

"Money's not a problem, Cuthbert. I need non-American weapons. Iron Curtain countries if possible. Antihelicopter, antitank, something that packs punch on the one-man missile line. The Kalashnikov sounds good as a rifle. I'll leave the pistols, grenades, and so forth to you. Give me the best available. For seven men plus two in reserve."

"Then not everything will be of Iron Curtain manufacture," Cuthbert pointed out. "Peshawar is a good marketplace. It's in Pakistan, not far from the border. As I said, it's expensive, but I'll get you what you need."

"I also need a contact inside Pakistan, someone who can evaluate our contacts for me and talk with me about crossing the border. I'm using someone called Aga Akbar for the crossing. He brought in three Americans not long ago. Have him checked out for me. You know someone?"

"A good man. I've known him for years. He spent a few days with me last year. We went coon hunting every night."

Mike had already been through that a few times, and he knew that Cuthbert's invitation to go with him and his dogs was his supreme tribute to any man.

Mike smiled. "I'm trying to imagine what a Pakistani thought of tramping the Alabama backwoods with you and your hounds in the dark of night."

"This man's a Pathan warrior. He shot them damn raccoons out of the trees before I could properly get a light on them. If it had been up to me, I'd have made him a U.S. citizen on the spot."

"Okay, okay, Cuthbert, that's enough."

Mike waited at the small airstrip outside Santa Ynez. He saw a single-engine plane approach and lower its landing gear. He recognized it from the high-wing design as a Cessna 210. The plane made an awful landing, its left wheel touching before the right, and the pilot managed to steady the craft only by almost aborting the landing by lifting both

COBRA STRIKE

wheels off the ground and touching down again. The Cessna stopped with only about twenty feet of runway to spare.

Campbell drove out to meet the plane, hoping this landing was not a sign of things to come. He watched while the pilot seemed to be having difficulty extracting himself from the cockpit. Finally a six-foot-four, extremely thin, bony man jumped out and walked toward him, hand extended.

"Jedediah Crippenby," he said, introducing himself.

Mike nodded and shook his hand. "That was some landing."

"Not bad for my first time at the controls of a plane," Crippenby said in a pleased voice.

"Your copilot let you land first time at the controls?" Mike asked incredulously.

The second man, looking a bit shaken, joined them. "Not the wisest thing I've ever allowed. But Jed here has made such progress in the last few days, I thought we might deliver a skilled pilot as well as everything else to you. That was a little premature, I'm afraid."

"Wait!" Crippenby said enthusiastically, and rushed back to the plane. He drew out an Armalite rifle, snapped a magazine in place, and wildly looked around him. Mike took the pack of Kent Golden Lights from the copilot's hand and threw it out on the grass. Crippenby hit it with his second shot on semiautomatic fire and then blew away the fragments with an automatic burst of four shots.

"Okay," Mike called, and gestured to him to put the rifle back in the plane. Campbell looked around. They were at the end of the runway, and probably no one noticed them or even heard the shots. When Crippenby rejoined them, Mike said, "Last I heard of you, all you could do was swim. Besides rifle shooting and flying planes, what else have you learned in the past few days?"

"I've fired a thousand rounds each from a Smith & Wesson .38 revolver and a Colt .45 semiautomatic, five thousand rounds from an Uzi submachine gun, two rifle grenades from an M16, and thrown more dummy hand grenades than I could count. I watched movies on antihelicopter and antitank warfare, but I didn't get a chance to fire any rockets. Still, I didn't do so bad for someone who never even got to shoot a BB gun as a kid. The instructors said I have a natural aptitude for target shooting, but then, that's the story of my life. I seem to have a natural aptitude for everything."

He said this like someone admitting a flaw in his personality, and perhaps Crippenby regarded his unusual abilities as such. Mike liked his lack of coyness and forthright assessment of himself.

"You'll do all right with us, Jed," Mike said, "so long as you always remember one thing. We need you as a member of a team, not as a solo star. That's what I'm going to be watching for. One thing I don't understand is why you want to quit your nice air-conditioned library and climb around on the hills with us."

"Concepts and ideas are one thing, climbing hills is another. I've had too many concepts and not climbed any real hills."

"I think both of you guys are off the wall," the copilot said. "If you need me, you have the emergency phone number, and I'll touch down here in exactly two hours from receiving your call. Do either of you happen to have any cigarettes?"

Campbell and Crippenby shook their heads. The copilot picked out a bent cigarette from the torn-up pack of Kents on the grass.

Andre Verdoux, Joe Nolan, Bob Murphy, Lance Hardwick, and Harvey Waller stood on the Camino Cielo, the road that ran along the top of the coastal ridge of the San Rafael Mountains. On one side of the narrow road they could see the houses of Santa Barbara sprawled far beneath them, the Pacific coastline, and, out on the calm blue water, the offshore platforms for drilling oil, the hulking, flat-topped silhouettes that made Nolan think they were aircraft carriers. On the other side of the road the ridge dropped steeply down to a wide valley, at the bottom of which was a ribbon of lake and a huge dam. The rugged folds of the San Rafael Mountains formed the other wall of this valley, and beyond them, in the wilderness, the last of the California condors still soared somewhere on their huge wingspans.

"I got to admit," Nolan said, "we don't have anything like this in Ohio."

"In New Jersey neither," Waller confessed.

Hardwick wasn't impressed by the natural splendor. "I still can't see why I had to take a plane from L.A. to New York, only to have to turn right around and have to come back again. I could have driven here in three hours from my place in West Hollywood. Instead I have to drag my ass back and forth across the continent—"

"You joined Mike Campbell's mission at my apartment in Manhattan," Verdoux snapped. "You're getting paid a hundred thousand dollars to do what Mike orders. If he wants to fly you from coast to coast nonstop for the next month, you shut up and do it. You've been warned before about mouthing off and second-guessing, Hardwick. The reason you do it is you know nothing, and since you know nothing, you're an expert on everything."

"I was in the Rangers, Verdoux," Lance spat back. "I was trained for special operations forces."

"Peacetime army, mon vieux," Andre said with disdain.

Lance was stung into silence as Andre touched his weak spot; he was the only member of the team who did not have combat experience outside Campbell's missions. Lance raged, but like the others, he accepted Andre as second in command to Mike without question. Like the others, he feared Andre verbally more than he did physically. What made the Frenchman's acidic remarks all the more deadly was their timing and accuracy. To attempt a punchout with him would only confirm the truth of what he had said. Campbell left it to Verdoux to maintain his own dominance over the others as second in command, except for one phase in the mission, which was this one. During training Andre Verdoux was in command and Mike Campbell had to rough it on the same terms as the others. Andre reserved his cruelest, wittiest observations for Mike, so that by the time training had ended, the other team members had formed close psychological bonds with their leader under the shared physical sufferings imposed on them by the merciless and precise French military man.

They stood on the Camino Cielo, waiting for Mike to

show with the new man. Apart from Andre and Bob, all they knew about him was that his name was Jedediah Crippenby, which was enough to make Joe Nolan crack up. Bob Murphy joined in the general kidding around while he and Andre tried to keep out of one another's way. Each time they met at the beginning of a mission, they renewed their personal dislike of each other, but increasingly they found this mutual dislike tempered by a respect for each other as soldiers. Each would have been more comfortable not to have the other along, yet each knew he could totally rely on the other no matter how disastrous things got. They did some mental sparring but tried nothing serious on each other. Murphy had no problems with Verdoux as second in command, since the Frenchman never allowed personal feelings or power plays to influence his control over the others—something for which they all respected him, yet also something that made him into an even more formidable opponent.

After Mike arrived with Crippenby and the gangly six-foot-four intellectual was given a moment of unbelieving silence, Andre gave his orders. "We're at this spot because we can see both our departure and arrival points from here. We leave from down there"—he pointed to a crinkle in the ridge to the south—"and we arrive due north at that point. We go from the southerly high point down to Gibraltar Reservoir, which is the lake you see down there, and back up the ridge to the northern high point. Each man gets a snakebite kit and leaves his cigarettes and matches behind—this is brush-fire country. Don't walk through that thorn scrub, go around it or it'll cut your legs to ribbons. And don't feed the bears."

He sent Lance in one car and Bob in another, to drop off one car at the arrival point and come back to the departure point in the second car. All the others piled in the third car and set off for the departure point. Three cars were already pulling into the side of the road when they got there.

"Hang gliders," Andre explained. "There won't be anything odd about our two cars left empty here."

When they got out of the car, they were in time to see a guy step up on the bank of earth between the roadway and the precipice on the ocean side of Camino Cielo, balance his fabric glider over his body, wait for an updraft of wind, and hop off into the great blue yonder. He didn't sink at all; the updraft wafted the glider into an immediate upward spiral, and the pilot cleverly went from updraft to updraft, climbing all the time.

"That's not a way I'd choose to die," Joe Nolan said, and found that he spoke for the rest of them. "Maybe Lance would try this shit. When he gets back, I bet he says he's done it."

Waller picked up a Pepsi can on the other side of the road. He showed Nolan the claw punctures and scrapes in it and the teeth marks where one end had been chewed off. "I guess Andre wasn't kidding about bears."

Nolan nodded. "They got a taste for sweet things. You and me don't have to worry, Harvey."

While they were waiting for Bob and Lance to come back, five more hang gliders floated past at their eye level. One glider was piloted by a woman with an infant in a pack strapped beneath her. On another glider a man had a small terrier sitting in harness on a platform beside him.

Mike said slowly, "I sometimes think maybe I'm crazy, Andre, until I take time to look at what other people do."

CHAPTER 8

Campbell had only forty miles to go across land from Pakistan's Karachi International Airport to find Naseeb Amin, and one mile out to sea, where he stood on the bridge of the S.S. *Guadalquiver,* a rusty tanker sporting a Panamanian flag.

"*Izzat!*" Naseeb roared. "*Izzat!* What you English call honor! There is no more sacred word in Pushtu!"

"Where's that?"

"Pushtu is not a place. Pathans speak Pushtu."

"I see." Campbell looked out over the Arabian Sea, which extended south of Pakistan and into the Indian Ocean. It was oily and calm, without a breeze stirring or a seabird in sight. "I want to clear up things about our backgrounds. I speak English but I am an American, not English. My confusion about Pathans is that I sometimes hear them called Afghans and sometimes Pakistanis."

"We live on both sides of the border. You could say that the eastern half of Afghanistan is Pathan, and Pakistan's Northwest Frontier Province—it still goes by its old English name—is our land too. You have heard of the Khyber Pass?

We Pathans beat back the British Empire. They could never conquer us. *Izzat*! Honor! When your honor must be regained, what must you do?"

"Kill?"

Naseeb Amin nodded his head gravely. "I see you understand some things."

Campbell read through the paper Amin had given him. He looked wonderingly at the perfect copperplate lettering written with a nib dipped in ink. The whole thing looked like a Victorian document. Aga Akbar, the guide into Afghanistan offered by the Nanticoke Institute, received a good recommendation. An inventory of weapons and supplies was provided, along with a bill—payment in U.S. dollars specified—for his signature. A dozen letters of introduction to rebel leaders in English for Campbell's guidance and the message itself in what he presumed was Pushtu. He would have Crippenby look them over, although he had no doubt that they would all be in order.

"I knew I could rely on a friend of Cuthbert Colquitt's," Mike said. "He told me you and he went raccoon hunting when you visited him."

"Allah be praised He did not put raccoons in the lands of the Pathans."

"I live in the desert, not too unlike what you have along here, so there are no coons there. I've been out with Cuthbert a few times and didn't do so well, but he told me you were a crack shot and could rival an old hand like himself."

"Show me a pair of eyes shining up in a tree and I will put a bullet between them for you if you wish," Naseeb said. "I said a bullet. No Pathan could miss with a shotgun. But neither does a Pathan wish to walk around after a heavy dinner in swamps and woods, listening to stupid dogs bark and chase into a tree an animal that is not good to eat, I was told, and which is not dangerous and thus honorable to hunt. I tell you I would sit in their comfortable house after the large quantity of food I mentioned, hoping to watch shows on their television, sipping excellent coffee—as a Muslim, I did not share in Cuthbert's passion for alcohol— talking with a very beautiful girl who worked for him and a somewhat less beautiful but very acceptable female companion she brought along for me, when Cuthbert would suddenly insist that I hunt raccoons in the swamps with him. How could I refuse such an offer without offending my host? It was impossible. So I went. Every night."

"And the female companion?"

"She waited up for me each night. She was collecting the skins for a fur coat."

Campbell caught the sly, amused look the Pathan gave him. Mike guessed he was in his late fifties, a bull of a man with a handlebar mustache flecked with gray, a barrel chest, and a commanding presence.

Mike signed the cost estimate for the weapons and supplies after a cursory examination and handed the sheets back to Amin. The prices were much more exorbitant than usual, as Cuthbert had warned him they would be, but since the Institute had to meet these expenses, they could discuss any discrepancies themselves.

"That seems to be everything," Mike said. "I seem to have arrived at an awkward time for you."

"Yes, it's high tide. Man must bow before nature. But if you wait four hours for this tide to crest, my work here will be done and I will go north with you."

"I would greatly appreciate that, especially since it's not something expected of you."

"We Pathans can be depended on to do what is not expected of us."

"Such as teaching the Kremlin a lesson about straying too far south?"

"If Allah wills it, we will be pleased to oblige."

They waited another hour before Naseeb Amin rang down to the engine for full speed ahead. He had selected a niche hardly a hundred yards wide on the sandy beach between two beached wrecks. The S.S. *Guadalquivir*, emptied of its cargo of oil, riding high with its Plimsoll mark many feet above the water's surface, charged in on the high tide at a good fifteen knots and ground its prow and keel onto the sandy bottom forty yards from shore, at a right angle to the beach and exactly halfway between the wrecks on either side.

Crewmen on the foredeck set loose a winch, and the starboard anchor chain rattled out to lower its burden. Men on the beach wound a steel hawser around the anchor and, when it was securely attached, signaled to the operator of a heavy winch on the beach. This winch pulled the steel hawser and anchor chain tight. Then, at each surging wave, Naseeb gave the ship full steam, and the winch on shore pulled at full power, so that the thirteen-thousand-ton steel carcass of the beached ship crept up on land inch by inch. They kept this up for as long as the tide was at its peak, after which the ship's heavy bulk could be moved no more.

"My work is done," Naseeb Amin announced with the satisfaction of a master.

Mike looked up and down the beach, on which more than a hundred big ships were beached and in various stages of demolition. On the shore itself, huge stacks of metal parts awaited trucking away. Beyond them lay a ragged string of hovels, constructed of scrap lumber and other unsalable materials, and beyond the hovels stretched the empty desert.

Once the ship was settled as close to the beach as it could be brought, the anchors were allowed to drop to the sand. Men walked up the chains to the prow high above the beach as casually as city dwellers on an escalator. They carried oxyacetylene torches and cylinders, crowbars, sledgehammers, and wrenches. One group immediately began to lower the lifeboats over the side and throw life rafts and other deck fittings down to others waiting below, who dragged each item ashore and placed it in a pile with like items. Other men were removing the brass fitting of the portholes. The ship's radar scope, sonar, and compass were gone in minutes. They were already putting thirty-foot lengths of piping over the side. Mike could hardly believe the speed at which they worked. The ship was disintegrating before his eyes. A half hour previously it had been a vessel capable of sailing around the world. Now these human piranhas were devouring it. While some were still ripping out the fittings, others were cutting steel plates from its sides with torches.

With an ironic touch, Naseeb Amin saw the crew members and Mike safely down a rope ladder over the side before he, as the vessel's last master, abandoned ship.

When Mike looked back for the last time, they were lowering the ship's ceramic sinks and toilets over the side.

While they waited for a flight north from Karachi to Rawalpindi, Naseeb told him that all the workers at Gadani Beach were Pathans who traveled more than a thousand miles south to earn the equivalent of less than four dollars for a twelve-hour day of dangerous work. Naseeb himself earned about fifteen hundred dollars for each ship he beached, a task that required more skill than it might seem. Any ship that could not be brought close enough to shore could not be broken up economically.

"Do Pathans buy these ships to break up?" Mike wanted to know.

Naseeb laughed at the idea of Pathans buying something like an oceangoing ship. "We are mountain tribesmen. All we know how to do is work and fight."

"You are an educated man," Mike said.

"I work and I fight. These people who buy these ships and sell the steel are millionaire investors. They watch for ships more than twenty years old bound for Karachi or a nearby port and they make a bid to the shipowner, with or without the cargo included, depending on who owns it. But you could have a ship, say, bound for Bahrain with a cargo of Japanese television sets. These investors might buy the whole thing, sell the television sets in Muscat or Karachi, let most of the crew go, and have it run up to Gadani Beach for scrap."

Mike estimated from Naseeb's casually quoted figures in Pakistani rupees that an old ship could be bought for about $100 per ton, be broken up on Gadani Beach for $40 per ton, and its best steel, about half the ship's weight, be sold for $240 per ton with the investors about breaking even on the other half of the ship's weight. Estimating a $100 profit per ton for half the *Guadalquivir*'s 13,000-ton weight would give a $650,000 profit to whoever decided to end her sailing days. A Pathan working a twelve-hour day in a seven-day week earned less than twenty-eight dollars.

Campbell was beginning to gather that life was not milk and honey for the Pathans either inside or outside of Afghanistan.

*   *   *

"*La ilaha illah'llah, wa-Muhammadun rasul-Allah,*" the eleven Soviet prisoners repeated piously. "There is no God but Allah, and Mohammad is His messenger." They faced Mecca and bowed on their knees till their foreheads touched the prayer mats on the earthen floor of their prison hut. They had been doing this five times a day now for two weeks, and they all agreed that it was worth doing alone for the improved rations such devotion brought them. But they had more ambitious plans than that. Some of their guards had let slip that they were being held prisoner in a refugee camp in Pakistan. After being captured in an ambush in Afghanistan, they had been marched, blindfolded, for days. They had not even suspected that they had been brought across the border. This changed everything. If they could escape now, they would find themselves in neutral territory instead of among hostile Afghan tribesmen. The Pakistanis had reason to fear their great Russian bear neighbor and would go out of their way to see that the eleven men were repatriated.

Although the floor was of earth and the prison walls constructed of pine logs and dried mud, they could not tunnel or break their way out because of the constant vigilance of the guards. Boris, who outranked the others as a corporal and was thus their leader, reasoned that if they could not escape the surveillance of their guards, then they must find a way to deceive them. Boris selected Rasool as any easy mark. Rasool had studied in the Soviet city of Tashkent in the Uzbek Republic before the Soviet invasion of Afghanistan in 1979. Nine of the eleven Soviet prisoners were from the Uzbek Republic, too, and as Central Asians, they shared more in common with their Afghan enemies than they did with European Russians like Boris. Some could remember their grandparents and even their parents as devout Moslems in spite of Stalin's savage campaigns to stamp out religion. Even today this was something they did not feel comfortable talking about. They were familiar with the sound of the prayers in Arabic, having heard old people chant them in defiance of the great socialist revolution in towns and villages all over the Uzbek Republic, though the mosques had been closed and the Korans burned. Rasool, who was as devout as he was naive, led the nine Uzbeks in their religious revival and earned a high place for himself in the Garden of Paradise by also converting Boris and the other Russian to the Shining Way. And it was Rasool they disarmed during a spirited discussion of the Prophet's son-in-law Ali. They laughed at the Afghan as they beat and kicked him until he lay silent and unmoving on the mud floor of their prison hut. Rasool wept tears, not tears from the pain of his injuries but tears of shame.

They crouched in the doorway of the prison hut and looked out, eleven men with one Kalashnikov between them.

"Once we get clear of this refugee camp, we won't need weapons," Boris whispered urgently. "But first we must get out of this place."

They saw what he meant. The usual dirty children played on the dusty ground, and the usual women, clad from head to toe in burkas, scuttled about as if fearful to be out of their homes—but here the men, as they could not do in occupied zones of Afghanistan, walked around with rifles and bandoliers of ammunition.

One of the Uzbeks said, "They will take one look at us and..." He imitated the sound of automatic fire.

They remained where they were, hoping for something to distract the armed men walking around the mud huts and tents of the camp. They could not wait too long, since guards came and went from the prison on an irregular schedule that always baffled the Soviet prisoners. There was no way for them to slip out of the camp unobserved, because they would have to pass at least a dozen people to go anywhere in these congested temporary living quarters, and all it would take was a single shout to raise the alarm.

They could watch and wait no longer. They had to make their move. Boris saw the solution. A hut slightly larger and of the same construction as their prison hut lay diagonally across the ribbon of bare earth that passed for a street in this refugee camp. They all had noticed the men coming and going to and from this hut constantly, and it was Boris who noticed that the men went in with one weapon and came out

COBRA STRIKE   123

with another or went in with an empty bandolier and came out with one filled with cartridges. This hut was their armory!

"Look, there's no way we can sneak out of this camp unseen," Boris whispered to the others. "That means we will have to fight our way out. This is how we will do it. I will lead a charge on that hut with this Kalashnikov. I will go in the door first and you come in fast after me. Even if we are seen, we should all be able to get inside before we draw fire. Then we select the best weapons they have inside and come out fighting. If we move fast and do not give them time to organize, we will be out of this camp before they can do much. Use their children and women as shields if you can. They will be reluctant to fire on us even with one or two children as hostages."

Boris looked around at their drawn, anxious faces. They had all been prisoners for months now, and not one of them was backing down. He nodded to them with a confidence he did not feel. "We're going to do this."

He moved quickly across the street, the ten others right behind him. Boris heard children or women shouting but he paid no heed. He stepped through the open door of the hut and peered into its dim interior. Two, no, three men were inside. He sprayed them with bullets from left to right. All three went down and lay there twitching and groaning.

His fellow prisoners crowded in the doorway behind him, pushing him forward. They rushed past him to grab weapons from the stacks all over the place, climbing over half-filled wood crates of ammo and grenades to get at them. One man grabbed a light machine gun. Boris saw the fine wire attached to its trigger guard, saw the wire stretch off into the wood crates, saw it tauten as the Uzbek hauled the weapon along with him. Boris rushed to him, yelling at him to keep still, it was booby-trapped. The Uzbek jerked sideways, pulling the line taut.

Boris felt himself ride in the air and saw the inside of the hut turn yellow, white, then black.

"One of the things we've been discussing a lot recently at the Institute," Jedediah Crippenby was saying to Mike

Campbell as they walked through the Afghan refugee camp, "is how we ourselves create make-believe data about things we don't know. The Afghan refugees were high on our list. Every time they see us Americans coming, they think to themselves, 'Ah, numbers. They will want numbers, and if we don't give them numbers, they say they cannot help us.' So now, when we ask them how much of the refugee population has dysentery, they say thirty-seven percent without batting an eye. *They* know that no one knows how many people are refugees, let alone how many people have dysentery. But Americans want numbers and facts. So we are given numbers and facts, and very serious people compare these numbers and facts with the numbers and facts from one month ago and from this time last year, and they make graphs and pronouncements and are amazed when things don't turn out like they predicted.

"The plain truth, Mike, is that we don't know anything— or at least very little. The Afghans themselves don't know. The Russians don't care. The Pakistanis are overwhelmed with their own problems. And we Americans feel we have to have all the facts before we can act. Those three men from our Institute came out here to gather facts, which is why we are now here. You see what I mean? We send three men out to find out what the reality is here. The three men we sent out are the only reality we truly understand. Now we are here, not to ask questions about reality, but to try to find the people we sent to ask questions about reality, and so we become facts too. Meanwhile nothing is getting much clearer. Are you following me?"

"I take a more practical view of things, Jed," Mike said, amused. "All I want to know is, from the conversations we've had through Naseeb Amin and from what Aga Akbar has told us, how much can we believe?"

"We can take as authentic that up until last week, at least, Turner, Baker, and Winston were the three mysterious Americans wreaking havoc with the Russians, that they are not straying too far from Gul Daoud's territory, judging from the locations of the incidents reported—they're probably trying to keep him from direct reprisals—and that all their escape routes back here are cut off. That was the status a week ago, the amount of time it takes word-of-mouth information to travel from there to here. Everything else we've been told is unreliable—about their capture, about their being seen at Karachi Airport, and so forth."

"So we have a solid wall of Soviet and Afghan communist troops between us and them," Mike muttered to himself. "We'll have to breach their line once on the way there and once more on the way back. Now that you're in the soldier-of-fortune business, Jed, you're going to find yourself in situations where passive brainwork isn't enough. You have to walk deliberately into the unknown and depend on your brain to act in teamwork with the rest of your body. It's not the kind of thinking that gets done much in libraries, but don't expect it to be any easier."

Crippenby wanted desperately to say something, but he was learning fast that this was going to be no academic project, that his opinions would not be worth a damn in the mountains, and that keeping his mouth shut now and then seemed to be something everyone on the team except himself enjoyed.

Mike was treading very cautiously while in Pakistan. It was rumored that a blast in the Zangali refugee camp had killed eleven Soviet prisoners of war. The Afghans denied this, saying that they would never embarrass Pakistan by keeping Soviet prisoners on their soil. The Pakistanis denied all knowledge of the event and warned all Afghan refugees that Pakistan's neutrality must not be abused. Of course, the Pakistanis were a bit uncomfortable about the fact that the Zangali refugee camp, where the eleven Soviets were said to have died, was just a little way down a rutted road in a hilly area near Badabir Pakistani Air Force base. It was from Badabir that Francis Gary Powers took off in the U-2 spy plane that was shot down over the Soviet Union in 1960. The Pakistanis had claimed that they hadn't known anything about that, either.

If the rumored deaths of Soviet prisoners were not enough to give Pakistanis the jitters about their Soviet neighbors, the arrival of two Soviet-made Mi-24 helicopter gunships next day certainly was. The choppers were crewed by Afghan government servicemen who all asked for political asylum. The Mi-24, named the Hind by Western military experts, was the most powerful gunship in the Soviet arsenal. This was the first time the craft had fallen into noncommunist hands, and military attachés from the embassies of various friendly Western nations were insisting that they lend a hand in giving the two choppers a maintenance checkup before they were returned. Moscow was threatening to kick Pakistani ass if they let any degenerate capitalists near their clean machines.

Mike sensed that now might not be the best time for an expeditionary force of seven armed Americans (one of French and one of Australian origin) to be caught crossing the border into occupied Afghanistan.

In Peshawar and Hangu and all the other towns along the Pakistan side of the Afghan-Pakistani border, the story was the same. Floods of immigrant refugees had cleaned out what had already been a very spare and hardy existence. It was said that there were three million Afghan refugees in Pakistan, but no one really knew for sure how many. The people on both sides of the border were Pathans, there was a long tradition of smuggling and drug and gunrunning, and violence settled serious arguments. The Red Cross opened hospitals and did what they could for those living in the three hundred camps along the thousand-mile border. Mike Campbell was struck by the number of men, women, and children missing a foot or a hand. A Swiss doctor told him that people with head or body wounds rarely survived the long trek to the border, while those with injuries to their limbs often did and thus were seen more often. Nearly all these injuries were caused by Soviet land mines dropped on the fields where the peasants worked and the children played.

Before the team gathered to go into action, Campbell and Crippenby visited a number of the camps. Mike found the Institute's intellectual very useful here in neutral Pakistan, and since he was not fully sure how Jed Crippenby would hold up under fire, he decided to put him to work while he could. Crippenby's fluent Pushtu and his unbureaucratic manner and appearance warmed the tribesmen toward him.

COBRA STRIKE   127

During the time they journeyed around, some of the camps—though none of the ones they visited—were hit by rockets and mortars from the other side of the border, and others were strafed or bombed by MIGs. President Reagan announced that he was sending forty F-16 jet fighters so the Pakistanis could use them against these Soviet violations of their airspace.

But if Mike and Jed were having an interesting time, the rest of the team was going bananas. No booze and no broads was the general complaint.

"There won't be any in Afghanistan, either," Mike pointed out.

"We expect that," Bob Murphy said, "but at least we'll be doing something there. Here there's nothing to do, and all day and night to do it. Come on, Mike, why are we waiting here? I'm not getting acclimatized, I'm getting crazy."

For once Andre Verdoux was in agreement with Bob. "You know what the military dictator General Zia did? He stopped the Pakistan women's team from competing in the Olympic Games because men would be able to see their legs. You want to know his big problem now? Well, he put back in effect the Islamic code of justice—flogging and chopping and so on—but so no one can say that he is a barbarian, he does it with modern technology. The law says a thief gets his hand chopped off. General Zia agrees but says the hand must be surgically removed. Most of the surgeons here are Western-trained, and this goes against their ethics. So what is Zia to do? If he puts the surgeons in jail, there'll be no one to operate on the ruling class. Meanwhile all these thieves are waiting around with their hands still attached—"

"We'll go, we'll go," Mike said. "I can see that you guys are going to fall to pieces if I don't get you out of here fast."

Mike went alone to find Aga Akbar, who agreed to leave immediately. Together they went to the arms dealer in the market, the one Naseeb Amin introduced him to. They sat on cushions and sipped tea, surrounded by stacks of weapons available to anyone who could pay the price, following the ceremonial civilities before anyone mentioned business. Mike's weapons were ready. The dealer and Aga Akbar spoke rapidly in Pushtu, arranging the details.

They left Peshawar before dawn in a rented van with a driver. They reached a village in the foothills at first light and examined their weapons and equipment there. Cuthbert Colquitt had proved himself reliable once again—the agreed-upon list had been fully supplied. Mike paid two fighters from the village to cross the border with them. This was more a gesture of goodwill than a necessity, Aga Akbar explained. From here on they would be on foot. They climbed up into the hills, bitching and whining like troops always do when they initially head out. Mike listened to the complaints grow fewer and finally stop altogether as the hills got steeper and they had to save their breath.

CHAPTER 9

Bob Murphy had cursed loudest back in Pakistan about dyeing his beard and hair black. On Mike's instructions, all of them quit shaving as soon as agreeing to go on the mission. Then the night before crossing the border into Afghanistan, Mike had produced black hair dye. Only a few days later Bob was sporting a black beard with bright yellow roots! With the weapons and supplies Naseeb Amin had stored at the village for them were the Afghan ethnic outfits they now wore. They all settled for the flat woolen hats with rolled bottoms rather than the bulky turban of many windings that many Afghans favored. They also skipped the blanketlike capes, long leather tunics, and all the other loose, flapping garments the mountain tribesmen wore. Instead they adopted the obviously new style of dress of the modern fighting Afghan—combat boots, baggy pants, and an assortment of oversize shirts, loose vests, and a Western parka or windproof jacket. After a few days of trekking in the mountains, at first sight they looked just like any of the other guerrilla patrols that infested the mountains.

They had slipped across the border without incident, and

Aga Akbar led them to Sayad Jan's emplacement. From there they followed in the footsteps of Baker, Winston, and Turner, often using the same guides they had. Not being held up by a train of six burdened asses, they made much faster progress than the three previous Americans had. They were helped, too, by Jed Crippenby's knowledge of Pushtu, and none of the local tribesmen even considered tangling with this tough-looking bunch.

Each day they headed out at dawn and made camp at dusk. They bought what food they could along the way in order to conserve their C rations. They met no Soviet or Afghan communist ground troops while they were still being guided by local rebels, although they frequently had to throw themselves to the ground and remain motionless while Soviet jets or choppers passed over their position. If they were seen on any of these occasions, as they assumed they must have been, they were not attacked, perhaps because there were bigger and better targets available elsewhere. But this all ended early one afternoon when the four Afghans acting as their guides stopped, and all began talking volubly together to Jed Crippenby, who kept nodding his head to what they were telling him.

"This is as far as they will take us, Mike," Jed explained. "They claim that the Russians have sealed all the passes in the range ahead of us, and beyond that range the Russians have more or less cleared away all rebel activity because of their troop concentrations, sweeps, and aerial surveillance. And these are Soviet troops, not Afghan government forces who might be expected to be halfhearted about it. They have heard of attacks launched by these three mysterious Americans, but some of these are obviously just stories. However, since the Soviet troops are still in place to cut off their escape back to Pakistan, it is reasonable to assume that the Americans are still alive and on the loose."

"Do you know where Gul Daoud is?"

After another excited conversation with the four Afghans, Crippenby said, "Gul Daoud simply retreats back into the mountains when attacked. The more the communists attack, the higher he goes. Finally the communists give up and go away, and he and his men come down again to resume control. These men say that the Americans are with some of Gul Daoud's warriors, so presumably they stay in contact or at least know where to find each other."

Mike nodded. "Finding Gul Daoud's main force will be a hell of a lot easier than trying to locate the three crazy bastards we've come for. Do these men know anything about the Soviet troop deployments in the mountains ahead?"

"No," Crippenby said right off. "They've been keeping a safe distance from them."

Mike paid off the four rebels in Pakistani rupees, and after much traditional handshaking and embracing they went back the way they had come, leaving the merc team to face the forbidding-looking jagged peaks ahead with their pockets of hidden Soviet soldiers.

That night was their first night in the open, since they had always stayed in rebel huts before. Although they had ultralight nylon tents, each sleeping two men, Mike decided against erecting them in his dangerous terrain. Seven men sleeping concealed on the side of a mountain were unfindable, whereas the sight of even one tent told a whole story. The next day, Mike teamed Bob Murphy with Lance Hardwick, Andre Verdoux with Joe Nolan, and kept the unpredictable Harvey Waller and the inexperienced Jed Crippenby with him. Bob and Lance's task was to locate military posts, and the other two teams were to check the approaches toward two high passages to the north, which might be less well guarded then the main pass. They were to meet back at their starting place in two hours.

"If you're seen, even if you kill some easy target, you'll give our presence away," Mike warned. "Then we'll never break through. As it is, they'll be watching for someone coming through from the other side of this range, so we're catching them from behind. We need to keep that advantage. Don't blow it for us."

The man Mike was really afraid might blow it for them was in his own group. Harvey Waller could be hard to restrain when he was rarin' to go. Of all of them on the team, Waller was by far the best fighting man—he had an instinct and imagination in combat that made the others look second-rate. Off the leash, Harvey could qualify for one of those TV nature programs about magnificent natural predators; on the leash, he might start shooting at any time, regardless of consequences. But not with Mike. Harvey never tried to disguise the fact that he was in awe of Mike. Whatever Mike said was law to Harvey.

"I think Jed should be point man," Waller said. "He's so skinny, he'll be able to walk through a hail of bullets."

Crippenby swallowed and looked uncomfortable.

Mike pointed to Waller. "You lead, I'll take the rear." Mike saw that Waller, with his instinct for someone's vulnerability, had sensed Jed's fear—something that Mike himself had not noticed. Crippenby was no fool; he knew they could not hope to break through the Soviet line without some contact. Up until now all had been plain sailing, easy going, apart from sudden alarms caused by approaching aircraft. Now the danger was from something unseen on the ground, something from which there would be no easy escape, since they were the ones who were advancing. No doubt Crippenby had been through all this in textbooks a hundred times, only now he was finding out that the mind and muscles behave in a different way in the presence of a real threat. "Are you going to be okay?" Mike asked softly.

"Sure. Sure, Mike."

"Stay between Harvey and me and you'll do just fine. Do what you see us doing. Don't try to prove anything."

Jed unexpectedly grinned. "Prove anything? My mind's gone blank."

"That happens."

They moved out at a cautious walk toward some stands of timber that they might be able to follow up onto higher ground toward the small northernmost pass. It was still early in the morning, and they could see smoke and dust from activity in the valley and hear distant trucks change gear as they climbed the road toward the main pass. Up where they were, the soil was too poor to cultivate and the trees had not been cut for fuel because they were too inaccessible to make it worthwhile. They climbed awhile, keeping to the cover of the trees, until they came to an overlook above a winding dirt road that clearly led up to the small pass.

Mike and Harvey had spotted a machine-gun emplacement by the side of the road and were moving forward cautiously for a closer look when Jed started fluttering his hands at them in alarm. They stood still and looked around them into the heavy undergrowth, guns ready, but they saw nothing. Jed pointed, his eyes bulging in alarm, at what could have been the topless trunk of a pine leaning at an angle maybe thirty yards away. Only it wasn't a branchless pine, it was the long barrel of a heavy gun.

Now that Mike and Harvey could see that, they could also see the camouflaged tank to which the gun barrel was attached, emplaced in a thick clump of what looked like rhododendrons, its outline broken by boughs thrown on its top. The two men started walking backward, with Jed keeping his long, lean form doubled down and staying between them. After they had backed off to safety and were retracing their steps, both Mike and Harvey praised Jed.

"Last goddamn thing on earth I expected," Harvey said. "Shit, when I saw those tracked wheels through the leaves, I thought to myself that I must be going blind if I missed that. I just wasn't looking for it. I'd have walked right in front of it."

"That's how we nearly fucked up, Harvey, knowing it all," Mike said. "Jed here has no idea what to expect. His eyes are peeled for everything from a hydrogen bomb to an elephant trap. He sees, we don't. We were lucky to have you along today, Jed."

"You're okay, kid," Waller conceded grumpily.

Jed blushed.

"Just don't go thinking you know anything," Harvey added, "'cause you don't."

The other four were at the arranged meeting place when they got back. Mike just shook his head.

Andre Verdoux said, "Joe and I may have something. A lot of flatbed trucks with loads of cinder blocks are arriving along the road to the middle pass. The Russians must be building something in a hurry up that way. A truck ride up there would be just the thing to take the weight off our feet."

"What about checkpoints?" Mike asked.

"We didn't see any," Andre replied. "Maybe they feel that an uncovered truck with a small load of cinder blocks can't conceal very much. They have to keep the loads small because the road is so bad and the trucks are so ancient. One truck lost eight blocks on a bump as we watched. We hid them in bushes alongside the road for possible later use. Murphy says the trucks passed a checkpoint before they left the main road for the side road to the middle pass."

Bob nodded. "Lance and I went back the main road a bit because of the sound of engines. All vehicles, commercial and military, were being carefully checked by uniformed Soviets. When we tried to follow the road toward the pass, we'd gone no more than a hundred yards when we started seeing sandbagged dugouts all the way along. It looks like they're expecting the Marines."

"And they got the road covered by tanks in the hills, and, nearer in, mortar crews," Lance added. "We nearly ran headlong into one mortar crew on the way back here. They were just sitting there smoking and talking. We smelled the Russian tobacco before we heard their voices."

Mike was interested. "How many?"

"Three," Lance said. "One on the tube, one to reload, one with a mobile radio."

"Bob, Lance, Harvey," Mike said, and drew his finger across his throat. "Jed, you speak Russian?" Jed nodded. "So do Andre and I," Mike went on. "More or less, anyway. So be careful with the radio, it will come in handy. We will cover you three and come in to pick up the mortar tube and rounds. Jed will pick up the radio. Andre and Joe will then lead us to those cinder blocks on the roadside. Any questions? No? Good," he said without waiting. "Let's move out."

Mike's nostrils twitched. He smelled the sweet pungent smoke of Russian cigarettes. He winked at Bob Murphy, who undraped his Kalashnikov and backpack and pulled his flat wool hat down on his ears. Lance Hardwick and Harvey Waller quietly dropped their rifles and backpacks, too, and together all three men moved forward very slowly. Mike motioned to the remaining men to hold their ground and not

COBRA STRIKE

to cock their rifles—a metallic scrape or click could be heard a long way and was unmistakable.

Lance and Bob had peeped through the scrub and bushes last time to see who was there. It had been necessary then, but this time they had to go in blind in case a glimpse of them gave the mortar crew warning enough to fire a shot and raise a general alarm. These men had to die silently and fast. To do this the team members had to go in blind, and it was just too bad if there were more men than the three who had been with the mortar previously. The mercs drew their combat knives and advanced to the point where they could commence their rush.

Waller edged in front to form the spearhead of the three men. He held up his left hand. When he dropped it, they charged. They broke through the brush and into the small clearing in which the mortar tube was placed, rounds lying near it in an aluminum carrying case. The Russian with the radio backpack was sitting on a stone and reading from a magazine to the two others, also seated on stones, who were laughing. They could have been soldiers of any army, passing the long, dull hours of uneventful duty. As the three mercs broke from the brush and into the clearing, the three Soviet soldiers jumped to their feet with frightened faces.

Waller was in the lead and in the middle. He rushed at the middle Russian, who was in the act of cocking the Kalashnikov slung on his right shoulder, and hit him a straight right in the middle of the chest, like a boxer in the ring, only that in place of a glove, Waller held the steel blade of a combat knife in his right hand. The tip of the blade entered the Russian's solar plexus, and the weight of Harvey's shoulder behind the punch sank the blade all the way in until Harvey felt the tip scrape the inside of the man's backbone. The Russian gripped Waller's arm with both his hands and looked into his grinning face with imploring eyes as his body slowly collapsed and slid off the blade. The dying man's fingers clutched Waller's wrist even as his body crumpled to the ground, and the light faded from his eyes. Waller kicked him away and broke his death grip.

Murphy stood a good six inches above his opponent and weighed almost twice as much. He charged into the Soviet serviceman before he could free his automatic pistol from its holster. Both men tumbled to the ground. Bob knelt on his struggling victim's chest, grasped a handful of his hair in his left hand and twisted his head back and to one side. With a quick, easy motion he drew the blade of his combat knife across the man's throat. The slit on his throat opened like a wide mouth. As the Russian wrenched his body beneath the Australian's massive strength and weight, bright red blood squirted fom the severed arteries in his neck. He died slowly, struggling like a farmyard chicken.

The Russian with the radio backpack took one look at Lance coming at him with the combat knife and turned around to run. Were it not for the radio, Lance could have buried the knife in his back. Were it not that he had been warned to avoid damaging the radio, he could have grabbed on to it and use it to pull his prey down. Lance swung the blade in an upward thrust beneath the radio, trying to drive the knife into the soldier's right kidney, a few inches above his belt, but he ended by giving him only a superficial wound. This close call spurred the Russian on to a burst of speed. He made for the edge of the clearing, with Lance running right on his heels, thrusting at him with the blood-smeared knife. Suddenly the Russian came to a dead stop and Lance banged into him from behind. To Lance's amazement he saw the point of a knife emerge from the back of the Russian's neck and almost touch his own nose. The Russian fell lifeless at his feet, and Harvey Waller was standing there easing the blade out of the man's neck with the crazy grin on his face Harvey always got when he killed people.

Jed stayed in the scrub, monitoring Russian broadcasts, while the others got into positions on both sides of the dirt road where Joe Nolan and Andre Verdoux had seen one of the construction trucks lose eight cinder blocks on a bump. They pulled the blocks out from where Joe and Andre had hidden them and left them scattered on the roadway as they had originally fallen. They were not enough to act as a block to any truck, and indeed only a few minutes after they placed them, a loaded truck passed them, steering around them so the blocks were between its wheels. Then two empty trucks came from the opposite direction, without stopping either. Mike had told them that this would happen, yet they should not try to erect a barricade because this would cause gunfire, which they could not let happen because of nearby military positions. Mike said all they need do was wait for one driver conscientious enough not to waste the blocks.

Lance, Harvey, and Mike were on one side of the road. Lance was tying his combat knife to one end of a long, straight branch from which he had trimmed the twigs and leaves. He ignored the condescending smile of Harvey. He knew Waller would be giving him a hard time now because he had not managed to kill his assigned man when they took the mortar. Harvey would move on to making remarks about Hollywood stuntmen who looked great on camera so long as everyone was pulling punches. This would go on until something else distracted Waller or until Lance proved him wrong. Which was what he was about to do. He hoped.

They heard the grind of gears as the loaded truck downshifted to negotiate the long steady climb up the winding road. This truck was a flatbed with a load of cinder blocks, identical to the others. The driver swerved to avoid the blocks on the road, going to one side of them. For a moment he appeared to be going on without stopping, then they heard his brakes squeal to a stop, and more grinding of gears, and the truck slowly reversed back. Leaving the engine running, the Afghan driver got out on one side, a Soviet soldier on the other. The soldier was mistrustful and alert. He circled the entire truck as the driver began to load the blocks. His finger rested on the trigger of his Kalashnikov, and it looked like no one could take him without a firefight.

But as he passed Lance's position, squinting suspiciously into the undergrowth right where the men were concealed, he spun around to look at the road on the other side of the truck. Perhaps he thought he heard a sound. Lance noiselessly rose to his feet, drew back the javelin balanced in his right hand, then launched it forward with all his might. The long tapering branch with the combat knife bound to its heavy end hit the soldier in the small of his back. He staggered a few paces, dropped his assault rifle without firing it, and reached behind him to desperately try to pluck out from his back the blade and long spear whose end was trailing in the dust behind. He flopped down on his face, and the long stick drunkenly reeled upright on his back and then fell sideways at an angle, still supported by the knife blade deep in the prone soldier's flesh.

Lance heard Harvey give a grunt of satisfaction and felt an approving poke in the ribs before Harvey burst out onto the roadway and descended on the petrified, unarmed Afghan driver, who had been in the act of picking up a cinder block. Harvey hit him head down, arms outstretched, like an enraged water buffalo. He was screaming, "Goddam fucking traitor! Selling your country to the commie robots! I'll put some sense in your fucking head!" He began to smash the driver's face into the corner of a cinder block. "I'll learn you! You won't deal with no more Russian scumbags when I'm finished with you!" He kept on beating the man's head against the cinder black until it was hardly more than a bloody pulp upon a set of shoulders.

Andre walked out on the roadway and coolly watched Waller in his frenzy. He said, "That's really showing him, Harvey."

Mike told Jed to drive, since he spoke Pushtu well enough to fool a Russian. Although both spoke Russian, neither Mike nor Andre could impersonate a Russian soldier because of their black beards.

"Move out!" Campbell yelled as soon as they had thrown the bodies and bloodstained cinder block in the undergrowth. "We're going to have another truck along any moment."

The six men on the back of the truck worked feverishly to build themselves a hideout from the cinder blocks as the truck was in motion over the bumpy dirt road. They lost some blocks and threw others off to make room for themselves inside a rectangle of double-walled cinder blocks interlaced like brickwork and placed crosswise to provide stability. Gaps were left through which to poke rifles in this five-foot-high fortress.

They met no other trucks on the road, and Mike supposed

that this was because it was early afternoon. "Keep driving till I tell you to stop," he yelled up front to Jed, and situated himself so he could peer through the rear window and windshield to see what was ahead. Mike had no idea how soon they would come to the building site and what he would do when they arrived there. Although he and the others in the back of the truck were well fortified against enemy fire, both the driver and the truck itself were vulnerable to even the mildest form of attack. Campbell watched the road carefully and shouted frequently to Jed to make sure his voice could be heard.

The truck continued climbing up and up the winding dirt road, and they could feel the air become cooler and thinner. Joe Nolan cursed from the moment he felt pressure on his eardrums, and he yawned constantly to relieve the discomfort. They passed through a zone of heavy timber, mostly evergreen, and after that came increasingly smaller and stunted trees until there was nothing taller than foot-high heatherlike plants. Higher still were patches of snow and clusters of bright wildflowers nourished by the runoff of melted snow and which looked out of place on these barren, exposed slopes. On the right side the road fell away in an almost sheer drop, a slope so steep, it could not be climbed in many places without ropes. Down below they saw the blacktop road leading to the main pass with trucks or military vehicles moving in both directions along it. Although they had climbed high, it was only to a pass, and there were huge snow-covered peaks and entire ranges without a break that rose into the air many times their height.

The road swung sharply to the left and ran between two gradual upward slopes as it entered the pass. As they went deeper into the pass the mountains towered on each side of them and cast the road in deep shadows, which made the air chillier than before.

"You see them, Mike? Both sides."

"Yeah," Mike yelled back to Jed. They were coming to one rocket and machine-gun emplacement on the right side of the road, and another two hundred yards farther on to the left. He could see three or four Soviet soldiers in light blue uniforms in each of the sandbagged bunkers, their weapons pointing along the road in both directions. They passed the first emplacement, receiving only a glance, and then the second, with only bored, frozen, miserable looks from the soldiers inside. The truck continued on around a gradual bend in the high-walled pass and came to the highest point in the road, beneath a mud-walled fort that looked as if it had been there since the days of Genghis Khan. Six or seven hundred yards before the fort, they saw the construction site, which was composed of stacks of cinder blocks, two empty trucks, and a cement mixer next to trenches excavated in the ground. A circle of turbaned men gathered around a fire some distance back from the road—obviously workers and drivers on their lunch break. There would be no siesta at this cold temperature.

"Pull over behind the other trucks as if you were going to unload," Mike shouted forward to Jed. "The rest of you keep down out of sight. You can bet the Russians are watching from that fort. This building is probably living quarters for them. Andre and Bob, sight that mortar tube. Rest of you place blocks on the base plate to hold it steady."

When Mike had heard from Bob and Lance that they had seen a mortar, he guessed correctly that it was an M1937 medium one, the mortar popular with all Warsaw Pact countries though it dated back to the year of its model number. It was a simple tube steadied on the ground by a base plate and held at an angle by a bipod. It fired on the Stokes principle, invented during World War I by a British manufacturer of agricultural machinery: a loose-fitting bomb, with propellant contained in a cartridge in its tail, was dropped down the simple tube with a firing pin in its base. In older mortars the loose fit of the bomb within the tube, which, of course, enabled it to be dropped on the pin, allowed propellant gas to escape around the bomb, which caused variations in aim and range. The M1937 had been modernized, like most other present-day mortars, by adding a plastic driving band that expanded on firing by providing a close fit for the bomb within the tube. Since the tube, base plate, and bipod each weighed more than forty pounds, and

COBRA STRIKE

the bombs six pounds each, the other team members were a lot less enthusiastic about the M1937 than Campbell.

By now the truck had come to a stop next to the stacked cinder blocks. The workers were looking toward the truck, but none seemed anxious to leave the warmth of the fire. There was no sign of any movement from the fort.

"Keep your heads down," Mike warned again. "Andre, is she set? I'd say your range is a little more than six hundred yards. You agree? Jed, leave the engine running, open the door, leaving it open behind you. We got to have something from that fort—is it empty or are those bastards ready to blow us into dust? Walk around a bit, Jed, in front of the truck."

A steel door opened in the side of the fort, and a uniformed Soviet serviceman emerged. He turned his head, and another came out to join him. This one raised binoculars to his eyes.

"They're wondering where the soldier is who was with the driver," Mike said. "Okay, Jed, jump back in the truck. Andre, give 'em a taste."

Andre dropped a mortar round tail-first into the mouth of the tube, and they heard it rattle down inside for a second, then it whizzed out in an explosive burst and arced across the intervening space to the mud-walled fort. It hit the flat roof of the fort with a growling roar. Flames spat out the doorway behind the two Russians who were observing the truck. One man huddled to the ground, the flesh seared from his bones, his cheeks melted off his skull, while the other ran briefly, waving his arms, in an orange sheet of flame, before he, too, was consumed by the deadly combustion.

Bob had passed another bomb to Andre, who held it at the mouth of the smoking tube waiting for Mike's signal. Campbell nodded to him, and Andre dropped in the projectile. It, too, landed on what remained of the flat roof of the fort, five or six yards behind the first. This time the explosion was not triggered off until the bomb hit something inside the fort. The upper third of the heavy mud walls folded outward as everything inside collapsed downward. Tall, angry red flames mixed with dense black smoke, and a great cloud of gray dust rose over everything.

"Let's go!" Mike yelled to Jed, who seemed mesmerized at the sight behind the wheel.

The truck lurched forward and swung back onto the road. Mike knew one thing for sure now: They were not going to be allowed to pass the rocket and machine-gun emplacements that must lie on the exit from the pass. If these were in the same position as those they saw coming into the pass, with steep walls rising on either side of the road, they would find themselves trapped inside, unable to go forward or backward because of the bunkers, and unable to climb the walls of the pass with speed enough to avoid being picked off by sniper fire. But they were in luck. The road opened onto a high flat-topped ridge, which it followed for hundreds of yards before beginning its descent on the other side of the pass.

Mike guessed that the gun emplacements would be immediately below the ridge top. "Don't go down," he yelled to Jed. "Stay on this ridge."

"Goddammit, Mike, I can't. Look at the rocks."

"It's not your father's car!"

Jed laughed and whooped. He crashed over rocks and ran in and out of gullies, making the flatbed truck pitch like a sailboat deck on a rough sea. The cinder-block walls fell down on them, a whole wall of them burying Harvey Waller beneath them. Harvey took it personally and began heaving and kicking them off the truck. Lance laughed so hard, he fell off the other side of the truck at a sudden, extra-savage bump. Mike yelled for Jed to stop and loaded the mortar and the aluminum box of spare bombs in the cab beside him while the others cleared away the remaining cinder blocks. Then they all got firm handholds on the framework behind the cab, and Mike yelled for Jed to push on, only this time with a bit of speed.

Jed did his best, but the level top of the ridge was narrowing fast, an he came to a stop when he could go no farther.

"What's wrong?" Mike inquired.

"There's nowhere to go but down," Jed said, exasperated.

"So go down."

Jed looked out the side window at the steeply angled

COBRA STRIKE

slope and down into a dry riverbed hundreds of feet below. Then he looked back at Mike. Then once more down the slope. Mike could have sworn he saw Jed shut his eyes as he turned the steering wheel hard to the left and eased the truck nose first over the edge and down the side of the ridge.

He tried everything to slow the vehicle, but its momentum built and soon it was hurtling downhill at an ever-increasing speed. When he locked the wheels with the brakes or put it in reverse gear, the rear end of the truck fishtailed viciously, and the whole vehicle threatened to swing sideways, which, of course, would cause it to topple over and over down the mountainside. Jed wasn't helped any by the hollers and yells coming from the back of the truck; if he took their word for it, any one of them could manage this with one hand on the wheel and the other around a heavy-titted woman, doing twice the speed he was doing with only half the discomfort. Not for the first time since he had set out, Jed wistfully recalled his days of peace and plenty back at the Nanticoke Institute. But he had no time for regrets, not at the wheel of a truck plummeting down one side of a sizable piece of the Hindu Kush.

As the truck began to skid sideways he turned the front wheels into the skid and straightened it out again, to continue nose first at terrifying speed down the stony slope, accompanied by a miniature landslide of rocks and small stones. Jed pushed hard against the steering wheel to prevent himself from being thrown face first against the windshield. He jerked the wheel to one side to avoid massive rocks or sudden sharp drops when he saw them in time, which was not often. Finally, battered and dazed, he rolled the truck to a stop in the dry riverbed where the boulders were too big to allow further progress. He staggered out of the cab and found satisfaction in seeing that the other team members were in no better shape than he was.

Campbell made them hump the mortar and shells to a hiding place in the rocks almost half a mile away. He would not let Nolan blow up the truck, saying that the column of smoke would tip off Soviet planes to their location.

"Maybe they'll lift the truck out with a chopper if the

rebels don't get to it first. Saving it may distract them from us, but I doubt it. All right, we stay on the riverbed and keep moving till dark, putting as much distance as we can between us and the pass. After dark we put up our tents and eat C rations. Then sleep."

That got a cheer.

CHAPTER 10

Mike Campbell thought that Jed Crippenby was raving in his sleep. He was sitting upright in his sleeping bag in the two-man tent in the dry river bottom, his shape outlined in the moonlight from outside the tent. Mike couldn't make out a word he was saying, then realized he was talking—not talking, shouting—in Pushtu.

"Shut up, Jed. Calm down, for chrissake."

"Mike, they're out there! I'm telling you! I heard them!"

"You're having a nightmare," Mike said soothingly. "Now wake up."

"Fuck it, Mike, I wasn't asleep. You were." Then he went back to talking Pushtu in a loud voice.

Mike sat up in his sleeping bag, alarmed. He picked up the Kalashnikov beside him, but Jed forced it down with his hand.

Jed asked something that sounded like a question and then waited, listening to the silence.

A hoarse, raspy voice came back from somewhere outside, speaking Pushtu.

Jed, sounding relieved, went into what Mike could tell

was a long explanation of who, what, and why. The raspy voice held out for some minutes in reply.

Then Jed called out in English: "You guys awake? Put all weapons down. We're surrounded by people who say they are rebels and friends of Gul Daoud. Come out of your tents with your hands in the air. I'm not sure who they are, but we're in no position to discuss it with only nylon tent walls between us and them. What do you say, Mike?"

Campbell said, "Harvey, put down your gun. I mean it. If they are rebels, we don't want to blow it. Let's go."

At first they could see nothing. Then a small, tubby man appeared in the moonlight. He was dressed in what looked like white pajamas many sizes too large for him, his white turban half unwound and draped on his shoulders, the usual Kalashnikov banging on its sling against his right hip, the usual finger on the trigger. He went from man to man in the team, peering up into their faces, pronouncing his judgment each time with a single English word: "American!"

After checking the last man he beckoned into the surrounding night. At least thirty men, bristling with weapons, silently crowded in around them. Under Mike's direction Jed explained who they were and that they had come to find Gul Daoud.

The short, tubby man was adamant. They wanted no more Americans here. They wanted American arms, yes, but not American people. They could fight their own war. The team would have to turn around and go back the way they had come. There was no room for more Americans. Their presence made the Russians even worse. There were already three Americans in this region. No more!

"Tell him we've come to take them back," Mike said.

"I have, but he's not listening to me," Jed answered.

"Try again."

Jed explained over and over until he got his point across that the only reason they were looking for Gul Daoud was that he might know where the three Americans were. The tubby man conceded that this was possible. His truculence evaporated only when Jed told him where to find the mortar and the truck. The team had not been spotted by the Soviets while escaping, although they had heard choppers back where they had left the truck. They were given two men who would guide them to Gul Daoud, and the other twenty-eight or so left in a hurry for the mortar and truck.

Gul Daoud was about three inches shorter than Jed Crippenby, and both were tall, skinny, and bearded. The Afghan looked in amusement at the American. "You managed to get through the Russian blockade to come here because the last thing those Russians expected was for more Americans to break into, instead out of, their trap. Local rebels saw you and know why you have come. Communist spies will pass this information to the Russians, and they will behave like crazy persons. It will be a day or two before the Russians hear this information. You must act fast."

"You'd better tell that to Mike Campbell. He makes the decisions, not me."

Gul sighed. "I have spoken with him. I have explained to him that I do not control the movements of the three men you seek. I help them when I can, and that's the only time I'm in contact with them. It was their own idea to go away, because their presence was bringing so much communist military pressure on us. You speak Pushtu. You have a deeper understanding of us than the others. Try to persuade Campbell to move on and search for those men yourselves."

Jed looked puzzled. "I thought that's what we were going to do. What are you telling me?"

Gul Daoud looked uncomfortable. "When I tried to tell Campbell what I have told you, he knocked me to the ground and told me he would kill me if I didn't find Turner, Baker, and Winston for him. He means it. I can tell when a man decides to kill someone. You might ask him how he can kill me, since I am with my people in my own country. With one word from me they would kill all of you. But what would that look like? Gul Daoud murders his American friends? Impossible. So I have to bear this man's threats and insults, even when he knocks me to the ground. Now I can see that you are an intelligent man. I want you to speak with him for me. Tell him I am hurt and angry to be treated by him like this. Reason with him."

"I'll ask him what this is about," Jed volunteered unwillingly. "but you have to understand, what Mike says, goes."

"Of course. Of course."

When Jed told Mike of his conversation with Gul Daoud, Mike exploded. "That two-faced son of a bitch is going to get his if he tries to play games with me. We didn't beat our way through a line of Soviet troops just to get the cold shoulder from this mountain character who thinks he's a slick operator. He doesn't want to hand over Baker and the others. He doesn't want us around, but he has some use for them, I don't know what. I guess he picked on you as the softest touch on our team, Jed."

"Fair enough," Crippenby admitted. "I'm not a soldier like the rest of you. He's complaining that you knocked him to the ground and said you'd kill him if he didn't find Baker and the others."

"I knocked him down when he tried to threaten me, telling me he was headman and all he had to do was snap his fingers and I was dead."

"He didn't tell me that," Jed said.

"You bet he didn't. He wants us out of here in a hurry, and I told him we ain't moving till we get what we've come for. Go back to him and tell him that he's right to be angry. Tell him you think I'm going to assassinate him if he doesn't start to cooperate. And you won't be telling him any lies neither."

Joe Nolan was on guard and heard them begin to move out. It was a little after four in the morning, at least two full hours before dawn. Nolan roused the others in their sleeping bags on the dirt floor of the mud-brick house allotted to the team by Gul Daoud. They had slept with their boots and clothes on, guns by their side, ready to go. Mike led them out to where Gul was quietly assembling a group of rebels at one end of the compound that formed his base. Gul ignored their presence and went on with what he was doing. But gradually the rebels stopped talking in whispers and tiptoeing around, since there was no longer any purpose in their doing so. Gul left the compound with about sixty men, and the team tagged along uninvited. A few miles along a path in only faint starlight, they were met by another group of about twenty men on horses and carrying heavy weapons. Campbell and the others kept their places at the rear of the march and spoke to no one.

In the first gray streaks of day they saw Gul Daoud work his way back to them, stopping to talk and march for a while with the men down along the line. When he finally reached Campbell at the head of the team, his attitude was completely changed from that of the previous day. He shook hands and beamed.

"We did not tell you about our operation today," he said to Mike, "because it will be extremely dangerous and I did not want to risk the lives of you, my guests, in our fight for freedom."

"That's mighty considerate of you," Mike told him.

"But now that you insisted on coming along, I think you can be a big help to us."

"Helping you has to be a secondary objective for us. We can't let anything interfere with our primary objective—recovering those three Americans from your territory. Anything that comes in our way to prevent that—government troops, Soviets, or you—will be eliminated."

"Mike, I don't want to have differences with you anymore," Gul said in his cheerful voice. "You will rescue your three fellow countrymen today, you will see. Not tomorrow. Today. I had this attack planned for next week, but your arrival changed things for us. I changed it to today, even though I would have had more men available to me next week. If you had not joined us today, I would have brought back your fellow countrymen to you as a surprise gift."

"What's going on?" Mike asked suspiciously.

"You will see," Gul Daoud said, highly satisfied now with how things were going, and went forward up the line of men again, shouting a slogan or a prayer as he went, which was taken up by the rebel column.

* * *

Gul Daoud placed the team on a rocky bluff overlooking a flat valley lined with irrigation canals and pocked with bomb craters.

"The Soviets tried to destroy our food supply last summer, hoping starvation would drive us into Pakistan during the winter," Gul explained. "So they used high-explosive bombs on vegetables. But we will grow food here again this summer."

Despite everything Mike tried, he could get no hard information from Gul. It seemed that Baker, Turner, and Winston could be found not far off and that Gul wanted Campbell and his men's help in exchange for them. At least Gul was admitting today that he knew the whereabouts of the three Americans, which was progress of a sort in Mike's opinion. Just how they were all fitting into Gul's plans remained to be seen.

They had a long wait. Gul's troops were dispersed in the cover at the edge of the valley. On four separate occasions a jet overflew the valley, coming down low. It was past eleven that morning before they spotted movement on the far side of the valley. Mike trained his high-power binoculars on the spot, and what he saw made his fingers grip on the binoculars in rage. Winston, Baker, and Turner were setting out across the valley floor, mounted on the backs of three camels!

"Goddam shithead is using them for bait," Mike ground out. "I swear, I'll tear his balls off—"

Gul Daoud came rushing up through the rocks to their position. "Calm down, Mike! You don't know what's going on. Baker and Winston know all about it."

"What're you talking about?" Mike growled. "Better talk fast because me and my men are going out there to fetch them."

"That won't help anybody," Gul said pleasantly. "A spy for the Russians had been fed the information that they are crossing here. The Russians could have killed them twice already—your countrymen will tell you that—but want to take them alive. They will see this as their big chance to do that. If you rush out to meet them on the valley floor, the Soviet force will strike at you before you reach them. Leave them to us. We need you to cover us from air attack. Baker and the others know what to do. You'll see. It will work well."

"I have my doubts about that," Mike said.

They all ducked down as the jet passed over the valley for the fifth time. The plane swooped low over the three men on the camels, now some distance out into the valley.

"Very good," Gul said. "They are aiming for this spot. They should be near us before the Russians arrive. I have to go now, I have many things to see to. We can depend on you?"

"Yeah, yeah, go ahead," Mike muttered, not pleased to find himself outmaneuvered but, all the same, feeling that he had gotten somewhere by setting eyes on the three Americans they were looking for. In a little while he said, "Okay, you guys, get set up for visitors."

Gul Daoud had made no comments, but his eyes had been sharp: he had recognized the Blowpipe guided missiles in their canister, which the team carried. Each man carried a thirty-pound missile stored in its firing canister. In addition, Mike carried one fifteen-pound aiming unit, and Bob Murphy the other. The team members knew better than to complain to Mike's face about the weapon loads he assigned them to carry on missions. They all realized they owed their lives to the hardware he had forced them to hump over mountains and through jungles, yet that did not stop them hoping for a heavy contact fast so they could use the weapons and be rid of their burden.

"My back is going to feel different after this mother is gone," Joe Nolan said, unloading his missile canister. "I'm going to be lifting one foot higher than the other."

Mike fitted a canister to each of the two aiming units and handed one to Nolan and the other to Murphy. He set the other five canisters on the ground within easy reach. It took only a few seconds to discard an empty canister after firing and to fit a new one. Then they watched the three men approach across the flat valley floor on their camels.

"How did Gul persuade them to do this?" Andre asked in wonder.

"With all due respect to Jed," Mike said, "you'd have to be an intellectual at some think tank like the Nanticoke

Institute before you could think up an argument brilliant enough to convince yourself to do something so dumb."

Jed laughed and said nothing. He was remembering how Mike had thrown Gul Daoud on the ground instead of listening to his bullshit as Jed himself did. Jed's only problem with this was that in order to react so strongly himself, he would have to be more certain of his own opinions instead of seeing three or four different points of view to everything.

"We have action," Mike yelled. "Gunships coming along the valley. Get your heads down. We don't want them."

The choppers sprayed the rocks and small dried-up bushes with bullets from the flex gun mounted in their side door. They were just blindly softening up the terrain for a nearby landing zone. Each of the three gunships fired a rocket at nothing in particular and fortunately did not happen to hit any of the rebels, although two of the rockets came close, detonating with an earth-thumping blast that kicked up a high plume of dust and stones.

After the gunships left, they heard the drone of engines as the slicks came in, landing out in the valley about seven hundred yards, each chopper dropping down to unload eight men and then lifting up and heading back from where they had come. Four slicks dropped thirty-two men to capture three.

The three camels were close by. Obviously, if the riders did not obey orders to dismount, the beasts would be shot from beneath them. Before this happened, Gul's men started firing on the Soviet servicemen. Their first burst of fire took the Russians by surprise and exacted a heavy toll. Then the Russians found themselves cover and fired back at their attackers. The three camel riders veered away from the action, forgotten for the moment behind the backs of the Russians.

The gunships came back, clearly summoned by radio. One rebel hit one with an SAM-7 missile. The craft exploded in midair, and the burning bits crashed to the ground in a conflagration of destruction. The two other gunships backed off, dodged a couple more SAM-7 missiles, and left.

COBRA STRIKE

"Bob, Joe," Mike warned, "keep a watch out."

Both men readied their Blowpipes by placing on their right shoulder the missile-containing canister that projected backward from the aiming unit. Their left hands propped up the muzzle of the canister in front of the aiming unit. They peered through the optical sight and held the grip of the aiming unit with their right hands. No one had to warn them of the approach of a jet—the aircraft's noise did that.

"She's mine," Nolan told Murphy.

He picked up the streaking, low-flying aircraft in the Blowpipe's monocular sight and tracked its flight for a moment before his right finger pulled the trigger mounted on the grip of the aiming unit. His right thumb hovered over the control button. The missile's first-stage motor kicked it out of the launching tube, and after it was safely clear of the tube, the more powerful second motor ignited and accelerated the missile to supersonic speed.

As it dived down to rocket or bomb the rebel positions, Nolan continued to track the jet through the sight. The aiming unit sent radio signals to the missile to keep it homed on whatever was visible in the monocular sight. He used his thumb on the control button to guide the missile, which was an easier task than it sounded because he did not have to keep the plane on a set of cross hairs to hit it: so long as the aircraft remained visible in the viewer, the missile would hit it.

All this took place in seconds. Nolan fired, and the missile struck the midsection of the plane's fuselage. The pilot had no chance to eject from the fast-traveling jet at low altitude, and in a few seconds it buried itself at six hundred miles an hour into the valley floor. The gas tanks inside its wings exploded, a boiling orange ball of flame billowed and trembled for a moment, then shrank into licking, dancing flames and thick black smoke.

Nolan threw away the empty canister and was handed a full one by Hardwick.

"Nice shooting, Joe," Mike said real easy, just like someone might say to Nolan after he had hit a good shot on the pool table back in the Bunch o' Shamrock in Youngstown. Nolan almost felt like reaching over for his bottle of beer.

For Joe, Ohio was real. His only reaction to hearing that they were going to Afghanistan was, "We could have gone somewhere easier to spell."

Mike had said, "Joe, you're not going to be writing to anyone about it, anyway."

"He's thinking about his memoirs," Andre had put in, sarcastic as usual.

To Joe, nothing about these Afghans running around these bleak mountains made any sense, no more than it did for the Russians to try to move in on them. There was more fertile soil in one square yard of Ohio than there was in one square mile here, and Ohio was as flat as a pancake, with no great fucking mountains poking up all over the place, getting in everybody's way. He had no idea why these thoughts were floating through his brain after he had just downed a $20-million or so Soviet aircraft, instead of feelings of heroism and triumph or some such. He guessed that was just the way he was made.

Maybe the Russians thought the jet's downing was a fluke, being unused to having jet aircraft blasted from the sky by the rebels, whose best ground-to-air weapons up to this point had been the inefficient Soviet-made SAM-7s. In any case, they sent in two MIGs on another rocket/bombing run, one plane about five seconds in front of the other.

"I'll take the left," Bob Murphy said.

"You got it," Joe replied.

The big Australian squeezed his left eye shut and peered through the viewer with the other eye. He found the lead MIG, triggered his missile, and tracked his target. Nolan followed suit with the second plane half a second later. The two MIGs got it like a brace of pheasant from a double-barreled shotgun—left-right, one-two, big bangs—and the aircraft spun out of control, slammed into the ground at barely subsonic speed, and their tanks of fuel did the rest.

Murphy yelled and crowed with glee; Nolan said nothing. They both reloaded with fresh canisters and waited eagerly, like kids at a fairground stall who have learned the knack of zapping the moving target. The British Blowpipe was fun to fire because of the visual and manual control over the missile and also because the missile went off with a big bang on impact with the target; the operator really got to see his fireworks explode. This was because the missile's HE warhead was basically a blasting device with little armor-piercing capability. The Blowpipe missile worked not by destroying its target but by hitting it with such a wallop that it spun out of its high-speed trajectory and destroyed itself.

No more jets came in support of the ground forces. The slicks landed behind the protection of a bank of earth and left it to the ground troops to fight their way back to them. Still farther back, the two remaining gunships wavered up and down, shooting off poorly aimed rockets at the rebels and taking no chances of being incinerated themselves. The Russians had given up and were in full retreat back to their slicks. They had started with thirty-two on the ground, eight from each slick, and the way it looked now, they'd be lucky to fill two slicks. And Gul Daoud's rebels hadn't done with them yet, laying down a hail of fire on the crouching, zigzagging men darting from cover to cover and plainly wishing like hell that they were back in Mother Russia.

The three camels came up at a fast run to the rocky bluff the team held, seeking shelter from the bullets that by now were traveling loosely in every direction.

Waller looked up malevolently at Winston arriving on the lead camel: "Here comes fucking Lawrence of Arabia."

Lance Hardwick and Bob Murphy spent the next two days reconnoitering with Gul's rebel guides. They already knew that all the mountain passes had been sealed in a great arc to the east and south of them. It was still too early in the year to cross most of the mountains themselves because of snow, and those that could be crossed might involve, instead of day through a pass, a week's heavy trekking during which they were almost certain to be spotted by observation aircraft. If they were spotted, the passes in the next range of mountains ahead of them could be guarded, and the whole process would start over. Campbell's idea was for Lance and Bob to find a place where the team could cut a "window" in the Soviet line and go through it to the other side.

Murphy and Hardwick took care not to engage the enemy.

They had some close calls, mostly in detecting ambushes at the last moment.

"What we need to find," Murphy said, "is someplace where their troops are strung out in a long line. These mountain passes serve as natural funnels—they narrow our movements to channels they can seal off with a minimum of men."

Half a day's horseback ride to the south of Gul Daoud's camp they found a high plateau across which the Soviet troops were stretched thin in two-man units every five hundred yards or so. This looked good, but the more they observed the setup, the clearer it became that units could not be attacked without others seeing it by day or hearing it by night. If the mercs were detected during a struggle, they had no place to run on this high plateau and no cover to protect them from the gunships on regular patrol up and down the line. They tried some other approaches on the way back to Gul's camp, but nothing looked good.

"Maybe if we moved a day's journey south, we'd find something better," Murphy told Campbell when they got back.

"You won't," Gul said.

"There's nothing here, Mike," Murphy concluded. "No way out. Looking is a waste of time."

Campbell respected Murphy's experience in the field. He knew it took a hell of a lot to stop the big Australian.

"Well, the plain fact is that we can't stay here," Mike said. "If they've cut off our escape into Pakistan to the east and south, then we go some other way. To the north is Russia, so I think we can forget that. To the west is Iran. They'll never expect us to go that way."

To their surprise, Gul Daoud was supportive of this route. "In spite of what you hear about the power of Khomeini and the mullahs in Iran, they have a huge population of addicts. The poppies are grown in our Afghan mountains, and Afghans smuggle the opium into Iran. It's a big business. I don't know what you will do once you get inside Iran, but crossing the border into it can be done. The Russians will never expect Americans to head for Iran."

Gul spread out a map and traced a shallow inverted

semicircle across the entire country of Afghanistan. "The Russians hold the roads and the big towns and they control the air. We have the rest. I will mark this map for you with the names and territories of rebel leaders on your way. They will help, but you have to understand that spies will report on your movements and that the Russians and Afghan communists will be after you. When they find that there are ten Americans now instead of three, they won't mind killing a few of you, for something to show before they get live captives. It's going to be a long haul to the Iranian border, Mike, but I still think you've got a better chance of getting yourself and your men there than you have of breaking through the Soviet lines to Pakistan."

The other team members took it in their stride when they heard they were going back to the States by way of Iran. They knew Mike. If he had said they were going by way of the South Pole, that would have been okay with them. Turner, Winston, and Baker didn't take the news so well. Baker claimed that going from Afghanistan into Iran was like going from the pan into the fire. Winston suggested that maybe Campbell hadn't heard that Iran was a disaster for Americans. Turner just said they weren't going and that was that. They were even less pleased when Crippenby handed each of them papers from the Nanticoke Institute, which informed them that they now reported to Campbell until further notice.

"We could quit the Institute," Baker suggested.

"You try to quit and I'll kick your ass," Turner informed him. "I'm here to bring you turkeys back in one piece, and I'm going to do it whether you like it or not. I don't agree with Campbell that we should go through Iran, but I still follow orders even if I think they're cockamamie ones. We got to have a leader. So if I have to choose between you, Baker, and Campbell here, I gotta go with Campbell—maybe only because I don't know him as well as I know you, Baker."

"Thanks, Turner, I appreciate that," Baker snapped back. "I have no ambition to be anyone's leader. I'm quite willing to follow Mike's orders—when I think they make sense.

Any way you look at it, going through Iran makes no sense."

"It does if your only alternative is going through the Soviet Union," Mike put in. "Now, I'm not going to tell you the places this team has been, but some of them have been at least as hot as Iran. But this is all beside the point, Baker. Like Turner told you, he'll obey orders even if he doesn't like them. That's the way it has to be on a paramilitary mission. You try to hold a round-table discussion when you feel you have a point to argue, you're liable to get us all killed. When I tell you to get your head down, you don't ask why, or the answer may be on its way in the form of an enemy bullet. If I can't depend on you to do what you're told, I can't be sure that what I think is happening really is happening. We could all get hurt real bad if you're not doing what you're supposed to be doing at some point because you had a better idea. And I want to say something else. I came here to bring you three guys out, so you assume. Right? You're being brought out not because you're sweet guys and everyone misses you in the cafeteria at lunchtime—you're being brought out because you'd be an embarrassment to Washington if the Reds caught you here, dead or alive. So far as Washington is concerned, I've done my job as long as I erase all presence of you three in Afghanistan. No matter how I do it. If I have to, I'll shoot any one of you for not obeying orders and burn the body with gasoline so the Russians can't say it was an American. I'll get paid. No questions will be asked. So all this discussion is bullshit. You have your orders. You report to me. You make a problem for me, I'll make a bigger one for you."

Baker was shaken when he realized that Campbell would do exactly what he said he would do. No one had come here to rescue him personally—only to extricate three Americans from a potentially politically embarrassing situation for Washington, since everyone would assume that they were CIA agents if they were caught. Baker looked at the team of mercenaries and decided he had been wrong in his first impression of these men as good guys on a mission of mercy. They were paid assassins, irresponsible psychopaths or sociopaths, disturbed violent types who would have to be humored. It would be up to Winston, Turner, and himself to use them until they were no longer useful, then dump them and strike out on their own.

Gul Daoud gave them all a farewell meal of mutton-and-yogurt dishes washed down with tea. Baker and Winston promised him surface-to-air weapons as a special priority of the Nanticoke Institute. It was plain, Baker said, that when the Russians lost their total dominance in the air, this war would become too punishing in casualties for them to fight. Even as it was, they had taken an estimated ten thousand fatalities. Of course, this was nothing in comparison to the hundreds of thousands of deaths they had caused, mostly of civilians, and the approximately three million refugees they had made out of a total population of fifteen million. He said that the estimated one hundred fifteen thousand Soviet servicemen presently in Afghanistan were being used to prop up the unpopular puppet communist government and that they were totally dependent on their air power to destroy food supplies and houses in order to starve the population into submission or drive them into exile.

Gul Daoud thanked them all for their help. As they were leaving, he asked Baker and Winston, as a special favor, to check on the status of his loan at Chase Manhattan for his fast-food chicken place in the Bronx.

CHAPTER 11

Campbell saw Baker pointedly consult his compass several times, although the sun was full out and he didn't need a compass needle to tell him they were riding north toward Russia instead of west toward Iran. Campbell let him sweat it out. Winston and Turner were keeping their mouths shut also, leaving it to Baker to do any challenging that was to be done. Campbell waited for Baker to confront him, but the most Baker was willing to do was to whip out his compass from time to time, look at it and then at the sun in a puzzled fashion, shake his head as if the sun and his compass must be wrong and Mike Campbell right, yet keep his tongue quiet on the subject and submit to Campbell as leader. Which was all Campbell wanted. That settled, he had no wish to be unreasonable by demanding that anyone follow him blindly without hope of an explanation.

Mike rode his horse into a central position so they could all hear him. "Some of you must be wondering where in hell we're going. And you got to figure out that if you don't know, neither will the Russians." He let that sink in. "We all know the Russians are going to be able to trace our

COBRA STRIKE 161

movements, and our best hope is to keep a bit ahead of them. They'll find out from their informants that we're heading north. They'll figure out we're doing this so we can swing east toward Pakistan, and they'll respond accordingly, tying up a lot of their troops on the ground hundreds of miles from where we're going. Apart from ourselves, only Gul Daoud knows we intend to swing west toward Iran just short of the Russian border and follow that border, at a safe distance, all the way across the Iranian border.

"Why do this when there's a road running west to east across Afghanistan, from Kabul to Herat? Because as soon as we set foot on it, the Russians would know exactly where we were going and easily head us off. This way we'll keep them guessing. And I'm betting on getting a head start during the time it takes them to discover us. They have unlimited power and resources working for them, against our mobility and the surprise factor. Right now the Russians don't even know the team exists. They're still hunting three trapped Americans. I'd like to keep them believing that as long as we can."

Winston laughed. "That's not bad at all, Mike. Maybe the Russians will think we're on our way north to attack the Soviet Union."

Andre Verdoux said, "Don't put thoughts like that in Campbell's mind. We don't call him Mad Mike for nothing."

They all laughed, except Baker, who was resentful of having been put in his place and deserted, as he saw it, by Winston and Turner.

The three-man rebel escort, provided by Gul Daoud, had ridden ahead and now returned, gesturing to them to slow their horses. They explained things to Crippenby.

Jed said, "There's a lone Russian tank ahead, on the other side of the river. They only take us as far as this river, and we pick up our new guides as arranged on the far side. Instead there's a Russian tank sitting there. But our guides don't think we've been betrayed. They say that the river is swollen with water from the melting mountain snows, and judging by the banks, the flood was higher and is dying down fast. They think that the bridge must have been weakened by the flood and couldn't take the tank's weight, so it had to leave the main road and come to this ford while the rest of the truck convoy or whatever went on without it. The river water is still high and very dirty, so the soldiers in the tank can't find exactly where the ford is and can't find anyone to tell them. So they're just sitting there waiting, which is what we'll have to do, too, until they go away."

They hid the horses among a big clump of bushes, where there was grass for them to eat, and then went forward on foot to investigate the riverbank. From their hiding places they could see the tank dominating the far side. The river was about the width of a six-lane highway, and its fast-moving brown waters wove in and out in currents and eddies. It was plainly deep enough to swamp a tank's engine and probably drown its occupants as well.

While they were keeping watch, one of their rebel guides came back from a reconnoitering trip along the riverbank—Mike wanted all the non-Afghans to stay out of sight as much as possible. The rebel said that there were local people hidden on the same bank of the river as they were, wanting to cross but unwilling to reveal the location of the ford to the Soviet tank crew. He confirmed their earlier guess about why the tank had been left behind. The locals had seen Russians, not Afghans, in the tank, but there were no other soldiers remaining in the area. Mike was relieved to hear this and said they would wait for the water to subside and the tank to leave. They made themselves comfortable and opened their C rations.

A man arrived on a black horse at the far bank of the river, about three hundred yards upstream from the tank, which he ignored. They could see he wore a long brown robe, had a pointed black beard and a very large white turban, and carried a black lamb before him on the saddle. Behind his horse, on foot, a boy drove a black mother sheep and her second lamb. The boy waited with these two animals while his father rode his horse into the river. By keeping the horse's head upstream against the current, he walked the animal slowly across the ford. As he went, the mother sheep left behind answered the calls of the lamb midway across the river and ran back and forth between the water's edge and the other lamb she had with her on dry land, the conflict of both their calls driving her hysterically back and forth.

The man on horseback dropped the lamb close to where the team was hidden and then returned slowly across the river. His son caught the second lamb and handed it up to him. This time the ewe did not hesitate; she plunged into the water after the horse but, being a much weaker swimmer, was washed downriver a distance before gaining the opposite bank. The man on horseback dropped the second lamb and went back across the river for his son. While he did so, the ewe ran up the bank to have a loud, bleating reunion with her offspring. The son put his foot on his father's left boot, and together they forded the river on horseback. The whole thing was like something from an ancient era, were it not for the presence of the silent tank. The Russians waited for the man and his son to leave before they started the engine and eased the tank slowly into the water at the ford.

When it came clanking out of the water and onto the bank only fifty yards or so from where the mercs were hidden, a small boy, perhaps twelve at most, appeared from behind some rocks and stood directly in front of the tank, shouting something. This was not the same boy they had just seen cross the river with his father and the sheep. The mercs could not hear what the boy was shouting until the tank stopped six feet in front of him and idled its engine.

"Allahu akbar!" he was yelling over and over. God is great.

The standoff between the small boy and the tank lasted almost two minutes. Then they heard the tank grind into gear and inch forward. The boy did not give way, so the tank stopped again, less than four feet from him. The tank driver, obviously having to obey an order from his superior, lurched the tank forward. With a final *"Allahu akbar!"* the boy did not give way and went under the tank.

Campbell had to restrain Harvey Waller. "The rotten fucking commie whoresons!" he roared. "I don't believe it, Mike! I don't believe you're going to let them cold-blooded child murderers go so they can go on doing it."

Mike took his hand away from Waller's shoulder. "Okay, Harvey, waste them."

Lance lifted the shoulder strap of his RPG2 over his head and handed the Soviet-made missile launcher to Harvey. Waller pushed a six-pound fin-stabilized round into the muzzle of the tube. The tube had an awkward pistol grip near its muzzle end and was encased in wood so it could be safety placed on the right shoulder but not on the left, since there was a gas-ejection port on the right side of the tube. Harvey raised the large rear sight and selected the fifty-meter graduation. He operated the firing pin and bolt, then squeezed the trigger, releasing the HEAT round, capable of penetrating 180mm of armor plate.

Having ground the Afghan child into a boneless pulp in the dirt, the tank rumbled away from the river. The RPG2 round caught it at the base of the turret, ruptured the steel plates with its impact blast, and, inside the tank, melted the plastic insulation from the cables and the flesh from the bones of the crew. The tank went off to the right at a sharp angle until it came up against a big rock, could move no farther forward, and its engine stalled.

Harvey patted the RPG2 launcher tube affectionately. "It's not such a bad little weapon, even if it is Russian-made."

Colonel Yekaterina Matveyeva smoothed back her blond hair, crossed her legs in her military skirt, and whispered into the telephone receiver, "Lieutenant, if you don't find them for me, you're going to be guarding ice fields inside the Arctic Circle from American attack. And not only that, Lieutenant, but I'll be your superior officer up there, and I won't let you forget how your failure to locate three U.S. infiltrators in Afghanistan caused our military careers to end in the snowy wastes. We will have all those long, dark winters to think about it."

She had shouted at him on all previous occasions and it hadn't gotten her anywhere. In Yekaterina's opinion a fully meant and fairly dire threat should be spoken very softly so that the person being threatened had to strain to hear the details.

She went on, "General Viktor Mikhailovich Kudimov has sent for me, and one of his aides has warned me that it's about an assignment in the Arctic. I just want you to be ready, Lieutenant, to assume your duties under my command at this new location in the very near future."

She thought for a moment that there was no one at the other end of the line until a strangled sob confirmed for her that her message had been received and would be acted on. The lieutenant would have heard that that swine Viktor Mikhailovich had arrived. The general was the closest thing to Stalinist purges they had in the Red Army these days. His victims still disappeared into the Arctic but to army outposts instead of work camps. And like survivors of the Gulag, they returned after only many years, broken men and women, content to live in obscure villages on tiny pensions. The Arctic was no place for a woman of her beauty and brains, yet she knew that neither her beauty nor her brains would save her if she failed General Kudimov. It was typical of him to have the subject of his interview with her deliberately leaked to her by an aide. He would thus expect her to come prepared to defend herself.

She hung up the receiver while the lieutenant was in the middle of a long litany of reassurances, glanced at her wristwatch, checked herself in the mirror, and left her small private room in the military base for the office the visiting general was using. She arrived punctually and was shown in. The general sat on an easy chair, smoking a cigarette, glasses and a bottle of vodka beside him on a side table. He courteously asked her to sit down and offered her a drink and a smoke, which she politely refused. She tried not to look back into his gray eyes, magnified by his steel-rimmed spectacles, as he sat there and calmly looked her over.

"Tell me, Comrade Colonel," he finally said, "how your views differ from those of army intelligence on these three American infiltrators. Do you agree that they are Americans?"

"Without doubt, Comrade General. I generally support our intelligence profile of the three. They are not a unit trained specially to operate behind our lines. Their behavior is much too erratic for them to be regular soldiers; in fact, their unpredictability has helped them against us. If we have one fault as a military force, General, I think you will agree that it is our predictability. I have been trying to shake up our field officers to be more innovative in their search for these men, but all most of them do is come down with a heavier hand in the same old way. I say this to you confidentially, General, and it is in no way a criticism of the Red Army or of the brave and dedicated soldiers under your command."

"I appreciate your frankness, Colonel," he said. "Where are the three Americans now?"

"They have vanished, Comrade General."

"Vanished?"

"Into some hillside cave or a hut in a mountain village. We are using ground sweeps over the entire region to flush them out."

"With no results so far?"

"None yet."

"Perhaps they have left the region," he suggested.

"I hope they have," she responded. "Word will soon come to us. When they travel, they are most vulnerable."

"You agree that intelligence is right to discount the rumors of more armed Americans in the region?"

She smiled scornfully at this notion. "Already these three infiltrators are being credited with the most fantastic victories over Soviet forces, victories in which hundreds of our men have died—"

"Somebody is killing them," the general said, interrupting tersely.

"Gul Daoud is, and all the other bandit leaders loose in the mountains, yet these three Americans get credited with actions hundreds of miles from where we know they were definitely located on a particular date—"

"That would seem to support the stories of more Americans in the region," the general said, interrupting again.

"I'm certain it's merely a result of the myth that has built up around these Western adventurers. The Afghan bandits are religious and superstitious. They need to believe in a miraculous American intervention in this struggle, and so they multiply everything the Americans do in order to make them look like gods who can confront Soviet power."

"That may be so, Colonel," the general said in a voice that made it clear he was keeping other possibilities open. "Now you have spoken frankly with me, which I welcome, and so I will take my turn in being frank with you. The other senior officers here have all steered clear of any responsibility for the capture of these three Americans, leaving all the burden to you, as well as all the credit for success, of course."

"As soon as these three are captured, all those officers will be standing ready to accept congratulations for the success," Yekaterina said bitterly. "You will find me standing in the second row."

"Not if you are successful," General Kudimov said with a smile. "I will personally see to it that you get full recognition. Do you accept the assignment?"

Yekaterina saw the trap. These man were palming off an unfamiliar challenge on her, unsure of how to handle it themselves anymore. The general himself was covering his own ass as much as the senior officers by having her as someone to point at if things went wrong.

"Yes, I accept," she said, determined to show these slothful, cowardly men what she could do.

"You will have to go into the field yourself," the general said. "No more sitting at a desk and talking on the telephone."

Yekaterina knew in an instant that he had already heard a tape of her phone conversation with the lieutenant, just before she came to see him. That had been fast. "If I fail, I will be sent to Siberia to count the birch trees."

He nodded.

"But if I succeed—"

"Full recognition and promotion."

She smiled.

Without moving from the armchair he fiddled with the front of his pants and pulled out his erect dick. He beckoned to her to come and kneel beside him.

The mercs' rebel contacts on the far side of the river had been in hiding and had witnessed how the team avenged the boy's death under the Soviet tank. They embarrassed the mercs by their adulation and embraces, their constant singsong praise and instant willingness to do anything for their heroes.

"We've hit them right in a soft spot," Jed Crippenby

explained. "They saw us avenge a wrong against them. They feel like an American would if you walked up to him and handed him a million dollars in the street. Like the American, they are amazed, overjoyed, and not quite sure what it all means. For the Pathans, or Pashtuns as they are often called here in Afghanistan, we have behaved according to their code of honor, which they call *pashtunwali*. The three parts of this code of honor are *milmastia, badal*, and *manawatai*, namely hospitality, blood revenge, and sanctuary. We've all seen everyone's hospitality to us—they literally give a stranger the last piece of bread in the house and starve themselves. And since you can demand sanctuary from one group when another group is after you for blood revenge, I suppose everything works out in the end somehow. So what we did was *badal*, blood revenge, something they don't usually expect from Westerners."

While the men had joked at Crippenby's mini-lectures at first, they all now listened very carefully to them. Jed still might be a library-bound intellectual, yet he only opened his mouth when he had something interesting to say.

Harvey Waller urged his horse forward among the rebel guides and yelled, "*Badal! Badal!*" and waved his Kalashnikov.

The rebels repeated his cries and added some more of their own. Harvey dropped back to ask Jed what they were saying about him. These were just Muslim prayers and war cries, but Jed didn't want to let Harvey down.

"They say you're the greatest since John Wayne," Jed told him.

Harvey looked at him doubtfully. "They know who John Wayne was?"

"I'm telling you what they're saying."

After that, Harvey was smiling and friendly to everyone all day. At one point he told Mike he had developed a new respect for the Afghan people.

They moved slowly north on horseback. Mike had bought the horses from Gul Daoud and intended to give them as a gift to their new guides when the team switched to some faster form of transportation. All going well, their journey would involve two hundred miles to the north, two hundred

COBRA STRIKE

west, and another two hundred or more southwest to Herat, the Afghan city not far from the Iranian border. Twenty miles a day on horseback over this rough terrain would be good going, so this journey on horseback would take about a month. That was hardly Pony Express standards, but it was probably a reasonable estimate, considering unforeseen difficulties, lack of fresh horses, etc. The great advantage of going horseback was the ability to stay off the main roads, which were mostly held by communist forces during daylight hours.

But they could never expect to survive their Russian hunters for an entire month. Their loss of fast movement through going on horseback would give the Soviets plenty of time to prepare for their arrival in advance. They needed some kind of rapid transport and would have to use the major roads, depending on the Russians not expecting them to provide them with a clear passage.

Mike had asked the guides to bring them to the main road that led northward from the capital city of Kabul. Kabul, by far the most Westernized city in Afghanistan, was a stronghold of Afghan communists and their Red Army supporters. The team had stayed south of the city and then cut to the north about forty miles west of Kabul. The road north followed the course of the Kunduz River, and Mike planned to join it east of the Shibar Pass. They made their farewells with the rebels close to the road, gave them the horses, and had them wait in concealment at a distance until the mercs commandeered a vehicle north.

They watched at a steep uphill grade where trucks traveling north had to climb slowly in low gear. The traffic was sparse, and most of it was military trucks and personnel carriers traveling in small convoys. Then they saw what they wanted—a lone truck, painted green and white, with large Arabic writing on it. Jed grinned but said nothing. Harvey Waller stepped into the roadway in front of the approaching truck and looked along the sights of the RPG2 launcher tube on his right shoulder. There was no escape for the truck toiling uphill. The driver pulled onto the side of the road, and he and his coworker climbed down out of the cab and put their hands in the air, talking together in a frightened squabble in Pushtu to Waller. They were both Westernized Afghans, without turbans or other head covering and in the same T-shirts, jeans, and running shoes Waller would expect to see in Jersey City.

"I can see these bastards are commies," Waller snarled. "Why don't one of youse guys snuff them? Or do you want me to do it?"

"Harvey, they say they are for the rebels," Jed said. "They know we're Americans and they're pointing out that they work for an American company. This is a Coca-Cola truck that we've stopped. Coke had to change its usual red-colored trucks to the Islamic green and white because a lot of backcountry rebels would just assume that a bright red truck was Russian and open fire on it."

Waller wasn't convinced until he saw the crates of Coke in the back of the truck.

"Let's move out," Mike shouted. "We've been here long enough. Now that they know we're Americans, we'll have to take these two men with us and decide what to do with them at the other end."

Joe Nolan drove, Campbell and Crippenby beside him. The rest made room for themselves as best they could among the crates in the back of the truck, and the vehicle resumed its slow uphill pull toward the Shibar Pass.

Yunis Latifi and his two remaining children huddled in the bomb shelter he had dug with his own hands close to his house. His wife and youngest son had been dead almost a year now, from a bomb dropped on them while they walked in a nearby field. This morning he had heard a plane searching in the nearby valleys, and he had gathered his son of six and daughter of four into his arms and rushed to the hole he had dug with a massive, flat boulder for its roof. This bomb shelter was close neither to the house nor to his crops, both frequent targets for planes sweeping through the valley. At last they heard the plane scream down low overhead, and they put their fingers in their ears to deaden the sound of the bombs. But no explosions came. When it became clear that the aircraft was not returning, Yunis emerged and searched for an unexploded bomb. He found nothing and decided that the plane had not considered the place worth attacking. He called the children up out of the shelter and told them to care for the sheep and lambs while he worked in his fields.

Many of the people in the area had fled to Pakistan, although the men came back to fight and die for these hills, which belonged to them. Yunis had been one of those who had refused to move his family, preferring to die or live on the soil he and his forefathers had tilled rather than eke out an existence and dwell in a tent in a squalid camp across the border. He had been badly shaken when his wife and youngest child were killed. He blamed himself for not taking them to a refugee camp. But still he did not take his two remaining children to a camp, feeling deep down that they would all be happier defending what was theirs at any cost, rather than scavenge from day to day as refugees.

The six-year-old boy helped his four-year-old sister along the twisting sheep path on the hillside above the field in which their father stooped, weeding between rows of young corn. His sister was the first to see them. She struggled to free herself from her brother's hand so she could run and pick up one of the treasures that had appeared as if by magic on the lonely hillside. She wanted the small, brightly colored plastic butterfly; he, the toy truck.

The little girl was left-handed, and she picked up the butterfly an instant before the boy reached for the toy truck. The explosion of the miniature anti-personnel mine disguised as a butterfly blew her hand off at the wrist and burned her body. Her brother lost his right hand a fraction of a second later.

Yunis jerked upright from his weeding at the sound of the two detonations on the hillside above him. He saw his two small children sagging to the ground, clutching to them the bleeding stumps at the end of their arms. With a hoarse cry to Allah he clambered wildly up the hillside to them.

Mike saw the turbaned Afghan holding his two blood-soaked children by the side of the road. Jed listened to his story as they were helped into the back of the truck, then rejoined Campbell and Nolan in the cab as the truck set off again. Andre Verdoux was tying tourniquets to stanch the bleeding in the children's arms and giving them small doses of morphine to deaden their pain.

"The man says there's some sort of medical unit off this road farther north," Jed told Mike. "He says a government hospital will refuse to treat his kids because they only treat pro-communists. One of the truck drivers says he knows the place, that it's at Zari and he'll show us where to turn off."

Mike nodded grimly. "We Americans say a lot about talking peace with the Russians and having to rely on their word in negotiations, but you can't talk peace with a nation's government that is willing to manufacture mines in the shape of children's toys. It's not just a matter of differences in political philosophy, it's a matter of one side observing certain limits of decency and the other side none. We Americans had instances of individual misconduct in Vietnam, but the manufacturing of mines with the aim of crippling children is a government policy, not the act of an individual. If you learn nothing else while you're with us, Crippenby, I want you to remember what you've seen here today."

They slowly had to round two landslides that almost blocked the road a few miles before the pass. Nolan barely accelerated out of the way of one of several large boulders that dislodged themselves from the glue of liquid mud and rolled rapidly downhill. The Shibar Pass was at an altitude of ten thousand feet, and there were still large unmelted patches of snow everywhere. On the far side of the pass the corn was just emerging on the bare brown hills. The village of Shibar was a lonely group of windswept houses beneath massive faces of rock. They met frequent convoys of army vehicles and passed through some inactive checkpoints without being challenged. Dugouts and emplacements by the side of the road at first made them hold their breath till they had passed by, but after a while they drove nonchalantly past everything, waved cheerfully back when waved at, or looked ahead stonily if that was the treatment they received.

All of them, except Turner, had full beards and had freshly dyed them black. Under Campbell's orders Turner had stopped shaving and dyed his hair, yet somehow he still managed to look like a U.S. Marine no matter how Campbell tried to disguise him. Winston did not have to be told to stay out of sight, since even a quick glance would have given away the black American's presence to observers. At first the Nanticoke Institute men kept to themselves and even shunned their fellow Institute member, Crippenby. Turner was the first to open up, and after him, Winston. Only Baker still held himself aloof from the merc team; he silently and sulkily obeyed Campbell's orders to the letter and gave nothing more. Baker had once been spokesman for his group, and now he found himself outclassed in leadership by Campbell and in linguistic knowledge by Crippenby. He had wanted to return a hero, not the object of a rescue mission. None of the three were aware that they were under the close scrutiny of Andre Verdoux. The Frenchman had given up many of his other team duties to keep a close watch on them. Campbell and he had not even discussed it. Andre just automatically took on a thing like this, and Campbell totally, unquestioningly, relied on him.

They turned off to Zari and found the hospital. It was run by a group called Doctors Without Borders. A young Belgian doctor was the only M.D. He had three nurses, all young. Like the doctor, one was a Belgian man, and the other two were women, one Belgian and the other French. The strict Moslems would only allow women to give medical attention to women. When the mercs arrived, supplies were so low that they were down to using veterinary anesthetics on humans. Mike donated a large part of the team's medical supplies. Turner and Nolan had the correct type of blood to give the two children transfusions. The doctor worked on his patients on a ramshackle kitchen table under a camouflage canvas awning.

Verdoux was ecstatic to meet others who spoke French. They told him that they volunteered for eight months duty and, on their return, would be paid three hundred dollars for each month.

"Would you treat a Russian?" Andre asked.

"Certainly," the doctor said. "Anyone who needs medical attention gets it. But I'm afraid no injured Russians have reached us alive. They always seem to slip off stretchers and take terrible falls before they get here. The Afghans apologize and say they slipped. What can I say? There are so many steep mountains."

CHAPTER 12

The team descended from the highlands into flatter, heavily Soviet-occupied country. The road wound down a sinking green plain covered with prickly clover and tall, bright yellow flowers. Horses and cattle were plentiful, and apparently the Soviets found less need to use their "scorched-earth" policy in this region. The team was aware that, in the event of trouble, they might find it much harder to find friends here than among the remote highlands. They passed through the old, fortified towns of Kunduz and Balkh, whose ancient walls were little more than crumbling mounds in places. All the same, sandbagged barracks and rolls of barbed wire around enclosures told a different story, that not everything was a charming antique. But they met no challenge and drove on their way right through enemy-held territory.

Nolan sensed that Campbell was becoming very edgy. "What's wrong, Mike? Think this is too good to last much longer?"

"Something like that," Campbell admitted. "So we just keep going until they try to stop us. That's when the shit hits the fan. I know they promised that word would not get out at the medical center, and I believe the two Afghan drivers who say that they will stay in Zari for three days before they report our seizure of their truck. But this many Americans is very tempting bait to anyone who needs to pick up easy money for information."

"I bet it don't happen that way, Mike," Nolan said. "You know what I bet will happen? Some joker on the roadside will decide to play the heavy just to do a little power trip on us—not because he's suspicious of us or anything, but just to give someone a hard time because he didn't get laid last night or couldn't get it up."

"You think you can handle that, Jed?" Mike asked.

"I'll try. This is no longer Pathan or Pushtun country here. The people are mostly Uzbek here. They speak a language that's close to Turkish, which I speak fairly well, and it's possible they may take me for one of the other ethnic groups speaking their tongue. I don't really know, Mike, what their reaction will be."

"I think that if anyone tries to stop us," Nolan said, "we should get Harvey Waller to 'speak' to him."

"You're right," Campbell allowed, and had the truck stopped so Waller could be squeezed into the cab along with them.

The road crossed and recrossed the Kunduz River at a few points on old brickwork bridges that showed much flood damage. The river itself was about sixty yards wide, filled with turbulent, pinkish, muddy snow water sweeping by at high speed, the banks lined by willows and reedy marshes. They came to one place where a string of more than a hundred loaded camels, many of them ridden by veiled women, crossed the road. Nolan eased to a stop some distance from them. A plump man in a silk cap and a long bright blue robe waved them closer. Nolan pretended not to see him. The man shouted and walked toward the truck.

"Here we go," Nolan muttered.

The plump man in the blue robe was clearly angry at having been made to walk to them. He shouted and gestured at them with an old bolt-action Lee Enfield rifle. Nolan stared straight ahead, as did Waller next to him, while Jed

COBRA STRIKE

leaned across them both and yelled back at the man in the Uzbek language. The man in blue seemed to be having a good time.

Jed gave them a quiet voice-over of what he was saying. "We Pathans are a very stupid, backward, belligerent people, and it worries Uzbeks like himself that since we are all Sunni Moslems, we will have to share Paradise together. In his opinion we Pathans will be in the bare, stony parts of Paradise, while Uzbeks will inhabit the river valleys and live beneath fruit trees with dancing girls. He doesn't seem to be joking."

Crippenby said no more in case the man heard him speak English, but the Uzbek was so preoccupied with his own concerns, he hardly paid any close attention to them. Finally something must have struck him as odd, because he climbed up on the footrest at the base of the cab door so he could peer inside closely at them. His eye immediately went to the Pakistani rupee notes Harvey held in his hand; he took them, stepped down on the road, made the notes vanish inside his blue robe with a gesture a professional magician would have been proud of, waved them on, and mentioned Allah several times. The last of the camels had cleared the road as the truck resumed its journey and began to pick up speed again.

Nolan said to Campbell, "I think our new boy Jed here is really getting the hang of things."

"That was smooth, Jed, real smooth," Waller allowed.

Jed grinned and waited for Campbell to compliment him. Campbell didn't.

They had not much farther to go down the road before they ran into real trouble. This was in the form of a communist government military checkpoint consisting of two machine gun nests about a hundred yards apart, one on each side of the road, and a soldier with a white piece of cloth, which he waved as he stood in the middle of the road at the first machine gun position. These were not dugouts like they had seen before in rebel-infested areas. The soldiers squatted behind a double layer of sandbags, protected from the sun by galvanized zinc sheets resting on metal rods, supported in turn by four-foot pillars of empty metal boxes marked 81 MOR HE.

"Slow to a rolling stop," Mike ordered Nolan. "See if you can drift past the first gun before stopping." As he spoke, he passed a wad of rupee notes to Harvey Waller.

Nolan braked and let the truck roll. The soldier, used to the varying quality of Afghan brakes, quickly stepped out of the way and trotted alongside as the truck ground to a stop. Nolan took it a couple of lengths past the first gun. The soldier jumped onto the footrest and poked his Kalashnikov inside. He spoke in Uzbek. When Jed replied, the man switched to Pushtu. Jed said in Pushtu, knowing he couldn't fool this man into believing he was a native speaker, that they were Tajik and changed to Dari, the Afghan dialect of Persian.

The soldier wasn't buying this, and he wasn't taking the cash in Waller's hand. Unfortunately for him, he had a face that revealed his emotions. The hand that only a second previously had offered him a small fortune in Pakistani rupees now grasped his throat. Nolan tore the Kalashnikov from the soldier's grasp and lifted his foot off the clutch pedal. The truck lurched forward, fishtailed, and skidded broadside off the road so that it knocked the galvanized zinc roof on top of the soldiers in the second gun emplacement. Nolan kept the truck off the road, keeping the roadside bank of earth between him and the first gun.

Waller was still holding the soldier by the neck in his right hand as the truck went back on the road, but the man was no longer feeling anything, as evidenced by his bulging eyes and protruding tongue.

"Let him go, Harvey," Mike said.

Waller released him unwillingly, like a dog wanting to hang on to a tasty bone, and the soldier's body flopped on the blacktop road.

"Those soldiers will have radioed ahead," Mike said to Nolan. "They'll be waiting for us along the road and searching for us by air. Joe, turn off the road as soon as you can. See if we can cut across country for a while before they pinpoint us."

They were now heading west, no more than thirty miles

south of the Soviet border. Nolan pulled the truck onto a dusty pair of tracks heading across the undulating land more or less to the west. They had gone maybe ten miles when they came to a long irrigation ditch and had to travel alongside it till Nolan found a bridge made of poles and turf. The truck's wheel base barely fitted onto the primitive bridge, and Nolan inched the vehicle across. Equally slowly the bridge sagged under its weight. As Nolan felt it giving way beneath him he accelerated forward. The dry poles snapped like shots, and the bridge collapsed in a rumble of lumber and dust. The truck fell on its side into the ditch.

"Some fucking driver," Waller muttered, trying to separate himself from the others and get out of the muddy water flowing into the cab.

Nolan growled from the bottom of the heap. "Know what broke the bridge, Harvey? The weight of your fat ass."

Colonel Yekaterina Matveyeva kicked the shin of her driver to make him stop. She nodded to the two Afghans in the back and said in Uzbek, "Ismael Rasool and one other."

The two Afghans ran through the village and came back in ten minutes with two worried men trotting in front of their Kalashnikovs.

"Which is Rasool?" the colonel asked.

One of the Afghans nodded to his right.

She directed her attention to the other man. She asked in Uzbek, "Are you the one who saw these many Americans?"

"No."

She drew her 9mm Makarov pistol, slid a round in the chamber, and drilled a slug into his forehead. He fell stiffly over, like a length of wood. She pointed the smoking muzzle at Rasool.

Rasool looked her in the eyes and said, "He died honorably, speaking the truth. He did not see the Americans. I saw them. Many of them."

"Who else in this village saw them?"

He spread his hands. "No one. Only me."

The pistol spat flame, and the lump of lead stove in his forehead above his right eye. He sprawled across the body of his fellow villager.

Yekaterina put her gun in its holster and felt better. This was the third of these Afghan rumor-mongers she had silenced, along with one or two others each time in order to test that they were telling her the truth. She intended to stop these unfounded reports of there being more than three Americans. She had assured the general that these stories were nonsense. The Americans were here all right—close to the Soviet border! The Red Army was on full alert on its own side of the border, and in Yekaterina's considered opinion these three Yankee provocateurs had already crossed onto Soviet soil for their own private vicious purposes. There were three of them. No more.

Having hid for the rest of the daylight hours in long rushes not far from where they had concealed the toppled truck in the ditch with the same rushes, they walked all night to reach a point on one of Gul's maps, covered Crippenby while he inquired alone at a shepherd's hovel for the local rebel leader, and followed the shepherd down a dry ravine in almost total darkness.

"Tell him he'll be the first to die if he leads us into a trap," Mike instructed Jed, "and that we'll all go back and violate his wife."

Jed talked to the man and reported back, "He says he's not afraid of death and he has no wife. He has nothing in this world except his sheep."

Waller said, "Tell him I'll violate his sheep."

Winston and Murphy, the only two who had been badly knocked about in the capsizing of the truck, were being allowed to take it easy, which in Campbell's unit meant that Mike might be inclined to listen if they claimed they could go no farther. Andre Verdoux added their care to his duties and, on a number of occasions, called a halt when he decided Winston needed a rest.

"The fucking frog has never once called a break on my account," Murphy complained.

"I was afraid that by doing so I would insult your manhood," Verdoux explained. "We all know how vulnerable Australians are about their manhood."

"You rotten *eau-de-cologne* Paris faggot," Murphy roared.

COBRA STRIKE

"Mike only takes you along to do the bookkeeping. You don't have any right to talk to a fighting man."

This was a low blow, touching as it did on Verdoux's status as an aging warrior, and Bob Murphy regretted saying it as soon as it was out of his mouth.

"Sorry, Andre," he said, suddenly subdued. "You know anything awful about Australia you want to say to even us up?"

"You'd have to give me time to think up something," Andre replied gallantly, touched that his enemy had such respect for him as a soldier. Then the Frenchman turned to the black American. "How do you feel, Winston? Ready to push on?"

"I'm okay, Andre."

"Great," Andre said. "All right, Mike, we're ready to move out."

"What about me?" Murphy demanded. "Why not ask me if my leg is rested enough so I can walk?"

"Australians are good at hopping," Andre answered.

Masood Haq was a steely-eyed giant with a big floppy turban and a loose brown pajama suit. "The Russians say there are only three of you," he said. "They shoot people for saying there are ten of you. What do you want of us? I mean, of course, beyond a place to stay and food to eat. What can we do for you?"

"We need transportation west," Campbell said, using Jed as an interpreter.

"West?" Haq smiled. "I will not ask where you are going. I know someone who will go part of the way with you. This man has excellent transport. But you must remain here for a few days until my present work is completed."

Mike said to Jed in English, "I'm not sure we can trust him. We could do with a rest, but I don't want to stay put here unless I know the reason for it. Be diplomatic, but insist on finding out why we must delay."

Jed and the rebel leader fenced verbally for some time before Jed was able to tell Mike, "They've dug a tunnel under the local army barracks, and they're preparing to blow it up. The people we travel west with are part of this plan, and so we have to wait. It sounds to me, Mike, as if it's going to be one helluva lot harder to get out of here even with their help, after they pull this caper, than it would be to leave right now and forge ahead alone."

Mike shook his head. "We'll be leaving with their people. He said we would be going with people involved in this project. They take care of their own. No matter what goes down, we're better off sticking with locals. If they've survived against the Russians this long, they've got to be doing something right. Tell him I want to see this tunnel."

"He says that's not possible," Jed translated.

"Hang on to him here while I fetch Nolan."

Mike returned with Nolan, who showed Masood Haq some Tovex TR-2, an underground mining explosive, and C-4, the powerful military plastic explosive, along with sophisticated detonators.

Haq's attitude changed instantly.

"They have been using the scrapings from artillery shells and mixtures of artificial fertilizer and sugar," Jed translated. "Masood Haq hereby appoints you chief fireworks-maker in the kingdom, Nolan."

The rebel leader escorted the three Americans across waste lots to a small house at the edge of a town. The four men crawled on their bellies all the way. The tunnel led from the floor of the house in a steep incline down beneath the town. It ran level for about a hundred yards and then angled gently upward for another twenty yards or so. No timbers shored the hard, dry earth in which the tunnel had been constructed. It was barely wide enough for a man's shoulders to fit without his turning sideways, and it varied in height, without apparent reason, from five to seven feet. The air was stale at the far end of the tunnel. Nolan checked the explosives already in place.

"Not bad," Nolan said after he had examined the mixtures and their placement. "What they have here would have caused the buildings above to collapse. When we mix in the C-4 and Tovex TR-2, we'll blow their asses sky-high. Where's the wiring?"

"That has been the holdup," Jed translated. "They expect it tomorrow or the day after."

"Ask him if he knows any communist who lives alone in a nice new house," Nolan said.

Masood did, and Mike agreed that they would drop by to visit him. Joe slid the catch of a back window with his knife blade and climbed in. He tiptoed across the unlit back room and peered through a doorway into the front room. A young Afghan in Western-style gray pants and a blue shirt, with heavy-rimmed spectacles, sat cross-legged on the floor, leafing through a pile of documents.

Nolan walked silently across the carpet toward him. The knife, blade horizontal, point forward, was held at his right side. The Afghan was suddenly startled to see a pair of boots beside his documents on the carpet. He looked up to see who was in them. The knife blade swung in an arc the length of Nolan's right arm. The point of the blade penetrated the man's voice box, and its edges sliced through his trachea. Nolan savagely jerked the blade from side to side to sever the arteries and veins and was immediately rewarded with splashes of blood on himself, the carpet, and the nearest wall. But Nolan had already lost interest and was on his way around the house, warm, sticky weapon in hand, to make sure it was empty before signaling to Masood and Jed to come inside. Mike would stand guard while they worked at stripping the house's entire electrical wiring from the walls.

The explosion was set for six that evening, when the soldiers would be eating their meal. Masood Haq insisted that it take place during daylight, and Nolan agreed to humor him. The mercs and Institute men slept late, and most passed the early afternoon listening to an older cousin of Masood's, Rahim, who spoke good English and had been a career officer in the Afghan army before the Marxists took over. He had been to the United States three times, taking courses at Fort Knox, Kentucky; Fort Benning, Georgia; and Fort Leavenworth, Kansas. He told them it was a "real pleasure" for him to speak to Americans again and that he was "mighty pleased" they were here.

What interested them most was what Rahim had to say about life under the communists in the capital city of Kabul.

Unlike Masood, Rahim did not consider himself one of the *mujahidin*, or holy warriors, fighting a *jihad*, or sacred war, against the infidels. He had even gone along with the leftist takeover, prior to the Russian invasion, because it promised modernization and new prosperity. The communists had not fully trusted him and transferred him from his active duty post to a desk job in Kabul.

"The government compound where I worked had three gates. The Khad—the secret police—used two of them, and everyone else used the other one. Even the prime minister, whose office was at the center of the compound, could not use the two Khad gates. One day someone must have observed me looking overly long at the Khad buildings, and I received orders to avert my face from them every time I was entering or leaving the compound. After that I was assigned a new typist, a sixteen-year-old girl who had been trained to type in Persian in Moscow. The typists had a meeting every day from two to four, and she always carefully locked her desk drawer before she left. One afternoon I had a cousin visit me, and he picked the lock while I kept watch. He found that she had a miniature tape recorder and a pistol in the drawer. Then I knew my days were numbered."

"She was a member of the Khad?" Verdoux asked.

"Probably not a member," Rahim said, "but she certainly worked for them. She was one of the many young people they send, some very young, for training all over the Soviet Union. They come back brainwashed and think they are being patriotic by informing on their less convinced countrymen. I know for a fact that they transport orphan boys to Moslem parts of the Soviet Union. There they teach them that Russia and Afghanistan are just two friendly countries that belong on equal footing to the Union of Soviet Socialist Republics. They teach them that the *mujahidin* are heretic Moslems and train them to use the AK-47 and TT 7.62mm pistol so they can come back here, shoot men in the back whom no adult could approach, sneak up to buildings and toss grenades through windows, distribute bombs disguised as toys to rebel children—"

"We've seen the result of that," Andre said. "They were dropped from a plane on a hillside."

Rahim nodded sadly. "You see things in this war that no one has stooped to before. Our Russian brothers have many things to teach mankind if they are given the chance. We know that because we have always lived alongside their empire. I think you Americans know it, too, but can't really believe it because you want to feel you can make trustworthy friends of the Bolsheviks. Only remember what they say—they say *they* never change, that the only thing that changes is other people's opinions of them."

Harvey Waller smiled warmly at him. Harvey was getting to love Afghanistan. This mission was working out like a vacation for him. He was meeting interesting people who talked common sense, and there was something new to do every day. He felt no doubt at all that he'd fill his quota for this trip—a dead commie to show for every day he was in the field.

"You knew your days in the army were numbered?" Andre prompted Rahim.

"Yes. Influential communists here all belong to what they call the Sazman Iwalia, or First Organization. One by one they appointed each other to all the key posts in the armed forces. Officers who did not belong were not invited to key meetings and in time found themselves transferred, like I was, to paper shuffling and donkey work. I was suspect because my brother Masood was emerging as an active rebel leader. I did not spy for the rebels while I was in government service because that is against my principles. I am a soldier, not a spy. I was loyal too. I did not leave until I saw that they meant to murder me."

"That's always a valid reason for leaving," Harvey assured him very seriously.

Colonel Yekaterina Matveyeva did not realize as she sat at a borrowed desk in the town's military barracks that she was less than fifteen feet from an American whose presence in Afghanistan she had strenuously denied. Almost directly beneath where she sat, in a narrow womb sunk in the hard earth, Joe Nolan jabbed detonators into explosive charges that were planted in a pattern to gain maximum effect. He linked the detonators together with wiring from the slain communist's house. He worked carefully, neatly, methodically, leaving no room for error, insulating against the rare chance of damp in the desert-dry soil.

Above him, the colonel carefully sifted through her information inputs. She yelled for the lieutenant. When he poked his head in the doorway, she said, "They're right here. In this town. I know it." She waved one hand toward the reports. "All independent sources, and they all say the same thing."

The lieutenant approached her cautiously. "Certainly they all agree, Comrade. All the reports say that two non-English-speaking Westerners with camera and sound equipment—"

"I can read for myself, Lieutenant! Why are you so dull? So totally unimaginative! Let me answer all your objections. First of all, there are two, not three, men. Why? Because they have to keep the black one hidden since he would immediately identify them as the group with Red Army priority notification status. The local people think they do not speak English because they are used to the British-sounding English of Pakistanis and Indians; they are unfamiliar with American accents. You know what their television cameras and sound equipment are? A shoulder-mounted ground-to-air or antitank rocket launcher plus wire-guided missile gadgetry. These peasants here are too stupid to tell the difference. You see? This shows I was right about only three Americans being involved, and not ten or eleven as some idiots have been claiming. I admit I was wrong about one thing—they have not yet crossed the border into the Soviet Union. We have to get to them before they can do so. This town is their staging area for the run across the border.

"Now listen carefully, Comrade Lieutenant, this is what I am going to do. Under the special authority extended to me by General Kudimov, I am countermanding all other orders issued to local troops and canceling all leaves for officers and men. I want all available regular forces to fan out between here and the border. Have all units assemble here in the barracks in four hours time, at eighteen hundred hours precisely."

Beneath her, in his clay womb, Joe Nolan was setting the

COBRA STRIKE

automatic timer before connecting up the electrical circuit powered by four heavy-duty car batteries.

Op van de Bosch hefted the video camera on his right shoulder, and Jan Prijt moved his mike around while he checked dials on a leather case suspended against his left hip. Mike Campbell looked at them and cursed Masood Haq first as a deceitful bastard and then himself as a credulous loon.

Campbell said to Crippenby, "Tell Masood I thought he meant he would be leaving with his men since he said they would be involved in the tunnel explosion."

Jed talked with the rebel leader and told Mike, "Masood says the Dutch TV crew is here specially for the explosion, which is why it has to be done by daylight. He says you must talk with the Dutchmen yourself about leaving town. Masood says you will be pleased with the arrangements."

Campbell glared at the cameraman and soundman, who were halfway through a bottle of Stolichnaya vodka, regardless of the anti-alcohol feelings of Masood and his rebels. He walked over to them and picked up the vodka bottle. "If we go with you, don't touch any more of this." He replaced the open bottle on the table between them.

"Ya, ya, no more today," Op van de Bosch agreed cheerfully. "We must see straight."

"And hear straight," the slightly drunk soundman put in.

Mike looked from one to the other of the half-sloshed reporters and asked, "You really need us along with you? We don't have the protection of international press passes."

"The present Afghan government does not recognize press passes," Op responded. "If we get caught, they'll either shoot us to get rid of us quietly since we are free-lance and not with a network, or they will sentence us to twenty years as spies if they want to annoy our government. Either way, it does not work out as much of a choice for us. You are going west from here, ya? Jan and I have spent weeks shooting many meters of tape out that way. Masood will tell you that I know more of the rebel headmen in these regions than he does. You know how we escape from here after the big bang, nay?"

"No."

"I will tell you." The Dutchman was about to reach for the vodka bottle, but he saw Mike's look and stopped. "All right, then, I tell you. Two weeks ago, up near the border, some rebels ambushed a Soviet tank convoy. All they got was one truck, and they, being good Moslems, were disappointed to find that all it contained was vodka and not ammunition or guns. Big disappointment! Jan and I were there and filmed everything, including the look on the rebels' faces when they saw all the vodka. Jan and I, we hid the vodka and bought an armored personnel carrier with it from Russian soldiers here in this town."

Mike prided himself on being a hard man to surprise, but when someone did so, he did not begrudge them his admiration. "You paid some Russian soldiers..." He just let it trail off.

Op nodded his head vigorously. "But we don't know how to drive it. So we need you along."

Mike was tempted to reach for the vodka bottle himself but resisted the urge.

Privates Valery T. Timofeyev and Sergei V. Prokopchik figured they had enough Stolichnaya to keep them and their friends pickled for the remaining four months they had to serve in this hellhole. The personnel carrier had already been listed as "damaged beyond repair" and "stripped and abandoned," a casualty of a flash flood with no attendant human casualties. That paperwork alone had cost them thirty-six bottles, and the two privates were becoming appalled at the greed of their fellow servicemen who thought nothing of extorting such heavy payments for a few moments of their time.

This new problem was more worrying. The pretty blond woman colonel, who was said to be hard as nails, thought the Dutch reporters were the Americans she was hunting. Timofeyev and Prokopchik steered reports her way, at the cost of more bottles, reports that stated things clearly enough, while understandably, they themselves were not in a position to volunteer more personal information because of regulations against trading with the enemy, which, of course, in reality had no application here because the men were Dutch, and vodka was vodka; but a woman could not be expected to understand that, and even if she did, they would end in irons at hard labor, anyway.

The problem was what to do now so this colonel would realize that these two were not the Americans she was looking for. The privates did not want the Americans to escape while the colonel was distracted by the Dutchmen. Another nagging worry was that the Dutchmen knew their names and might talk if captured. That was the essence of their problem: how they could put the colonel back on the right track after the real Americans, for the good both of Russia and themselves.

"There's nothing we can do, Sergei Vladimirovich, except shape up at eighteen hundred hours along with everyone else," Timofeyev said to Prokopchik. "If something turns up after we move out, we can steer it her way. We stand to lose too much by volunteering information we're not supposed to know."

Prokopchik nodded. "You know we could be out for days in the field before we come back to town. If both of us were to take a couple of bottles along to help pass the time for us, they'd fit easily in our packs and would be hardly any extra weight to carry."

Timofeyev thought this a brilliant solution to all their problems. They still had half an hour before shape-up time at eighteen hundred hours, just enough to go outside the town and take four bottles from one of their numerous stashes.

Bob Murphy and Lance Hardwick had left the area earlier with two of Masood Haq's men and moved down the personnel carrier from its hiding place. The Dutchmen were to be picked up at an agreed location precisely at 6:07, giving them five minutes to film the effects of the explosion. They had wanted twenty minutes. Mike gave them five, plus two to move their ass. Whether they were there or not, the mercs were leaving town at 6:07 in the personnel carrier. The Dutchmen sighed and said, "Ya, ya."

Nolan was confident of his timer, so the rest of the team

was to be picked up outside the town precisely at 5:55. The personnel carrier would remain at that spot until the explosion, at 6:00, and then proceed to the rendezvous with the Dutchmen, which would take them five minutes to reach at most. After that, nothing short of antitank missiles could stop them, and they could depend on the damage and confusion caused by the blast to cripple all serious opposition.

At 5:50 Prokopchik and Timofeyev, hurrying back to the town barracks with their vodka bottles safety stowed inside their packs, saw eight heavily armed Americans waiting in a group outside the town. They got away without being seen, ran to the barracks, and shouted to the colonel. She was sitting in a vehicle next to a driver, and so they piled in the back and shouted directions and explanations as they went.

"Eight Americans?" the colonel asked guardedly.

"Yes, Comrade, including the black one. They were all dressed as Afghans, but they are Americans."

"Maybe three of them were American and the rest Afghan," Colonel Matveyeva hinted in a cold voice.

"No, Colonel. All of them. All Americans."

Well, if she took them all prisoner, they could hardly criticize her because she had been wrong previously. She would establish visual contact with them from this vehicle and wait for the lieutenant to arrive with two platoons in the next few minutes. She knew better than to doubt the account of these two seasoned infantrymen. Later they would have to explain what they had been doing out here, but she took them at their word. Eight of these rich, grinning Americans! She'd wipe the smiles from their well-fed capitalist faces!

She did not see the looks of horror that spread over the faces of Timofeyev and Prokopchik behind her when they saw, instead of the eight waiting Americans, the personnel carrier they had sold to the Dutchmen and had listed as damaged beyond repair.

The carrier lumbered forward at surprising speed and headed straight for their vehicle. The driver could not at first understand why he should flee from a Russian personnel carrier, not comprehending how eight Americans or more could be inside it. This delay nearly cost them their lives as the heavy carrier tried to ram them. The driver pulled out of the way at the last moment, but not far enough, because the personnel carrier twisted toward them and sideswiped their vehicle. All four occupants were thrown clear as the open-topped vehicle flipped over, its wheels in the air.

The colonel lay on her side in the dust, gasping for breath and allowing tears of rage to stream down her cheeks as she gazed after the armored vehicle heading slowly toward the town.

As she watched, the barracks erupted in a blinding light, and she clearly saw bodies and large sections of buildings lifted high into the air as shock waves traveled through the ground beneath her and the deafening blast resounded in her ears.

CHAPTER 13

Murphy drove the personnel carrier at high speed westward across Afghanistan, never more than thirty or forty miles below the Soviet border. With the two Dutchmen they now amounted to a force of twelve heavily armed men in a heavily armored all-terrain vehicle, mounted with two heavy machine guns and topped up with fuel. One well-aimed rocket could take care of all that. But at least it beat slogging up and down mountain slopes and throwing themselves facedown on the bare rock every time they thought they heard a jet or a chopper.

Sheep grazed on rich grasslands here, roses grew in front of houses, jays and squirrels squawked beneath poplar trees. They fitted Op van de Bosch into a Russian uniform discarded inside the carrier, and he spoke rapid Dutch to the local peasants and paid for lamb kebab, milk, yogurt, bread, tea, and other supplies in Afghan currency supplied by Mike. Campbell had always paid the highland rebels in Pakistan currency, for that was where they made their purchases, but this part of the country—Afghan Turkestan—was a very different place populated by very different

COBRA STRIKE 193

people. Many of the men were strongly Asiatic in appearance and wore long, striped or flowered robes.

Fierce mountain warriors they were not! In one town the local government soldiers walked around each with a flower in the muzzle of his Kalashnikov. They refueled the personnel carrier at the base there, letting the Afghan doing the work see Op in his Russian uniform and hear, but not see, Jed Crippenby talk Turki to him in a Russian accent from inside the carrier.

"Op, all you have to do is sign for the fuel," Jed said softly in English. "The Russian officer in charge here has been down with dysentery for five days, the Russian sergeant has been drunk for three days, the radio receiver and transmitter have never worked properly but haven't worked at all in two days, and none of the soldiers have gotten laid in more than a year. Sounds like our kind of town, Mike. You think we should settle down here?"

She had always warned the slow, rotten son of a bitch that he would freeze his nuts off in the Arctic for not catching these Yankee terrorists, and once again he had evaded her by burning to death in the American-engineered explosion. If the lieutenant had obeyed her promptly and followed on the double with two platoons, he and they would have been clear of the barracks when the explosion took place. But, as always, he had dithered. She was well rid of him. Only now, when the kicks were passed down to her, she had no one to pass them along to.

"We have work to do," she snapped to the driver of her damaged, but still operable, vehicle. "Those two privates have given me the slip. To hell with them. And we have no time to bother with what's happened here. Take me to the main highway."

"But, Comrade Colonel, many of these men were in my unit. They were all under your command. Some are still alive. We must help—"

The driver stopped talking when she pointed her Makarov at him. He started the engine and pulled it onto the road to the highway. The vehicle's transmitter had been smashed, and the chaos and destruction around the town barracks would make another difficult to locate. On the highway she could commandeer the first suitable transport and communications she saw.

She halted a small Afghan army provisions truck traveling east, and the driver told her he had seen a lone Red Army personnel carrier traveling against him at high speed not long ago. She sent the truck into the town to help out at the destroyed barracks. The next vehicles were a convoy of eight Afghan army trucks going west. They had not seen a personnel carrier on the road, so it went west. The lead truck had a powerful transmitter, on which she called in first the data on the eight plus Americans in the carrier, arranging to be picked up in a slick at her present location, and then put in a call for emergency medical assistance for the destroyed barracks. She placed a warning that the medical evacuation efforts must not be allowed to interfere with the ongoing military effort to apprehend the American provocateurs and enemies of free workers. She ordered the eight trucks to the barracks.

Despite his pleas to be allowed to return to help rescue his buddies, she kept her driver and vehicle with her in case the chopper didn't arrive. Yekaterina paced up and down, deep in thought. When the chopper arrived, she would have three to four times the speed of the land vehicle at the very least, with the added ability to take shortcuts. The personnel carrier could leave the road, too, but where could it go? Head for Russia? Or the high mountains of Afghanistan's interior? No. It was plain now to her where they had been headed all along and that this was a carefully staged wild goose chase. First three Americans. Now eight Americans. Maybe even more. This was an elaborate morale-boosting tour, which was just the kind of thing she had read that Americans believed in. They thought that they could rush around Afghanistan and stir up trouble, like they had in Poland and Hungary and Czechoslovakia, trying to make simple working people discontent through their elaborate lies and false promises. No wonder the Moscow authorities wanted to capture them so desperately. And she herself would have failed the cause of world communism if she did not cut out this cancer that was threatening the healthy tissue of Marxist society, which was in the process of being grafted onto Afghanistan. She knew now where they were headed. Herat. That hotbed of revisionist superstition and banditry, where brave Soviet lads gave their lives every day to bring the class revolution to these backward, ungrateful people.

"Sure we're going to drive this tin can into Herat," Campbell said, "unless someone comes at us with a can opener."

"Or unless we don't find more fuel real soon," Murphy added, who was still driving the personnel carrier, his injured leg long forgotten.

"Don't forget your promise to drop us off at our assignment," Op said. "We don't take one inch of tape on you. That shows we keep our part of the bargain."

"That shows you know you'll get a bullet up your ass if you do," Waller commented.

"Ya, I think that is a possibility too," Op admitted with a grin. "Harvey does not like us because he thinks he is a brave man to spend days in Afghanistan with his guns. Then he sees us, with no guns, and we spend weeks here. He won't admit I am a braver man than he is."

"You fucking tulip-sucking cream puff!" Waller bellowed. "You're some kind of fellow-traveling half-assed leftist from a welfare state that the Russians can't arrest or kill in case it shocks all your pinko friends back home."

Op howled with laughter. "I'll tell them that, Harvey, if they catch me."

"You're even crazier than I am," Waller muttered.

"We'll stop with your rebel friends tonight, Op, provided we reach them," Campbell told him. "We can't travel by night in this carrier, since we could be ambushed at any point by unseen enemies, either communists or rebels."

"Mike, problem ahead!" Murphy snapped. "Two personnel carriers, same model as this, at roadside ahead. Too late to turn off."

"Pull in alongside them," Mike told him calmly. He fetched one of the Stolichnaya bottles he had confiscated from the Dutchmen, "so there would be no misunderstandings," and unscrewed its cap. He undid some buttons on the Red Army tunic Op was wearing, mussed his hair, and handed him the bottle. "Drink," he said. "Lance, you and Joe take that clear plastic tubing." When the carrier eased to a stop next to one of the others, two young Russians left to guard the carriers while the others ate in a tea house came around to see who had arrived.

"You're real drunk, Op. Part with the bottle," Mike said as he pushed the Dutchman out the hatch. Campbell closed the hatch and said softly, "We should all be wondering why we are not having to bust through roadblocks by now, and why we're not having rockets shot at us by gunships, and why the soldiers that belong to these carriers have not been warned to look out for us."

Winston knew the answer to that. "They want to take us alive, Mike, and they know that these guys out in the boonies would fuck up. They'll have the elite squads stretching steel nets for us where we don't expect it, but certainly well before Herat."

The soldiers were just kids too dumb to demand to know why this drunk had been pushed out the hatch to them and why he was bearded to look like an Afghan, but they were not too young to have developed a taste for high-quality vodka. Op muttered at them and made a futile effort to hide the bottle from them. They grabbed it and pushed him away. He stood with them, grinning foolishly when they gave him an occasional toke from his own bottle.

While the guards were distracted, Hardwick and Nolan siphoned the fuel from the empty carrier into their own vehicle and got two-thirds of a tankful. Nolan signaled Op with a knock on the steel plate when they had finished, and Op left, unnoticed, to climb back in the hatch. The two young soldiers waved cheerfully after them when they pulled out.

Colonel Matveyeva rode in the Mi-24 helicopter high and to the east of the road to Herat, which at this point ran due south before swinging to the southwest at Maimena. Here the road left the northern plain and became more difficult to control. It did not make her happy to allow the Americans free passage all this way—and she wouldn't permit it if she was in full control because they had already shown themselves to be very slippery—yet there was nothing she could do about it except watch them far below her, as a cat watches a bird in a cage.

She had waited impatiently for this chopper, anxious to climb to an altitude where she could have good direct radio contact with HQ in Kabul, forgetting that once such contact was established, she might be taking orders rather than giving them. That swine Kudimov had maneuvered her into taking full responsibility for the capture of these American adventurers, and now he was ordering her to take them alive without harming a hair on their heads. After they had blown up a barracks and maybe two hundred and fifty men!

She knew General Kudimov's game. If he took all of these eight to a dozen Americans alive and put their trial on international television, it could earn him a place in the Moscow power structure, a big apartment, an official car, and a *dacha* for country weekends. Clearly he was not going to let her stand between him and all that. But she would benefit, too—in a more modest way, of course. No, Viktor Mikhailovich was right: These Americans could not be harmed. These Americans, if handled right, could be her and the general's tickets to a life of power and prestige in Moscow's top military circles. If she failed, she could see that the general had it all set up so that she alone would be disgraced. That was the risk she had to take. But she would not fail.

She would track the personnel carrier unobserved from this height until it crossed the Murghab River, about a hundred miles farther on. Then she would signal the armored column to leave Moghor, to the south, and the Americans would find themselves with an easily guarded barrier behind them in the form of the big river, with wild mountains on all sides, and a Red Army column of tanks eating up the road toward them. This was going to be something the White House would remember with a shudder, and strangers would smile at her in the Moscow streets, near her apartment in a fashionable section, recognizing her as a people's hero.

* * *

Mike Campbell didn't like the looks of what he was seeing. Something smelled wrong. The other team members seemed happy that things were going so easy for them. Mike sounded out his old friend Verdoux.

"Are you noticing some of the things I'm noticing, Andre?"

"You mean how soldiers at the checkpoints along the road conveniently look the other way when we pass through?"

"Things like that."

"There's been no general alert put out for us," Andre said. "Those military transports we pass don't know us from Adam and don't care. But I have a feeling that the soldiers at the checkpoints do and have been ordered to let us pass. It's just not natural that some tight-assed lieutenant or regulations-minded sergeant hasn't stopped us by now to check that our papers are in order, that we're in the zone we're supposed to be in, that our faces are shaved and our boots shined, that we still remember how to stand at attention. No, Mike, it's just not natural."

Campbell nodded, pleased to have his suspicions confirmed. Together they pored over the map inside the bouncing, swaying personnel carrier. Mike put his finger on the crossing of the Murghab River and shook his head. Andre nodded his head to show he agreed that it would be suicide for them to attempt a crossing. Mike was suddenly restless now, fidgeting in the crowded, enclosed space of the carrier. He poked Lance Hardwick in the leg, and Lance, who had been riding with the top half of his body out of the personnel carrier, took the binoculars from his eyes and drew inside.

"What do you see?"

"I dunno, Mike. Once, a while back, I thought I saw a high-flying speck behind us to the east. Now I could almost swear I glimpsed it to the west of us, making use of the sun setting in our eyes. I don't want to sound paranoid, but I think we might—no, hell, I think we *are* being tailed by either a light observation plane or a chopper that's really hanging back and giving us room to move. I wasn't going to sound the alarm till I caught another look at it, because what

COBRA STRIKE

I saw might have been a hawk or even a goddamn pigeon, just a high-flying dot—"

Mike pointed upward. "Look out for a track for us to pull off this road." Then he went back to intensely studying the map, a silence spread among the men cooped inside the armored vehicle, who realized that something was about to happen now to change the tedium of the journey. Baker, who had been in an almost wordless sulk for days, looked carefully around him and began to take close note of things.

General Viktor Mikhailovich Kudimov had flown in by Mi-24 to inspect the bridge over the Murghab River for himself. Things were set up as he ordered. Two heavy trucks waited to the side at each end of the bridge. When the personnel carrier mounted the bridge, the trucks would seal off both ends, leaving the armored vehicle trapped on the spans. Coils of barbed wire had been laid according to his instructions on all the parapets of the bridge to stop the Americans from jumping into the water. Floodlights were strategically placed, since the crossing would almost certainly be attempted after dark.

The general was not particularly concerned when Colonel Matveyeva's helicopter radioed a coded signal that the personnel carrier had left the road. They were nearby and stopping to wait for dark. Her helicopter could not just stay out there without being spotted, so he ordered it to Moghor. This pleased Yekaterina, who thought she was still communicating with him in Kabul, more than four hundred miles to the east. No doubt she expected him to be present for the confrontation between the tanks and the personnel carrier, a scenario she still believed was in his serious planning.

He would personally trap these Americans on that bridge. They would probably try some dramatic stunt, like holding out inside the armored vehicle and raking the bridge with fire from their two machine guns. The bridge walls were too strong for them to break through and topple down into the water. He would let them strut and storm for a while. It would only make their final personal surrender to him all the more sweet.

* * *

Bob Murphy peered through the grating and into the fading light, and Lance Hardwick yelled down directions to him from on top.

"Just keep pushing south any way you can," Mike urged them, "and we got to hit the river."

Waller had fitted the machine guns with tracer bullets every fourth or fifth cartridge. He manned one gun, and Turner the other. Harvey expected company on the riverbank. It would be fully dark when they got there. If there was going to be a firefight, they would need the glowing tracers to indicate to them where their bullets were hitting.

But the riverbank was deserted. Campbell inflated the rubber raft from inside the carrier. He sent Op van de Bosch along with Joe Nolan to make contact with Op's friend the local rebel leader and kept Jan Prijt, Op's very quiet soundman, behind to make sure Op came back. Lance paddled the raft across the wide river and brought it back. Waller and Turner removed the two machine guns from their mountings and collected the ammo for them. Mike wanted to present them as a gift to the rebel leader and ordered Lance and Harvey to ferry them one at a time across the river. Each of these KPV heavy machine guns weighed about a hundred pounds and fired 14.5cm shells from a hundred-round metal-link belt-feed system. Campbell wanted the rebels to have these weapons because he knew their value as antiaircraft guns—the Cong and North Vietnamese had used these Soviet weapons very effectively against U.S. aircraft in two- and four-barrel models known as the ZPU-2 and ZPU-4.

Everyone else stripped everything of use from the inside of the personnel carrier, and each man was ferried with this merchandise and his own weapons across the Murghab. Campbell and Murphy were the last to cross in the rubber raft, paddled by Hardwick. Before leaving, they selected a deep stretch of water close to the bank, and Bob set the personnel carrier heading for the river at about 20 m.p.h. He jumped off and removed his hat in respect for the machine as it trundled over the edge of the riverbank and tipped over into its watery grave.

The rebels, thirty strong, came by horseback to the far

bank with spare horses for the newcomers and their equipment. Some of them took the machine guns and equipment scavenged from the personnel carrier to hiding places in the steep hills that rose south of the river, while the main body of men rode with them to a temporary camp the rebel leader was not using and which was not far from the main road to Herat. He had promised the Dutch TV team that he would let them film an exploit of his, which Op suspected was blowing up the river bridge. Joe Nolan had ridden back with the rebels and assured Mike that things looked good at the other end. There were about a hundred men in this encampment, in addition to the riders with them, and all were armed with automatic rifles, according to Nolan. The leader's name was Noor Qader.

He met them on their arrival, welcoming each of them individually with hugs and handshakes but no English. He was a big man, not unlike some of the mountain Pathans they had come across near the Pakistani border, although he was not Pathan but a Dari-speaking Tajik. He wore the Afghan rebel's usual collection of loose garments. Instead of a turban he wore a pale blue synthetic-fur Soviet army hat with the red star pulled off. They could see why Op had been anxious to come here. This Afghan was photogenic.

Two riders galloped in out of the darkness, jumped from their mounts, and ran, breathless, to Noor Qader. Jed Crippenby elbowed his way in close so he could overhear. Seven tanks had left Moghor earlier. They had stopped at darkness, were now blocking the road less than ten miles away, and could be expected to start forward again and pass close by at first light. Groups of rebels immediately began to hurry around. At first the mercs thought they were abandoning the camp. This was not the case. Men hurried back and forth all night as the team rested on full bellies in their sleeping bags to one side of the cooking fire. Campbell was insistent that his men all rest, regardless of the preparations taking place around them.

They heard the tanks before they saw them, clanking along the road, deep roars from their powerful engines. When Campbell saw them, he knew they were T-54s, which the Russians had supplied to the North Vietnamese. These were Red Army tanks, and although they were not the latest thing in Soviet tank design, they carried a powerful 100mm cannon. It was clear to Mike that they had come in search of the Americans in the armored personnel carrier. A direct hit from one of these cannons would have left the carrier looking like one of those ultralight compacts after being totaled by a Mack truck.

The mercs were enjoying this. For once their asses weren't on the line. They could scrunch down and watch Noor Qader's men do their stuff. They hadn't been told exactly what was going on; they hadn't seen any weapons or mines heavy enough to do much more than scratch the paint job on these tanks, and they thought it a reasonable possibility that they would be running for their lives in the next few minutes with 100mm shells ripping craters in the ground behind them. But no one had asked for their help, and as Campbell said, they weren't going to force themselves on anybody. They caught sight of Op van de Bosch and Jan Prijt from time to time, with their camera and microphone, as the two men moved themselves closer and closer to the road edge, only to be pulled back by Noor's rebels.

The tanks descended from the higher mountains, rumbling down the center of the road, one behind the other, awkward and careless and capable of crushing all in their path. The first tank drew level with the team's position and passed them. Then they saw the road give way beneath its front end. The lead tank fell nose first into the deep trench that had opened up across the road. The tank's weight had broken through the light timber that had been used to support the light skin of road surface stretched over the trench. The second tank bumped into the first from behind and drove it deeper into the pit. The other five tanks ground to a stop with several yards between them and shifted into reverse as their guns swung around to bear down on anything that might try to stop them from backing out of this situation. At that moment three heavy pine trees fell across the road almost simultaneously, each more than five feet in diameter and weighing at least twenty tons. The last tank began to butt against one trunk to try to roll it out of the way.

Noor's rebels swarmed out onto the road and up on the tanks. They smeared mud over all the slits so that the crews inside were blinded. Then these men scattered, and the first bottle with a blazing rag stuck in its neck arced through the air and smashed on the top surface of one tank. The gasoline inside spread as the bottle smashed and was ignited by the flaming rag, so that it covered the tank with a leaping carpet of flames.

More bottles were thrown in a constant series upon the lumbering, blinded tanks, so that they constantly remained engulfed in fire and the men inside began to scream for mercy. Some burst through the escape hatches, their hair and skin immediately catching fire. The rebels let some die slowly, half in and half out of the tanks, clawing the air and hoarsely roaring. Others they cut to bits with automatic fire as soon as they showed themselves.

A helicopter flew in from the south to observe the action but did not present itself suitably for a rocket shot.

Yekaterina knew they should have stopped those Americans while they were still on the plains. Now they had been allowed to regain rebel-held high ground again, and this was the result of it! Seven totally destroyed T-54s and crews! But, needless to say, wily old General Kudimov had covered his ass again by ordering her to proceed the previous night to Moghor, from where the tanks had set out. As colonel, she had found herself to be the ranking officer in the town. She saw now why that had been arranged. Viktor Mikhailovich Kudimov had not remained a general in the Red Army all these years without having found a way to dispose of unwanted mistakes. She knew his immediate action, once he heard about the tanks, would be to suspend her from active duty and that after that she would have no means of restoring her reputation. So she might as well be hung for a sheep as a lamb.

"Maintain radio silence," she told the two pilots of her chopper, "and make for the Moghor landing zone with all speed. If either of you mention a word to anyone of what you *think* you *may* have seen down there on that road, I'll have you executed for treason. You've heard what they say about me. I'm pretty, so I've got to be extra mean to make dumb bastards like you believe."

"We two saw nothing," the senior pilot assured her, "and neither did the engineer or door gunner. I'll talk with them."

"Be sure you do."

Her plans began to fit into a more logical framework as she turned them over in her mind on the flight back. She had met a lieutenant the night before and spent an hour in bed with him. He'd been coarse and brutal; he had even imagined he was her master because she had permitted him in her bed. He had soon learned he was mistaken there! He would be perfect for this job she had in mind. By the time she had finished, the general would have something to criticize her for—or she would have succeeded on her own where he had failed, by bringing in these Americans. At this stage it mattered little to her whether they were dead or alive. So long as she got them, she was off the hook.

She watched impassively as her gunship raked the field and workers crumpled in the rain of bullets. She glanced at Lieutenant Tokar. The oaf was grinning. The slick carrying eight infantrymen followed the gunship as it headed north through fertile valleys in the bare red mountains. Lieutenant Tokar would do all right.

She did not want to travel too far north, and yet the progress of the Americans would be slowed now that they had to stay off the main road into Herat. Also, she would need fairly fast results since she was operating without clearance from her superiors. In a short while she spotted an ideal village in the sheltered end of a valley. The Americans would not have lingered after the tank attack. If they had not passed through this place, they could not be very far from it.

"Soften it up and signal to the other chopper to prepare to put the men in," she said to the senior pilot, who had to swing around to make himself visible to the slick pilots and use hand signals to them. He then dove the gunship on the village, rocketed a few of the houses, and strafed the streets as they filled with fleeing people. The gunship then pulled back and hovered to give cover to the slick as it selected an LZ and went down to put in the men.

After a while, when no resistance was offered, the gunship touched down beside the slick and waited for the infantrymen to bring back prisoners for questioning.

The colonel had a basic working knowledge of Dari, the Afghan dialect of Persian. She kept her question simple. "You see Americans?" "No." "No." What else did she expect them to say? She told the lieutenant what she wanted him to do and waited for his reaction. He grinned again.

"Take them over by their houses so they don't damage the choppers or mess us up," she told him.

The lieutenant tied the thumbs of five people together behind their backs, after selecting an old man, two mothers who had to be separated from their children and from whom he ripped their head and face covering, two children of eight or nine who had to be separated from their mothers, and one youth he would use as a demonstration to the others. He had the five set twenty yards apart, close to the houses, and had the soldiers keep back their family and other villagers at about forty yards. Then he bound a single stick of dynamite to the belly of each of the five, set a cap at one end of each stick, and connected a twenty-foot fuse to each cap. He stood by the youth and waited for the colonel to ask her question.

"You see Americans?"

The youth might have been retarded; the lieutenant couldn't tell. Or maybe just filled with hate, as so many of these rotten Afghans were. Anyway, he didn't answer the question, so the lieutenant touched the end of the fuse with a match flame and moved away fast.

The youth remained for some time, watching the long brown fuse turn to white ash as the point of ignition crept nearer to the stick tied to his belly. Then he tried to back away. He even tried to run, his thumbs tied behind his back, but his long tail of creeping death was attached to him and went where he did. He spent his last moments standing still with his head bowed.

The dynamite blast knocked him on his back, splitting open his chest cavity and splashing his blood on the mud-brick wall of the house behind him.

The lieutenant next selected a nine-year-old boy whose mother the soldiers were having trouble keeping at a distance. He waited for the colonel to ask her question.

"No," the boy replied in a firm voice.

The lieutenant lit the match but did not yet touch it to the end of the fuse. He looked at the colonel.

She walked over to the boy's mother. "You see Americans?"

"There are none! I would tell you if I had!" the woman screamed.

The colonel herself had to knock her to the ground when she saw the match light the fuse leading to her small son's body.

CHAPTER 14

"The crazy bitch!" General Kudimov shouted to the major. "Are you sure she's on this rampage?"

"Certain, Comrade General. Do you want me to send forces to restrain her?"

"Absolutely not! Maybe she'll get them this way." The general knew the major resented having a woman for a senior officer in a combat zone and would do anything to get rid of her, which might come in handy later if Yekaterina did not succeed. On the other hand, if she did succeed, he would have no choice but to give her some of the credit. He said aloud, "Right now Colonel Matveyeva is the only senior officer making what I regard as a serious effort to apprehend these American outlaws. I think that instead of finding ways to try to block her efforts, Major, you might attempt to initiate some of your own."

After the major had left, suitably chastised, Viktor Mikhailovich Kudimov began to worry again about what she might be up to. She was crazy enough to capture the Americans, load them into those two choppers, and fly them across the border into the U.S.S.R., all on her own, taking all the credit. No, as little as he wanted to be associated with her campaign of torture and terror, he would still have to pay her a visit in the field, if only to remind her who she still reported to, like it or not.

He would give her a little more time and try to keep a watch on her. Then he would pay her an unexpected visit himself and see what she had to show him.

The colonel and lieutenant had refined their technique. Their early methods had been too time-consuming. They had wasted huge amounts of time on people who had no idea what they were talking about—country people who became confused when strangers dropped out of the sky and demanded to know about other strangers these people had neither seen nor heard of. But she could never be sure if they were lying until she tested them physically. Their new technique involved fewer victims in a greater number of locations, so that she could mark off the grids in her military map of the area as having been thoroughly investigated. Coming into villages was dangerous. They had drawn fire in two of them, and now they approached people in fields just as readily as those in villages. They had run out of dynamite but had discovered a safer and even more effective replacement—kerosene. Few of the houses here had electricity, so kerosene was in plentiful supply everywhere they went.

"There!" The colonel pointed down to a group of women working in a field. The gunship and the following slick made fast descents and touched down in the field, close to the women, before they could scatter very far. The infantrymen from the slick knew their job by this time: they rounded up two of the women whose small children clung to them like lambs to a ewe. One soldier seized a girl about five, and another poured kerosene over her head so that it ran into her eyes and over her skin and soaked her clothes.

"You see Americans?" the colonel asked the struggling mother.

"No! No Americans!"

The lieutenant tossed a match on the kerosene-soaked child. The flaming figure ran toward her mother, who was dragged away by the infantrymen and then held so she could watch her now blinded child die an agonized death before her eyes. They did not release the woman until the fire-blackened little torso lay still on the ground.

Then the lieutenant seized a child from the second woman, one of four who clung close to her. This mother managed to hang on to her boy by one arm as the lieutenant pulled him away by the other.

"I see Americans!" she shouted. "I see Americans!"

The lieutenant immediately released her boy and stepped back from her.

The colonel walked over, looked her in the eyes, and said in her slow, deliberate Dari, "If I think you are lying to me, I will burn *all* your children."

"I see Americans! I will tell you where they are!"

Campbell had abandoned the idea of going as far south as Herat because of the communist forces now being set up to intercept. Word was coming in to Noor Qader's men of major troop movements just north of the city. The main road into Iran went from Herat, and in time it, too, would be blocked. Along with Verdoux, Campbell studied the maps and listened to the advice of Qader's men. They were presently about thirty miles south of the Soviet border and about a hundred and fifty miles east of the line with Iran. Old smugglers' routes ran due west for hundreds of miles, and these were still used today by Afghan opium smugglers.

It seemed that in spite of all the Islamic fervor in Iran, the country still had a huge population of opium addicts. The Afghans grew the poppies, as they had done for centuries, and smuggled in the sticky opiate they drained from slits in the pods. Campbell refused to go in as an armed escort to a drug train, and instead exacted a deal that made it worth the smugglers' while to transport the team in place of opium. They would travel by horseback one day's ride and wait there for a truck to bring them the rest of the way.

The team moved out of Noor Qader's territory as quickly as they could because word of the savagery of the Russian search methods had spread, and Mike did not want to have those who helped them punished like this. Once the team had moved out, the Russians would follow. But they were back in the mountains now; there any movement in a horizontal direction could involve strenuous and time-consuming climbs and descents. Still he was satisfied to have put more than ten miles between themselves and the place of the tank ambush in only a few hours, and to the west rather than the south, where the Russians would expect them to be headed. Campbell was less pleased about having to stop in one place to wait for the truck to transport them, but there was no way around this at such short notice.

Who exactly these opium smugglers were, and what their relationship was with Noor Qader's men, remained vague.

Noor Qader had broken up his temporary camp after the attack on the tanks, and the team had left with a body of almost fifty rebels. Sixteen were still riding with them as they neared the place where the team was to wait. The lead riders spotted a Russian infantry patrol and prepared to attack. Campbell did not want this, since it could easily draw attention to the team's present whereabouts, but he had no control over Noor's men and they were clearly going to attack the Russian unit whether or not they got help from the Americans.

The Russians were spooked. Some of them had made visual contact with the mounted rebels, but they had no way of knowing how many were in the area and whether the ones seen had fled or were waiting in ambush for them. When the unit called in air support, none was available because all aircraft were engaged in looking for the Americans toward Herat. So the patrol of eight soldiers moved out in a regularly spaced line with a case of the jitters as they wound their way through steep-walled gulches and skirted massive outcrops that could have concealed a whole enemy battalion.

Noor's men followed at a distance, until they knew the route the Soviets would take. They gave two men to the mercs as guides, and the fourteen others set out in a wide half circle to bypass the Russian patrol. The ten mercs and the Institute men, along with their two guides, set out in a similar half circle in the other direction. Where these two forces met ahead of the patrol would be the point of ambush. This turned out to be a broad low pass through which flowed a narrow stream. The hills rose only gradually on both sides, and at no point would the movement of soldiers moving through it be constricted by a narrowing. It looked safe enough, which, of course, was why the Afghan rebels had chosen it. What could not be seen from down in the pass were the trails high on its sides that would permit the horsemen to move out fast from concealment once the Soviet patrol was in the valley below. They could then pick off the soldiers on foot who could not move as fast as they could.

The mercs concealed themselves high on one side of the pass entrance, knowing that Noor's fourteen men were already hidden somewhere on the opposite side. In about half an hour the Russian patrol appeared and looked as if it were going to pass as planned between them.

The Russians stopped short. With an infantryman's sixth sense they detected that something was wrong. They took cover among some small rocks and carefully surveyed everything around them. Nothing stirred.

Mike Campbell felt sort of sorry for them. He knew that feeling well: knowing that to keep moving ahead meant certain disaster and not having any other choice but to keep going. A foot patrol like this one, without air, artillery or mortar support, was just so much condemned meat. Mike himself had survived situations like this, only just barely. No doubt the Russians would find it ironic that the same force they had lost their air support in search of was the one now menacing them. But the Russians didn't know that. Yet.

The uniformed men warily formed their line of patrol again and advanced into the pass. As they probed deeper into the pass and nothing happened, they started to move in a more relaxed fashion. This was when the horsemen appeared high on the far side of the valley. The mercs led out their horses and climbed onto their backs, and they, too, cantered forward along a narrow track high on the valley side.

The Russians sought cover. However, anything that protected them from one side of the valley exposed their backs to the other. They fired on the horsemen catching up with them on both sides. Bob Murphy felt his horse stagger. Its front legs doubled up beneath it, and the heavy Australian was thrown into the stony dirt. Joe Nolan's horse narrowly missed the fallen man's head with its hooves. Murphy climbed painfully to his feet and was about to yell at his horse, lying on its side, threshing its legs, making unsuccessful attempts to scramble upright, when he noticed a hole in its chest and blood washing down over its hide. Bob drew his pistol and put the animal out of its misery with a bullet in the forehead. The horse's head immediately fell to the ground. Bob collected his things and hobbled after the others, who had not waited for him.

Bursts of automatic fire from two directions toppled the Soviet foot soldiers like skittles. Three climbed to their feet again, their hands held high above their heads.

Andre Verdoux made an unwilling Baker double-up behind Turner on his horse and sent Lance Hardwick back with the free horse for Murphy. Verdoux had deliberately made the Australian wait to be picked up but knew that no horse could have borne his weight as a second rider.

When the mercs reached the Russians, Noor's men were finished off the wounded with their long knives and stripping the bodies.

"We are keeping these ones alive long enough for you to spit in their faces and tell them who you are," one rebel told Jed Crippenby, who translated it for Mike.

Campbell said, "Aren't they going to take them prisoners?"

"We have hardly food enough for ourselves," the rebel replied angrily. "Do you want us to feed our oppressors too? You take them with you since you care so much how Russians are treated in Afghanistan. We do not want them here!"

"We can't take them with us because of our journey," Mike explained. "They are your prisoners, not ours."

"Then they will die," the rebel announced, pleased that they had come to an understanding.

"If you guys can't make up your minds," Harvey Waller offered, "I'll shoot them for you. No problem."

"Stay out of this, Harvey," Mike snapped. "We got to

be moving on for our meet-up with the truck." He turned to the soldiers and said in his poor Russian, "If you have anything you want sent back to your families, you better let me have it."

The Russian soldiers, overcome with emotion at the sound of their language, pressed photos and papers on Mike, begged him to intercede for them with the rebels. All three were nineteen-year-olds, conscripts who had never even heard of Afghanistan before coming here. They claimed they had never killed anyone while here, and all they wanted to do was go home, forget this nightmare, and live peacefully.

Verdoux and Crippenby also spoke to them in Russian, and even Baker and Winston joined in. The Russians knew from the outset that their position was hopeless. It was their own army that was causing all the death and destruction and which had not provided them with air support or responded to their emergency calls.

The rebels looked on at all this fraternizing between the Americans and Russians with stony faces and unyielding stares. Harvey Waller stood apart also, glowering at the scene. As he left, Mike made sure to lead Harvey with him.

"They're just young guys who got pushed out to bear all the burdens while the clever ones stay home," Mike said. "They're not here because they're communists, Harvey, they're here because they're draft age. Go easy on them."

"You're getting soft, Campbell," Waller snarled.

Mike shook his head and sighed, resigned that it was hopeless to discuss this further. He turned around sharply when he heard a pistol shot and saw one of the three Russians sink to his knees, his face in a tight grimace of pain. The rebel then shot the second Russian prisoner in the belly, and they all watched in silence while he clutched his gut and staggered a few steps before falling. Mike exchanged a glance with the third man and turned away before the shot rang out, the shot that would leave him to die slowly, too, in this rocky Afghan valley.

To the west. Toward Iran, not Herat. So that's where the Americans were going. No wonder she hadn't been able to verify any sightings of them for so long. But now she was getting results! A little kerosene here, a little there, and she was hearing how ten Americans—now it was ten!—had ridden west through these parts with a force of Noor Qader's men. Then the infantry patrol's distress signals came over the air and the fool command refused them help because they were too busy combing empty hills far to the south. The Americans were about to strike again. It had to be them! She had almost been tempted to alert General Kudimov by radio and would have done so had she not been aware that the old fox would somehow have done dirty, gone there himself and sent her somewhere else. No, any credit she would get from comrade Viktor Mikhailovich Kudimov would only be what he couldn't deny her. But she was ahead of him now, beyond his control for the time being.

She had two choppers, recently refueled, two crews, the lieutenant, and eight men. The gunship had taken on more rockets, and both choppers had big ammo supplies for their door gunners. All she had to do was take some or all of ten Americans on horseback in rugged terrain. She would do it and take the credit for it back in Moscow. Viktor Mikhailovich Kudimov could go to hell.

The colonel told the senior pilot to head for the map coordinates given in the patrol's final emergency signal that they had monitored over their radio but to continue to maintain radio silence himself. She wanted to give Kudimov no clue as to where she might be. Hovering high over the valley, they saw the eight bodies below and no visible signs of continued rebel presence. The colonel was tempted to fly on without touching down, but for the sake of morale she ordered the two craft down. The men might have grown sullen if she had not tried to help their comrades. She walked around the eight bodies, half naked, their uniforms, boots, and weapons taken, lying twisted on the stones, eviscerated, slashed, their private parts stuffed in their mouths.

She had seen all this before and she would see it again. She was not nearly as upset by this carnage as her men, including the lieutenant, who could stand there grinning as a child burned to death in kerosene. Here he was on the verge of tears, calling the Afghans inhuman bandits and animals.

"The Americans did this!" she shouted, knowing this was not true but wanting to derive some benefit from the men's anger at the slaughter. "Are we going to let them escape over the border into Iran? I'm not!"

She ran back to the gunship, the men hurried back to their places filled with rage at the Americans, and the two choppers lifted off in a newly dedicated search for the monstrous capitalist brigands.

After a while the colonel recognized where they were. A heavily timbered area stretched ahead of them. "I know this place, Anatoly," she told the senior pilot. "Don't overfly it or you'll draw fire. Everyone will take pot shots at you, even with 9mm pistols, from the cover of the trees. Swing around to the left and follow the line of trees without coming too close. It would be better for us if the Americans don't know we're in the vicinity. There's a village somewhere along here in the next few kilometers—I will know the place when I see it. The opium smugglers on their way to Iran use it. We have tried to eradicate them in the past because they use their profits from the drugs to buy guns in Iran. Noor Qader sent them here. They must have only just arrived, or perhaps they haven't reached here yet."

The lieutenant looked unhappily at the forest. "We will have to engage them on the ground."

"That's right, Lieutenant," the colonel said. "You and I will take those eight men in after them. This gunship will stand by to provide us with air support, and the slick will stand ready to evacuate."

"Yes, Comrade Colonel," the lieutenant said obediently, if not very enthusiastically.

She sneered at him, saying nothing, but letting her face show that she could see he was not nearly so anxious to hunt down armed Americans in these woods as he was women and children in open fields.

It would be three hours, maybe four or even five hours before the truck came for them. Drug smugglers did not stick to strict time schedules. They would come when the time was right. Campbell pointed out that the longer things were delayed, the greater the chance of Russian intervention. There was nothing anyone could do, he was informed. The truck would come when it was ready—almost as if the truck were the one who was making the decision. Mike sent to a nearby village for warm food. When they had finished the mutton, yogurt, and rice dishes, he ordered the men to rest. When Lance Hardwick told him he wanted to look around, Mike told him all right but not to go far. Lance walked in the woods in the direction of the village where two of Noor's men had bought food. Any bit of urban action at all sounded good to Lance after all this time in the mountains. He knew that all he could expect was a tumble-down place built of mud where fierce, bearded men loaded down with daggers and guns would stare at him suspiciously. He reckoned he had hardly seen a dozen women since he had come to Afghanistan, and they had been so shrouded up in cloth that they looked like kids dressed up as Halloween ghosts. His expectations were low.

Two of Noor Qader's men had bought large quantities of hot food in the village. The informant pointed out to the Russians the direction in which the men had ridden away, less than two hours ago. The colonel felt her heart skip a beat. At last she felt she was close to her quarry. She would take them alive. At least some of them. Kill the others. Even if some escaped, so long as she had at least one alive to put on trial, her name would be remembered in military records and she would lack for nothing the rest of her life. Moscow knew how to reward its faithful, loyal ones.

The colonel, the lieutenant, and the eight men moved out of the village on the double. They were well armed, in radio contact with the two choppers, and making no effort to hide their presence in the village. This would frighten off any local rebels who might have ideas of attacking them. It would be essential to move with speed to reach the Americans before word of their presence did. They moved fast through the tree trunks parallel to the dirt road that Noor's two horsemen had taken with the food. In less than ten minutes they saw a lone American, heavily armed, walking along the dirt road. The Russians froze. They watched him amble along, kicking the dirt and looking around him as if he were on a country stroll. Realizing that her men wanted to mow him down, the colonel thought fast.

She eased her Kalashnikov from her shoulder and handed it to one man, undid her pistol belt, and handed that with its attached holster to another. She whispered to them, "I will take this one alive. He will tell us where the others are. So long as I have at least one alive, I don't care if you kill all the rest." She did care, because the more she brought in alive, the greater her triumph, but she knew she had to promise the men blood to keep them in line. "That house we passed farther on—two of you go and empty it and keep the owners away. I will bring him there."

She looked at her face in a small mirror and winked at the men. "He won't shoot at me because even though I'm in uniform"—she thrust one hip and thigh against her straight military skirt—"I'm not carrying a gun." She reached in the top of one cowboy-style boot and pulled out a tiny revolver.

The men were startled at the sudden transformation of this Amazon into a flirtatious lady.

"Don't disturb us until I give the signal," she whispered, and hurried off through the trees.

Lance's expectations were low, and the last thing on earth he expected to see while walking in these woods was a beautiful blond in a Russian uniform. He trained the Kalashnikov on her all the same, until it became evident that she was not carrying weapons. If Lance wasn't so horny, he might have wondered about the coincidence of meeting a beautiful Russian woman like this, but Lance was horny, very, very horny, way past being sexually frustrated, and she looked much too good to him for him to have any doubts about her.

She smiled and greeted him in Russian, showing that she was not fooled by his imitation Afghan costume and beard. For one terrible moment he thought about answering her in English, then it dawned on him who he really was, not the Hollywood resident with the phony name but Miroslav

Svoboda born in Minneapolis of Czech refugees, who had grown up listening to his mother speak to him in the old language and tell him about the old country.

"I'm a Czech, not a Russian," he told her in Czech. "Do you understand?"

"I spent two years in Prague with the Red Army," she said in passable Czech. "Imagine us meeting like this in Afghanistan!"

They both laughed at the world being such a small place. He told her about serving in a Czech army intelligence unit, one of several sent by the Warsaw Pact countries to show support to the Soviets in Afghanistan. She hadn't heard about these units but supposed she hadn't because they were in intelligence operations. He was grateful she didn't ask any difficult questions, such as how he could coordinate with the Red Army here if he didn't speak Russian. He decided that maybe she was horny too.

"I was on my way to the village," he said.

"I will walk back that way with you. I just passed an empty house a little way back and wanted to look inside, but I was too scared to go in alone." She took his arm. "Now, with you along, I will be able to see inside."

Lance wasted no time in getting her there. The house wasn't deserted, like she had said, but no one was around. He led her into a back room with a window looking onto the woods and a large straw-filled mattress on an ancient four-poster bed. They embraced and kissed passionately while lying side by side. She tried several times to get him talking about the other Czechs he was with, but he had other things on his mind. She would have to take care of those first before they got into deep conversation.

She was willing. He watched her as she undressed and revealed her beautiful, silky-skinned body to him. Only two things slightly disturbed the amorous atmosphere in the room. The first was a glimpse Lance thought he caught out of the corner of his eye of a pale blue uniform slipping behind a tree not far outside the window. The second was the sight of the wood grips on a steel pistol butt down inside one boot his blond angel had left next to the bed. But in his biological condition Lance was not going to let little things like those interfere with the great urges of life.

Viktor Mikhailovich Kudimov, general of the Red Army, touched down in his Mi-24 next to the waiting gunship and slick. He smiled at Anatoly and said, "Good work, Comrade. Where is she?"

The senior pilot said, "Not far. But there's been no radio contact yet."

"Make contact," the general ordered, "but no word of my arrival."

The lieutenant told the senior pilot to be patient. On the pilot's demand he gave his location.

A half hour later the lieutenant's jaw dropped when he saw General Kudimov, a major, and several other officers arrive on foot outside the house. He explained hurriedly that Colonel Matveyeva was interrogating an American captive inside and had left strict instructions that she was not to be disturbed until she gave the signal.

The general shrugged this off, and he and the other officers went to the house and walked in the door. In the back room they found the colonel lying facedown on the mattress, wrists and ankles bound to the four bedposts, gagged with her panties.

General Kudimov made no move to release her. Instead he beckoned to the major, whom he knew could read English, and asked what the characters lipsticked on Yekaterina's smooth and rounded buttocks meant.

The major read slowly in heavily accented English. "USA" on the left cheek, and on the right, "ALL THE WAY."

CHAPTER 15

The truck, a vintage model from the 1950s, rattled along trails a little narrower than its wheelbase, with dropoffs of hundreds of feet to one side at speeds that would have been dangerous in such a vehicle on a flat, modern highway. Campbell claimed that the only time he really thought he was going to meet his end on this mission was during this ride to the Iranian border. They crossed a main highway running north from Herat to the Soviet Union, where they had been seen by a spotter prop plane. The plane called in Mi-24s and MIG-25s, which seemed to concern the driver very little. He liked to pause before crossing a rise, look around like a prairie dog checking the sky for hawks, and then make a run for the next gulch, pass, or canyon in which he would wait, concealed again for an opportune moment to make his next dart forward.

They took three close misses from rockets and were strafed eleven times by gunship fire. The aircraft lost them at dusk. They kept going well into the night, the truck headlights being so weak that they hardly showed the ground ten feet ahead, let alone give away their position to the air.

Joe Nolan and Andre Verdoux were kind of mad at Lance for not bringing the Russian lady along. They refused to accept his explanation that he had been lucky to slip out the window in the woods unobserved. The mercs realized she had been a trap intended to lure them, but none realized she had been the chief Soviet officer in charge of their pursuit. It never occurred to any of them that she might in any way have been involved in the tortures and atrocities that had taken place in Noor Qader's territory as the Russians searched for them.

The constant stops the truck made kept the men on edge, since they never knew what to expect. One time, when the truck suddenly braked, they looked out and saw three gunships search a valley they had been about to enter. Not long afterward the truck came to an even more sudden stop, and the mercs piled out, only to find the driver at one of his five daily prayers heading toward Mecca.

They arrived at a staging area for convoys across the border. The driver ignored them from this point on, concentrating all his energies on collecting passengers and goods for his return journey. As a force of ten heavily armed men, the mercs were respected by the various groups trading and discussing the most favorable routes. As the acknowledged leader of the team, Campbell was offered cups of tea and shown other marks of respect by various eagle-eyed warriors. Crippenby was kept busy translating their compliments and well wishes and invitations to travel with them.

Mike and Andre Verdoux took a walk around to see for themselves what each group of smugglers looked like. Only very few were glassy-eyed and passive, indicating that they had been sampling their own wares. Most of them looked wild and irresponsible, the sort that, even if they made a successful sale of their opium, would linger on to find some other kind of trouble. Three of the groups were large, well armed, disciplined, and organized. These were obviously the professionals, the ones most likely to succeed and the ones most likely to survive.

"I don't want to be mixed up with any kind of drug

smugglers," Mike explained to Andre, "but if we have to, let's be sure they're not junkies and losers. We're going to have enough problems in Iran without that."

"Have you given up on us going ahead on our own without cooperating with any of these groups?" Andre asked.

"From what Crippenby has learned, we have no choice but to cooperate. The Iranian police and some army units are waging a big campaign against the drug traffickers. We may not care for the looks of these characters, but at least they know all the routes and where the Iranian police are most likely to be."

On Turner and Winston's advice they avoided one group that was bringing in its merchandise on packhorses. The two Institute men had not forgotten hauling arms on donkeys from Pakistan. They left with two groups, of six and eight men, all of whom carried large pictures of the Ayatollah Khomeini on their Western knapsacks.

One of the smugglers, who had learned to speak good English and Arabic while working in Saudi Arabia and Kuwait, told the mercs, "This can save you from being shot in the back by an Iranian policeman. He sees you and raises his gun, you turn your back to run, he aims at you—and what does he see? A picture of his spiritual leader, the holiest man on earth, the Twelfth Imam! He cannot hit that with a bullet, so he must adjust his aim—by which time you are gone, no? You need pictures of the Ayatollah to wear?"

"I think my men would prefer to cut their throats," Mike told him.

The Afghan thought this was very funny and told it to the others, who all laughed. They agreed with the Americans and said they were right to prefer death than to hide behind a picture of someone they hated.

"Do you like the Ayatollah?" Mike asked.

"I am not Shiite, but I think he is good for all Moslems."

"What about all the people he has executed?" Mike put to him.

"What about them?" the man answered. "The people needed to have revenge against the Shah, but the Shah escaped, so they had to have revenge against someone.

COBRA STRIKE

They took your hostages in revenge because you helped the Shah escape. What should they do with his supporters? If they put them in prison, they would bribe the guards, escape, organize an army, and come back to execute the people who put them out of power. So they had to be executed. Anyone sensible can see that."

Mike decided that, as a merc, he was hardly in a position to criticize people for seeking blood vengeance. He learned some interesting facts as he listened and avoided argument. Iran was still mostly owned by rich landlords, with the clergy owning most of the rest. The real menace in Iran came from the Revolutionary Guards, the Pasdaran, who were now 150,000 strong, rivaled the army in strength, and were used by ambitious mullahs for their own private ends. These were city mobs, jobless, without schooling, who now had power and status so long as they were blindly loyal to the mullahs.

"What about the police we are trying to avoid?" Mike asked.

"They are good men. Since the army has to fight the Iraqis on the opposite border of Iran, they have sent the police here to fight us. The army was well trained and made things very hard for us. The police do not have training to operate in wild mountains like this. You do not have to worry about them. But they are sending Revolutionary Guards here too. We don't like them. We kill them but they send more. For each one we kill they send three more. The Pasdaran are fools. They think that they have only to shout at us and we will run. That is what happens in Teheran and their cities where they beat women for not wearing modest dress. Up here in the mountains they shout at us, and we kill them for making too much noise."

Mike laughed at his joke.

They were in Iran. As the Afghan smuggler had said, the police were easy to avoid. They seemed to make lots of noise while moving around in tight-knit groups, almost as if saying, "Here we come, quick hide, then we won't see anything and won't have to fight you." The smugglers and the mercs lay low each time until it was safe for them to move on again. They met another group of smugglers, nine men, coming against them. The team covered them with their weapons until they were sure of who they were. The men showed the Afghans with the mercs their unsold opium. They were returning across the border and would come back again in a few days time when things were quieter.

"They say that there are thousands of Revolutionary Guards ahead of us," Jed Crippenby translated. "These men tried to break through but could not. They escaped only because they know the country here so well, while the Revolutionary Guards are strangers here, flown in by helicopters specially to search for smugglers. This is some mullah's idea, they say, and the Pasdaran will get tired of walking around in these mountains after a few days, of being bitten by snakes, of being shot at by mountain tribesmen, of being baked by the sun. Then the helicopters will take them back to the cities and things will be quiet again in a few days."

"Ask them how they know the Pasdaran traveled by helicopter," Mike told Jed.

When Jed found out, he answered, "There are forty to fifty choppers on a landing zone north of a small village ahead of us. We will be able to see them from the top of the next ridge, but that's also the point at which we can expect to run into these Revolutionary Guards. They say we should come back with them inside Afghanistan and return when this antismuggling crusade is over. The men who came with us are going back, too, I think."

"They should," Mike said flatly. "But we go on."

His men looked at him.

"Haven't you wondered why the Russians haven't pursued us over the Iran border?" Mike asked them. "It's hardly because they've suddenly grown scrupulous about borders. It's certainly not because they're afraid of the Iranians. I think they've made a deal with the Ayatollah. Khomeini has probably promised to return us to them in Afghanistan if the Russians don't cross his borders. The Russians believe he can keep his promise because he has no rebels to give us shelter and we have a nine-hundred-mile journey before us to get to Iraq. I'd say the Ayatollah's

COBRA STRIKE

chances were pretty good, too, except for one thing. He doesn't know us."

The mercs and Institute men all cheered except for Baker, who said now that they were in Iran, they should negotiate with the Iranians.

"Sure, Baker," Mike responded, "they would love to negotiate with us for two or three years in jail cells."

"The Iranians would never try a stunt like that again," Baker snapped.

"I agree, they probably wouldn't," Campbell conceded. "They'd hand us over to the Russians instead, and both they and the Russians would deny that we had ever entered Iran. We'd be back to being captured inside Afghanistan and the Soviets would be happy again. Jed, you tell our smuggler friends here that this is no antismuggling crusade. Tell them that these Revolutionary Guards are after us, not them. They should stay inside their own border until we get away."

The Afghans wished them luck and offered them weapons and ammo from their own meager supply. Instead Mike gave them some of the team's unneeded armaments, and they departed happy.

Mike asked in a serious voice, "Did any man accept any opium?"

"No, Mike," Lance said in a loud voice. "It was offered and I refused."

"Anyone else?"

Most had been offered some and all had refused.

"Good," Mike said. "That way maybe we'll stay alive."

They saw the landing zone from the top of the ridge. Mike observed it through his binoculars. His lenses traveled over the camouflaged fuselages of the Huey choppers. The red, white, and green "target" symbol on their sides and large national flags of the same colors in horizontal stripes near the tail rotor defeated the purposes of the camouflage but looked good, which was perhaps all that mattered. Mike knew how to fly a Huey, more or less, from some bad experiences in Southeast Asia when he had to fly one despite no training. They were not easy to fly, but then, no chopper was.

He didn't want a Huey. Ten men aboard a Huey was a heavy load. The chopper's range was 230 miles, or 460 miles one way, which was only half the distance they had to travel if they took the shortest way possible. He'd take a Huey in a pinch, but they needed something with a longer range.

His binoculars settled on a familiar shape, a Sikorsky HH-3. This chopper would be ideal, if it weren't for one thing—he wasn't sure how to fly it.

"Anyone know how to fly a Sikorsky HH-3?" he asked.

Silence.

"Damn. Too bad. Especially since we're going to use one. It's got a range of about seven-fifty klicks, as far as I remember. It has a twin turbine and can go up ten thousand feet or more. Last one I was in was a thirty-seat troop transport in Nam. But I'm fairly sure the Navy used them for air-sea rescues and as a submarine hunter/killer. You sure none of you can fly her? Too bad."

Mike's attention was called by Andre to a lookout point farther along the top of the ridge. From there they could see the Revolutionary Guards scouring the scrublands at the base of the ridge on which they stood. A few groups had climbed higher. They kept in constant motion, like restless gangs in a city park, not sure what to do with themselves. Despite their apparent lack of military training, they could still be dangerous because of their numbers and because they all carried automatic assault rifles. Mike selected the shortest route from the hills to the landing zone as a point about a mile north along the ridge. Accordingly he had the team retreat, make its way north, and then reclimb the ridge. While they were doing this Andre mentioned to Mike that Baker had started acting up again.

"He admits himself that he can't fly the damn thing," Baker said to Crippenby, Winston, and Turner. "Even if he knew how, he would have no chance of getting it across Iran to the Iraqi war zone. If the Iranians don't shoot it out of the sky, the Iraqis will. Campbell has been brilliant so far, I'll grant him that, but his success has gone to his head. He doesn't know when to stop. We don't need any more life-endangering heroics. Now is the time to talk. We're all

Institute men, so we have a deeper perspective than these soldier-of-fortune types, who are all brawn and no brains. Their only answer to every situation is violent action. I would hope you are more civilized."

"Stuff it up your ass, Baker," Turner said, and walked on ahead of them.

"Don't mind him," Baker said. "He's not part of the Nanticoke's brain trust."

"Turner has more horse sense than you'll ever have, Baker," Crippenby said. "All I've seen of you in Afghanistan is someone sulking like a kid and being a help to no one. Yet the moment Campbell gets you safely out of Afghanistan, you start mouthing off as if you were the one who led us through it all. If you hadn't been such a louse up to this point, I'd be tempted to listen to you because, yes, I think Campbell is being reckless. But if I have to choose between his crazy maneuvers and your bullying sulks, I'll have to go with the one who brought us this far, won't I?"

After Crippenby had walked away Winston slapped Baker on the shoulder, and said, "That was a reasonable response, and one you deserved, David. Better come along and hold your peace until something goes wrong."

"That Sikorsky HH-3 is what will go wrong," Baker predicted grimly.

But he wasn't thinking clearly. First of all they had to get to the Sikorsky.

Mike broke out a supply of Belgian HE-RFL-60N antipersonnel rifle grenades. "Remember, you don't have to hit someone. These are just as effective behind someone taking cover. It breaks into five hundred pieces and is lethal out to eight meters from the point of impact. But it will cut the shit out of them out to fifty meters. So spread them around. The range is about three hundred meters, so we'll flatten the bastards out as we move and empty our magazines into any that survive."

"Let's do it," Waller growled, his husky voice turned savage.

"Campbell, as soon as we kill them, we will have lost

our negotiating power." It was Baker. He stood up out of cover. "I am not prepared to sacrifice—"

Verdoux lunged at him, but Baker dodged him and ran forward, downhill, waving his arms to get the attention of the Revolutionary Guards below. "Peace! Peace! We come in the name of peace! We must speak with the Ayatollah Khomeini!"

Campbell pulled the rifle grenade from the muzzle of his Kalashnikov, fired a burst of three shots from the hip, and brought down Baker with two bullets in his right thigh.

"Winston! Turner! Carry him!" Campbell shouted, pushing the rifle grenade back in the barrel of his gun. "Verdoux! Nolan! Cover them and escort them! Hardwick, Murphy, Waller, Crippenby, ready your grenades! All right, men, see those choppers? Let's go!"

The team moved downhill at a run and enveloped Winston and Turner, who were carrying Baker, screaming with pain, none too gently between them. They took some light, wildly aimed fire from the surprised Revolutionary Guards, but the mercs used their time and energy in covering ground. Only when they were quite close did Campbell release the first antipersonnel rifle grenade. It burst a couple of hundred yards directly in front of them, and its hundreds of white-hot metal fragments tore through the flesh of the surrounding Iranians. Four other grenades followed, each man finding his own area, cutting a swath in front of the team.

They were soon running among the screaming, dying, struggling Pasdaran. They had asked to be martyrs for the Islamic revolution, but it seemed to Campbell that most seemed not too happy to have their wish granted. Having emptied and replaced a thirty-round magazine, he replaced it and fitted another grenade in the barrel.

The second wave of grenades was even more devastating than the first, because the Pasdaran were thicker on the ground. It was no longer possible to avoid stepping on the dead and dying.

As always, Campbell was astounded at the multiple slaughter it was possible for a trained, disciplined, small unit with a defined objective to inflict on a large, undisciplined,

COBRA STRIKE

poorly trained mass that did not possess a clearly defined plan of action to meet the circumstances.

They gained the chopper landing zone without sustaining any casualties and used the fuselages of the parked Hueys as cover.

"This way!" Lance yelled, having found a Sikorsky HH-3.

As they ran, they passed two Iranians in flight suits. Mike noticed that IMPERIAL was poorly inked out on their prerevolutionary badges. They had holstered pistols on their hips, but they made a show of putting their hands behind their backs and looking away. These armed forces men seemed less than upset at the beating the Revolutionary Guards had taken and probably resented having had to ferry them here.

"Bob! Lance! If I can't get this mother started, you two go back for them!" Campbell shouted as he ran to the Sikorsky.

Mike sat in the cockpit and tried to "think helicopter." He got the twin turbines started with no trouble while the others were still climbing in and passing Baker on board. It was the disk formed by the revolving rotor blades that actually flew. The fuselage or main body of the chopper went along only because it was suspended from this disk by a mast. That was the big difference between flying a chopper and a fixed-wing plane. Here you were flying a spinning disk with dead weight hanging from it.

Mike reached to the left of the pilot's seat and gently pulled up on the collective control stick. This increased the pitch angles of the main rotor blades and caused the disk, along with the chopper attached to it, to rise.

"Check the gauges, Andre," Mike commanded. "How are we on fuel?"

The throttle twist-grip was on the end of the collective stick, and Mike had to give the engines more throttle as he raised the stick for takeoff. Too much or too little could produce dangerous effects. Needless to say, Mike had no idea what was too much or too little in this Sikorsky.

The cyclic control stick was placed vertically between his legs. Moving this stick in any direction caused the rotating blades to increase in pitch and move higher on one half of their cycle and feather on the other half. This in turn caused the disk to tilt in the direction in which the cyclic stick was pushed, and thus the chopper moved in that direction.

As the main motor spins, torque revolves the fuselage slowly in the opposite direction. The tail rotor controls this movement by pushing the tail sideways against the torque. The left pedal increases the tail rotor pitch and pushes the tail to the right and the nose to the left. The right pedal produced the opposite effect. The left-hand throttle had to be adjusted in time with these maneuvers, more power with the left pedal, less with the right.

That was it. Nothing much more to it.

Andre yelled that they had full fuel tanks, and as far as he could see and understand, everything was in order.

Mike gave it throttle with his left hand and gently eased up the collective stick. The big chopper jumped off the ground like a person stung by a hornet. The rotor blades roared crazily over their heads, and the entire craft began to vibrate and rattle. Then it began sinking and rising in sharp stomach-churning jerks. The more Campbell tried to correct this up-and-down motion with the collective stick, the more pronounced it became.

Mike decided that the only way out was up, so he raised the collective stick and gave it more throttle, trying to keep it straight with the left pedal as he eased on the cyclic stick to see if he could stop the now violent vibrations. About twenty feet above the ground, both engines cut out and the chopper began to fall.

Campbell pushed the collective stick all the way down. This flattened the pitch angle of the rotors and allowed them to continue spinning, which provided lift. If he had not gotten the collective stick down instantly, the chopper would have dropped like a stone. As it was, they bounced hard on their three wheels onto the ground.

"That's called an autorotation," Campbell said in the calm voice that signaled things were going bad. "Anyone who wishes to discuss things with the Ayatollah Khomeini should leave the craft now."

The others were too shaken to understand a word he was saying.

The engines roared to life again, and Campbell gave them the throttle and raised the collective stick in his left hand. As the Sikorsky lifted off the ground this time, its nose made an abrupt right-angle turn. Then it started moving in odd directions in short, fast darts, as if hysterical—yet all the time it kept rising. At length it moved westward, unsteadily but definitely under way by this time.

A bullet ripped up through the floor near Mike's right foot. "Hey, we're under fire!"

Andre smiled and pointed to a number of other bullet holes in the sides and floor. "Mike, we have been for some time. Nobody wanted to mention it in case it distracted you."

"Is everyone all right?" Campbell asked anxiously.

"So far, Mike. Please keep your eye on what you're doing. Why is the ground rising up at us so quick?"

As they passed south of Teheran and north of Qom, only two hundred feet above the rolling, sandy wastes, two Tomcats searched for them above.

"Last time I was in a Tomcat was with a crazy bastard called Glasseyes, and he practiced a night landing on the U.S.S. *Constellation* off San Diego. Now we have the same planes up there looking to destroy us. I guess we sold some to the Shah."

The Iranian pilots did not pick out the camouflaged helicopter against the sandy wastes, and the chopper was either flying too low for the aircraft radar to pick it up or the radar was defective, as so much Iranian-owned American-made equipment was these days because of America's refusal to sell Iran spare parts.

They knew they had it made when an F-14 Phantom jet also failed to spot them. They saw a river ahead, and beneath them they saw shelters constructed of corrugated zinc, sandbags, and metal ammo cases. Clothes hung out to dry, people went here and there on motorcycles, and no one on the ground paid any attention to them.

This changed fast when they crossed the river. Antiaircraft shells exploded around them, and flak tore the metal skin of the fuselage. They had no chance to establish radio communication because of the suddenness with which they crossed the battle lines from one side to another. All the Iraqis could see was an invading Iranian helicopter. It would be only a matter of seconds before they took a direct hit.

Mike switched off the twin turbines and yelled, "Autorotation!"

He remembered to push down the collective stick as far as it would go.

The Iraqi officer had a clipped mustache, freshly pressed fatigues, and a British manner.

"Certainly I was surprised to see Afghans emerge from an Iranian helicopter," he said as they watched a medical evacuation chopper move Baker to a field hospital, "although you have to be the most unconvincing Afghans I've ever seen. When I heard your American accents, I thought, 'My God, this is publicity for some film these people are making.' That fellow we evacuated seemed a bit upset at you."

"He was disappointed at not having met the Ayatollah Khomeini," Mike said.

"I don't think he missed much." The officer took them aboard a chopper for the ride to Baghdad. When they were seated, he looked over their Afghan garb. "Appalling," he said with a smile. "I take it you have been in Afghanistan."

Mike nodded.

The officer laughed. "You know, we don't much like Americans here in Iraq. But now I think we're slowly coming round to the opinion that anyone who is hated as much as you are by the Russians and Iranians must have some good in them."

"Nice to know," Mike said, and dozed off.

GREAT MEN'S ADVENTURE

__DIRTY HARRY
by Dane Hartman

Never before published or seen on screen.

He's "Dirty Harry" Callahan—tough, unorthodox, no-nonsense plain-clothesman extraordinaire of the San Francisco Police Department . . . Inspector #71 assigned to the bruising, thankless homicide detail . . . A consummate crimebuster nothing can stop—not even the law!

__DEATH ON THE DOCKS *(C90-792, $1.95)*

__MASSACRE AT RUSSIAN RIVER *(C30-052, $1.95)*

__NINJA MASTER
by Wade Barker
Committed to avenging injustice, Brett Wallace uses the ancient Japanese art of killing as he stalks the evildoers of the world in his mission.

__SKIN SWINDLE *(C30-227, $1.95)*

__ONLY THE GOOD DIE *(C30-239, $2.25)*

WARNER BOOKS
P.O. Box 690
New York, N.Y. 10019

Please send me the books I have checked. I enclose a check or money order (not cash), plus 50¢ per order and 50¢ per copy to cover postage and handling.* (Allow 4 weeks for delivery.)

_____ Please send me your free mail order catalog. (If ordering only the catalog, include a large self-addressed, stamped envelope.)

Name _____
Address _____
City _____
State _____ Zip _____

*N.Y. State and California residents add applicable sales tax.   14

Mystery & Suspense by GREGORY MCDONALD

___FLETCH AND THE MAN WHO___ (B30-303, $2.95, U.S.A.)
(B30-868, $3.75, Canada)

America's favorite newshound has a bone to pick with a most elusive mass murderer! From the bestselling author of FLETCH'S MOXIE and FLETCH AND THE WIDOW BRADLEY.

___FLETCH AND THE___ (B34-256, $3.50, U.S.A.)
___WIDOW BRADLEY___ (B34-257, $4.50, Canada)

Fletch has got *some* trouble! Body trouble: with an executive dead in Switzerland. His ashes shipped home prove it. Or do they? Job trouble: When Fletch's career is ruined for the mistake no reporter should make. Woman trouble: with a wily widow and her suspect sister-in-law. From Alaska to Mexico, Fletch the laid-back muckraker covers it all!

___FLETCH'S MOXIE___ (B34-277, $3.50)

Fletch has got plenty of Moxie. And she's just beautiful. Moxie's a hot movie star. She's got a dad who's one of the roaring legends of Hollywood. She's dead center in a case that begins with a sensational on-camera murder and explodes in race riots and police raids. Most of all, she's got problems. Because she's the number one suspect!

___CARIOCA FLETCH___ (B30-304, $3.50, U.S.A.)
(B32-223, $4.50, Canada)

It's Carnival in Brazil, and Fletch is fast becoming a *carioca!* He's stripped down to his shorts because of the heat, carries his money in his shoe because of the thieves, drinks *guarana*, and is just watching the women walk. But, some people think that he's the reincarnation of a murdered Brazilian. And, worst of all, the man's murderer thinks so too—and wants to stop Fletch before he remembers too much!

WARNER BOOKS
P.O. Box 690
New York, N.Y. 10019

Please send me the books I have checked. I enclose a check or money order (not cash), plus 50¢ per order and 50¢ per copy to cover postage and handling.*
(Allow 4 weeks for delivery.)

_____ Please send me your free mail order catalog. (If ordering only the catalog, include a large self-addressed, stamped envelope.)

Name _____

Address _____

City _____

State _____ Zip _____

*N.Y. State and California residents add applicable sales tax. 18

DETECTIVE PETER BRAGG MYSTERY SERIES WILL EXPLODE OFF YOUR SHELVES!

Tough, gritty, authentic, packed with action and loaded with danger, Jack Lynch's BRAGG novels are American hard-boiled detective fiction in the grand tradition of Hammett and Chandler.

___**SAUSALITO** *(B32-083, $2.95, U.S.A.)*
by Jack Lynch *(B32-084, $3.75, Canada)*

Peter Bragg, working on a blackmail case in the quiet community of Sausalito, senses something else simmering beneath the ocean-kissed beachfront. Residents are being "persuaded" to give up their homes to the developers of a glittering new hotel complex. Bragg smells a conspiracy so immense that his own life isn't worth a paper dollar if he doesn't bring the criminals to justice. And if anybody can, Bragg will.

___**SAN QUENTIN** *(B32-085, $2.95, U.S.A.)*
by Jack Lynch *(B32-086, $3.75, Canada)*

It's mayhem in maximum security at San Quentin State Prison. Right now, it's a battlefield with guards on one side of a barricade and a group of hostage-holding cons on the other. Their incredible demand? Let their leader's kid brother off a murder rap—or else . . . The case is a natural for Bragg. It's a dangerous, down-and-dirty job—and only Bragg can stop the bloodbath.

WARNER BOOKS
P.O. Box 690
New York, N.Y. 10019

Please send me the books I have checked. I enclose a check or money order (not cash), plus 50¢ per order and 50¢ per copy to cover postage and handling.*
(Allow 4 weeks for delivery.)

_____ Please send me your free mail order catalog. (If ordering only the catalog, include a large self-addressed, stamped envelope.)

Name _____
Address _____
City _____
State _____ Zip _____
*N.Y. State and California residents add applicable sales tax.   108

By the year 2000, 2 out of 3 Americans could be illiterate.

It's true.

Today, 75 million adults... about one American in three, can't read adequately. And by the year 2000, U.S. News & World Report envisions an America with a literacy rate of only 30%.

Before that America comes to be, you can stop it... by joining the fight against illiteracy today.

Call the Coalition for Literacy at toll-free **1-800-228-8813** and volunteer.

Volunteer Against Illiteracy. The only degree you need is a degree of caring.

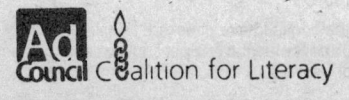

Ad Council — Coalition for Literacy

Warner Books is proud to be an active supporter of the Coalition for Literacy.